A TASTE OF HEAVEN

"Oh, what is that which smells so sweetly?" Miranda asked, as Jonathan helped her down the shallow steps which led to the garden.

"Lily-of-the-valley." He bent down to the sheltered corner near the steps and broke off several stems. The touch of Miranda's hand as he placed the blossoms in it was galvanic. He almost dropped the stems as her hand closed over them.

Miranda caught her breath as Jonathan touched her. Then she bent her head and inhaled the fragrance of the flowers. "Like a bit of heaven," she said softly, not quite certain whether she meant the blossoms or his presence.

"You're quite right—although I doubt I could have said it so poetically."

A sharp breeze made Miranda shiver, despite the warmth she had felt in his presence, and she looked about her. "It's quite dark," she remarked in surprise.

"Yes—so it is. I shouldn't have kept you here so long." He rose, taking her hand which did not hold the flowers and drawing her to her feet. He kept her hand in his as they walked the short distance to the door through which they had come out, both certain this must be the loveliest garden in the world.

As they closed the door behind them, Jonathan drew her fingers to his lips, then dropped her hand as they strolled into the drawing room where the others were awaiting them.

ELEGANT LOVE STILL FLOURISHES —
Wrap yourself in a Zebra Regency Romance.

A MATCHMAKER'S MATCH (3783, $3.50/$4.50)
by Nina Porter

To save herself from a loveless marriage, Lady Psyche Veringham pretends to be a bluestocking. Resigned to spinsterhood at twenty-three, Psyche sets her keen mind to snaring a husband for her young charge, Amanda. She sets her cap for long-time bachelor, Justin St. James. This man of the world has had his fill of frothy-headed debutantes and turns the tables on Psyche. Can a bluestocking and a man about town find true love?

FIRES IN THE SNOW (3809, $3.99/$4.99)
by Janis Laden

Because of an unhappy occurrence, Diana Ruskin knew that a secure marriage was not in her future. She was content to assist her physician father and follow in his footsteps . . . until now. After meeting Adam, Duke of Marchmaine, Diana's precise world is shattered. She would simply have to avoid the temptation of his gentle touch and stunning physique — and by doing so break her own heart!

FIRST SEASON (3810, $3.50/$4.50)
by Anne Baldwin

When country heiress Laetitia Biddle arrives in London for the Season, she harbors dreams of triumph and applause. Instead, she becomes the laughingstock of drawing rooms and ballrooms, alike. This headstrong miss blames the rakish Lord Wakeford for her miserable debut, and she vows to rise above her many faux pas. Vowing to become an Original, Letty proves that she's more than a match for this eligible, seasoned Lord.

AN UNCOMMON INTRIGUE (3701, $3.99/$4.99)
by Georgina Devon

Miss Mary Elizabeth Sinclair was rather startled when the British Home Office employed her as a spy. Posing as "Tasha," an exotic fortune-teller, she expected to encounter unforeseen dangers. However, nothing could have prepared her for Lord Eric Stewart, her dashing and infuriating partner. Giving her heart to this haughty rogue would be the most reckless hazard of all.

A MADDENING MINX (3702, $3.50/$4.50)
by Mary Kingsley

After a curricle accident, Miss Sarah Chadwick is literally thrust into the arms of Philip Thornton. While other women shy away from Thornton's eyepatch and aloof exterior, Sarah finds herself drawn to discover why this man is physically and emotionally scarred.

Crossed Hearts
Monette Cummings

ZEBRA BOOKS
KENSINGTON PUBLISHING CORP.

ZEBRA Books are published by

Kensington Publishing Corp.
475 Park Avenue South
New York, NY 10016

First Printing: October 1993

Printed in the United States of America

Chapter One

"But I've barely begun to write my new book," Miranda Drake protested faintly, wondering how Mr. Warrington could expect so much of her. "The first chapter isn't even finished! I couldn't possibly hope to bring you another manuscript so soon."

Actually, she had done much more than that, but it was all preparatory work—descriptions of her characters, a rough sketch of the countryside where the story was to occur. Not that the sketch would appear in the book; it was only for her own reference, so she could imagine where all the events would take place.

She always did these things before she started upon the book itself. There were weeks of work involved; yet, even with all of this already done, the writing itself would take her some time.

"I hadn't thought you would wish it quite so soon." The words sounded lame to her, as if she were attempting to excuse herself for being so lazy. She hoped they didn't sound the same to the two gentlemen. In fact, she had been quite surprised when she'd received the message asking her to come to London for a meeting. Always before, Mr. Warrington had been willing to wait until she was ready to send him her completed manuscript.

One of the gentlemen was Edward Warrington, who was her publisher; the other had been introduced to her as his younger brother. Miranda didn't understand his presence at today's meeting, but he had been most polite.

For today's meeting with Mr. Warrington, she had—as she had done when she'd called on him in the past—hoped that her gray merino gown with the darker spencer and the matching riband on her cottage bonnet were enough to make her seem more business-like. If only she didn't appear to be so young! Even drawing her curls into a bun at the nape of her neck didn't seem to help.

How could publishers think her capable of writing good stories when she looked as she did? Still, she was able to remind herself that, although she was barely two-and-twenty, her last two books had sold extremely well. Of course, her readers didn't know of her youth.

Upon her first visit to Mr. Warrington's office, made more than a year ago, she had thought that it would give her a more studious appearance if she were to wear spectacles. She had borrowed the ones her companion customarily wore in recent years, although Sammy had told her they would do her no good. When she tried to wear them, she found that they blurred her vision until she could barely make out large objects, instead of making things clearer, as she supposed they did in Sammy's case.

Reluctantly, she had discarded the idea of wearing them. Having a studious look might be a good idea, but it would never do for her to be stumbling about the office, bumping into the furniture, or even falling. Mr. Warrington might think that she was one of those terrible females who were given to drinking.

The two gentlemen who faced her today were aware

6

of her youth and accepted it—not only accepted it, but appreciated it. Nor could they find anything in her appearance that was not pleasing. Not even the "businesslike" gray gown could successfully disguise her svelte form or the graceful way she moved.

Neither of them cared for bluestockings, although they were careful to share that opinion only with each other. They frequently published the writings of such females and appreciated the income these writers provided them and, as the elder brother had often remarked, "Even if one does not appreciate its looking like an iron fist that would break our teeth, it would be foolish to bite the hand that feeds us."

The neatly clad young lady with the large blue eyes and brown hair that curled despite all her attempts to make it lie smoothly against her head was an agreeable change from the hard-favored females with whom they often had to deal. Many of these ladies were doubtless of the opinion that it would make a better impression upon their publisher if they appeared belligerent, doubtless confusing belligerency with a businesslike attitude.

The two gentlemen thought quite otherwise; they much preferred a softer and younger look, like that of the young lady who sat across the desk from them. Nor did they object to the fact that the exceptionally pretty face had a equally clever brain behind it. It was that brain which had been making an excellent profit for several years for Edward Warrington and, they hoped, would soon be doing the same for his brother.

"That will be quite all right, Miss Drake," the elder man, who had been publishing her books, hastened to assure her. "We didn't ask you to call on us for that reason. Although both of us are eager to begin with our little scheme, we don't wish to press you unduly for your next manuscript. Creative ability can't be

7

rushed, we know, but must be permitted to develop as it will."

"That is kind of you, sir. I shall, of course, work upon it as soon as I return home."

"Excellent! When you have written several chapters, please let us know. That will be enough for a start, for we have a brilliant idea, and we hope that you will agree with us. My brother Herbert," he indicated his companion, who was almost as rotund as he, "has, for several years, been the editor of a small periodical. Small, but growing—growing rapidly, I may say," he amended, as his brother, who had been beaming at Miranda, turned to scowl at him.

"Although it will be some time," he continued, "before it rivals the *Times* or the *Gazette,* he can already boast a number of discerning readers."

"The number is greater almost every day," the younger brother stated. "It is being noticed. And by a number of important people, I may say."

"Quite right. And it is our thought that it would be the thing for Herbert to publish your new novel a chapter at a time, before I bring it out between covers. You must have noticed that this is being done more and more often now—although a great number of the writers are so old-fashioned as to prefer to use the more established newspapers."

This remark earned him another scowl from his brother. The younger man was quite proud of what he had accomplished and disliked having it belittled in any way, even by the more successful book publisher, from whom he had learned his trade.

To Miranda, there seemed to be little difference in the two men. Of equal height—each little more than her own five feet four inches—their bulk made them almost spherical in appearance, causing a smile as she thought they were much like the little dolls which would right themselves whenever they were placed on their sides.

She was well acquainted with the elder of the two, having called upon him several times since he had begun publishing her books. He had somewhat less hair than his brother, and wore a pair of square-framed spectacles which constantly threatened to slip down his nose, so that she wondered how much use he got from them.

When he beamed at her, as he did now, she felt she was in the presence of Father Christmas. Not the gaunt, fierce figure of a saint which was so often seen, but a plump, kindly gift-giver. One who had given her much in the way of self-confidence, as well as some very welcome money during the past two years.

"I must confess that I've paid but little attention to such matters," she owned, in answer to his comment about the serialization of other works. "Although I do make an attempt to keep up with the works of other writers, I must confess to you that I seldom appear to have enough time to read the newspapers."

She was aware of their surprised and somewhat pained expressions at such an admission, and hastened to add, "Or at least, any of the larger ones. Although many in our area do subscribe to them, I do not. Living in the country as I do, I find it impossible or even unnecessary to remain *au courant* with matters occurring in London."

"Ah, but you should make an effort to do so, my dear lady," Mr. Edward Warrington told her. "London is, after all, the nerve center of the world." A true Briton, he chose to ignore such spots as Paris, especially now that it was in the hands of Bonaparte. He couldn't see anything good coming from the city controlled by that Corsican. "Being aware of day-to-day affairs of the *ton* would be a help to you in your

9

writing—although I must own you do very well now."

"Very well indeed, if one may judge by the many orders you continue to receive for her books," the other said in a sharp tone, wishing for a slight revenge upon his brother who had spoken of his *small* newspaper—although that, for the present, was no more than the truth. "He may not tell you, Miss Drake, but *I* have no hesitation in saying that you are one of his best-selling authoresses."

"That is certainly no secret."

"I was not certain that you had informed the lady of that fact. And you know, Edward, that Miss Drake's writing—profitable as it may be—has nothing whatsoever to do with matters of the present."

"True enough, Herbert—and I can see that current affairs would mean little, my dear young lady, unless you should decide to branch out into a different type of story. I wish you will not do so at this time, however, as your Gothic romances are so very popular. Still, I should suppose that, wrapped up in your work as you are . . ."

"No, I should not be able to write anything other than I am doing at present, I fear." Her tone held no regret that she might be unable to do other than she was doing now. These tales had begun as childhood fantasies, such as many others might use to amuse themselves. However, instead of fading as she grew older, these dreams had developed into the sort of Gothic tale which now was so popular, and Miranda discovered that she had a talent for putting them down on paper.

"As for writing about current affairs," she continued, "it seems to me that many of the books of that kind—at least, the ones I have read—have a tendency to moralize and instruct, rather than to amuse."

"Yes, some of our authors feel that they ought to be

teachers." Some of the more successful ones, he would have been forced to own, although personally he didn't enjoy such books as much as those with more exciting themes. And few of these writers had made such an immediate success as had the young lady facing them.

"Or else they wish to mock at people in high places. And I prefer to entertain my readers if I can do so. Most modern themes simply do not give me ideas for stories. Too, there are so many other things for me to think about without being too concerned with what is taking place at the present time."

"But—"

"Oh, I don't mean that I'm unaware of the war. I am neither so blind nor so stupid as that, I assure you. And if I thought that I could write seriously about such matters as the effects of war upon the average person or the plight of poor people in today's world, I might venture to do such a tale. But I don't feel that I could do so successfully, and I should never attempt a *roman à clef,* for I have found that the frivolous lives of the *ton* don't interest me, even to the point of satirizing them."

"Quite right of you to feel that way about them," Mr. Herbert Warrington agreed. "Why should you go so far afield searching for a theme, when the books you do write are so popular?"

"Thank you. I'm happy that it is so. But as for your idea of publishing the story serially—I confess it sounds quite interesting, but don't you fear it will detract from the sales of the printed book, since people will have had an opportunity to read it as it appears?"

"Not at all. Quite the opposite, in fact. We're certain that it will stimulate interest in the completed volumes, and we expect to receive enough orders that the first printing will be sold out by the time the last chapter appears in the newspaper."

"That would be wonderful!" Miranda could envision the new income, not quite so badly needed as it had once been, but still extremely useful.

"Also, I think I can assure you that it would create a new demand for your earlier books. Readers who have been enjoying the serialization of your present novel will look about for similar books they may have missed. If only you would permit us to use your name—"

"Oh, no," Miranda said quickly, half rising from her chair in her concern. "As I have told you before, it would never do to have anyone know who I am. Although I'm no one of importance, and the disclosure of my identity couldn't harm me personally, I do have several well-known relatives living in London, and it would not be the thing for them to learn that I am 'Madame V.' I mean, it might do them harm to have it known they were related to me."

Edward Warrington shrugged and spread his hands in a gesture of defeat. "Very well, we shall continue as we have been doing."

"Thank you, sir. I'm happy that you can see my point."

"I can see how important it is to you, although I'm not certain I agree with you. Yet it may be that you are doing the wisest thing to conceal your identity—that the mystery which surrounds your authorship is actually a help to your sales. But what do you think of our suggestion? You would be paid for each chapter as it is printed, then a lump sum when the book appears, as you are now."

Miranda looked at the two eager faces across the desk, and smiled her acceptance. "Then I must certainly agree, gentlemen. It will make the task of writing go more quickly when I have to look forward to doing only one chapter at a time, and I can't deny that the additional money will be welcome."

Both men nodded. They weren't aware of her true situation, but they knew that additional income was always welcome. Even the wealthy never seemed to have quite enough money.

"There's only one problem." Herbert Warrington spoke forcefully, not wishing to be overshadowed by his elder brother. It had been *his* idea to print the story serially, and although he had no trouble in convincing the other of the wisdom of his plan, he did not wish it to seem that his brother and the authoress were merely doing him a kindness by permitting him to print her work. "You speak of looking forward to only one chapter at a time, but I must have each chapter promptly before we go to press, which will call for more looking forward than your words imply."

Miranda thought for a moment before answering. "I understand. And I believe there should be no problem about that once I have completed three or four chapters to give you at the start. For months—actually it's been several years since they first asked—my London cousins have been urging me to pay them a lengthy visit. If I were to arrange to stay with them for a time, I could manage to bring you each chapter as it's finished. Or perhaps even several chapters at one time. That would be better than trusting them to the post."

"Much better, indeed. The post is too often dependent upon the weather, although not so much so now as during the winter, but still it may cause a delay in our receiving the material. Also, it will be useful for you to be near at hand, if I should find it necessary to get in contact with you about anything in the manuscript."

"I think you will find that Madame V's work seldom makes it necessary for you to have a consultation," Edward Warrington commented. "I have had no difficulty with it."

"I merely said it would be useful for her to be near, should something arise."

"Yes, but you must remember—if I am staying with my cousins, you must be very discreet in any communications you might make. Nothing can be said which will give them any suspicion of the truth. My cousin Lucy is to make her comeout this Season, and it would not be to her credit to know she is related to a writer of Gothic novels."

"Not even one whose books are as popular as Madame V's?" the elder Mr. Warrington said teasingly. "I don't doubt that one or both your novels may be found in every important household in London. If they're not there at present, they will be by the time the next volume appears."

"Especially for that reason, it would not be wise to have my identity known," Miranda said firmly. "As both of you are quite aware, a young lady *may* be permitted to read a book now and then—although, with a few exceptions such as yourselves, it seems that most gentlemen would prefer that ladies never look beneath the cover of a book. But actually to have it known that I had written such a novel . . . I doubt if I should ever be able to live down the scandal! Not that it would matter greatly to me, living almost in seclusion as I do, but I fear my cousin would suffer as well."

Both men laughed at her fear, although they were forced to own there could be a deal of truth in what she said about the gentlemen who preferred ladies who did not read. They were thankful that a great many of the ladies disagreed with that opinion or their sales of

14

novels would be considerably smaller. It was well known that the greater number of their readers of romances and Gothic tales were female. Men who read such books were careful to keep their activity quiet, lest their companions should think them unmanly.

"Very well," her publisher agreed, "we shall continue to keep your secret. But how soon may we expect to receive the first chapters of your new novel?"

"It will be a fortnight or so, I think. Perhaps as much as a month. I must return home, then write to my cousins, asking if this will be a good time for me to accept their invitation to visit them. Then, in addition to the writing I must do, Sammy and I—"

"Sammy? A pet?"

The young lady laughed. "Not at all—although I might call her a pet. I mean Miss Sampson. My old—I should say, my former governess, who is not at all old, and who is now my good companion. There will be a deal of packing and preparation, although I realize that I shall have to purchase a more stylish wardrobe once I come to London."

She gathered up her reticule as she spoke, shook hands with both gentlemen, and waited while one of them sent a boy to summon a hackney to return her to her hotel. In fact, she felt as if she could have danced all the way, but refrained from saying so. She would not wish such kind people to think she was given to queer fancies.

Chapter Two

As soon as she had returned to their lodgings from Mr. Warrington's office, Miranda told a jubilant Sammy all of the good news she had received from her publisher about the serialization of her upcoming book and what it would mean to them in the matter of additional income. She also disclosed her hopes that she might stay with her cousins while she sent in her manuscripts.

"I had feared, when he asked me to come to London, that something might be amiss. But this is excellent news, is it not? And if we can stay with the Owens family while I write the book . . . I shall write them as soon as I return home, to ask if we may come at this time."

"It *does* seem a long distance to travel, only to return again in so short a time," Sammy objected. She had never been fond of making the long journey to London, but had done so whenever Miranda needed to meet with her publisher, for it would have been unthinkable for the young lady to travel alone.

"Yes—it will be tiresome, and I can't say I shall enjoy it more than you do. But we shall have a great deal to do before we can leave. If I were to write to them while we are here, it would cause them to wonder

16

why I didn't do so before I came to London, and why I am here. Also, if their reply is favorable, they'll expect us to come at once. And, as I said, I'm not quite prepared to do that. Nor are you, if I know you—and I should, by this time."

"You are correct, of course. I was thinking only of the length of the journey itself, not of the preparations we must make. But I can see that we ought not to create a mystery about our present visit. The younger children, especially, would attempt to pry into your reasons for being here. And you're correct, too, about all we ought to do before undertaking so great a change as making a long stay in the city."

"More things than I like to think about—planning a long visit is a great deal of work. Of course, you'll be doing the greater part of it, as you always do."

"That makes it sound as if you're lazy, which I know you're not."

"No, but I do tend to leave most things to you, because of my work. I have the first part of my story written, plus all my descriptions and so forth. I couldn't leave all of it and begin again. That would take some time, and it would be the wisest thing if I were able to take Mr. Warrington some material as soon as we arrive."

Knowing how important this new venture was to Miranda, Sammy agreed, putting to one side her own thoughts about the discomfort involved in the double journey, and the pair departed from London as quickly as could be arranged. As soon as they were at home, Miranda dispatched a letter to the cousins she hadn't seen for several years, asking if this would be a propitious time for her to pay a visit.

She hoped to receive a favorable reply. If it was not suitable for her to come to them now, she would have only the choice of trying to keep Herbert Warrington supplied by post with the chapters he wished to receive regularly or to take lodgings at an expensive hotel in London.

She wasn't certain how long she would be able to do this, for she knew the cost of rooms for herself and Miss Sampson, even at one of the smaller London hotels, would certainly be more than she was expecting to receive for each chapter as it was delivered. A short stay such as the one they had just made was one thing; it allowed time for them to enjoy a bit of the city, aside from Miranda's interview, and they thought it worth the expense.

It would be a far different matter if she must remain there until the book was finished. Miranda disliked having to use the small amount she had been able to save from the sale of her earlier books.

As young as she had been at the time, it had appalled her to learn the load of debt she had faced following the death of her improvident father a dozen years ago, debt that had been resolved only by her disposing of the Drake property, except for the tiny house she and Sammy occupied and the pittance of an income which barely prevented the pair from starving.

Now that she was earning money from her writing, she was determined that she would never find herself in that position again. When she learned that she could actually sell her writings, she greeted the additional income with a feeling close to ecstasy.

To her delight, the answer she received from the eldest of the cousins in London was most enthusiastic.

"Of course, my dear Miranda, you must come to us at once," Lucy had written. "We have been eager to have your company for months—no, it has been years. I'm certain that Charles first invited you during the time he was at home from university. But unfortunately, you would never come."

18

Miranda recalled the many invitations Charles had sent—and her evasive replies, as she had been unwilling to allow her cousins to know that the cost of a journey of that kind was then beyond her reach.

"And of course you must bring your Sammy as well. Mrs. Hemphill, our wonderful housekeeper, assures me that all will be ready for you whenever you arrive. Cousin Augusta, too, is eager to see you again. Please send word when we may expect you. It will be such fun, having you here. I shall be able to share my secrets with you, as I cannot do with the children—even with Diana, although she considers herself no longer a child, being thirteen years old. Still, there are some things she is too young to know."

Although she told herself that the secret about the book she intended to write while she was in London was one she would never be able to share—and especially with the cousin who was busy with her plans to come out this Season—Miranda agreed it would be nice to have a confidante, about some things, one who was much nearer her own age than her companion. She sent an immediate reply that they would come in a fortnight's time; then she and Sammy indulged in a veritable whirlwind of preparations for their visit.

To anyone who was unfamiliar with the Owens family, the fact that seventeen-year-old Lucy was the one who made the decisions would appear to be unusual. But it was an unusual family. Professor Owens' second wife, Laura, had dutifully provided him with three children. As soon as the youngest, Giles, was out of leading strings, however, she had begun to accompany her husband on all his trips to explore various parts of the world, most of them supposedly uninhabited and quite possibly inhospitable.

It had been this similarity of interest which had first drawn them together, and she was delighted to learn that he still welcomed her company on these expeditions, rather than expecting her to remain at home to care for their family. Whenever anyone accused her of being an unnatural parent to desert her children, and there were many who did so, Mrs. Owens only laughed.

"Perhaps I am," she owned, "but I feel that my place is with my husband. Besides, Augusta and Mrs. Hemphill do a much better job of raising the children than I should do if I remained here, and I believe both of them would actually resent any attempts I might make concerning the children's upbringing. The children do not truly need me; I feel that my husband does."

During the next several years, the three children saw their parents so rarely that when the professor's yacht was lost in a storm at sea two years past, it made almost no difference to the way they had been living. Since they—and especially the younger ones—could scarcely remember their parents, they could not truly feel that they had lost anyone.

Augusta Owens, their father's spinster cousin, had come to live with them some time before this catastrophe, with the expectation that she would serve as a guardian to the children in their parents' absence. She was so shy of meeting strangers, however, that she seldom ventured from the house, so her guardianship was so lax as to be nonexistent.

Their elder half-brother, Charles, had been away from home since the time of his father's remarriage—although the two events had no connection: he and his stepmother had managed very well together. He had first been at school, then at university. Because of that, he had little in common with the younger members of the family. It was he, however, who had first invited Miranda to visit, thinking that she would be good company for his young half-sisters, and that they would profit from having someone nearer their own age beside them.

He was now in Wellington's army, so—despite the frequent arguments of ten-year-old Giles that he was the man of the family in Charles's absence—Lucy ran the household quite efficiently. In this she received the guidance of Mrs. Hemphill and the occasional advice of someone to whom she referred as "Cousin Jon."

"It seems that Miss Augusta is willing to allow Lucy an entirely free hand in running things," Miranda said to Sammy, when she read Lucy's letter. "I wonder who this cousin may be."

"Doubtless some connection of their mother's," was the sensible reply, "since he doesn't appear to be related to Miss Augusta. I don't recall the name."

Not being truly interested in the unknown gentleman, Miranda nodded and returned briskly to her writing. The story on which she was working was much more important to her than any vaguely named "cousin." She wished to have as much of this new tale finished as she was able to before their departure for London. Herbert Warrington ought to have several chapters in hand, lest some unforeseen event should arise to prevent her from writing as regularly as she planned to. Even now, with Sammy attending to most of the details, there were things to take her away from her work.

One of these was the matter of suitable clothing for the visit. "What I now have will do well enough," Sammy had declared. "But you, child, must have a better wardrobe if you're to meet your cousins' London friends! You won't want them to think you a country bumpkin."

21

"But I don't plan to meet them. I'm going to be working," Miranda protested.

"Of course that's what you prefer to do, but Lucy's friends will be about, and you won't always be able to retire to your room if they should come to call. Not if you wish to prevent any curiosity about your reason for being there."

For almost as long as Miranda could remember, Sammy had been her guide and mentor. Aurora Sampson had been a young girl scarcely out of her own childhood when she'd entered service. She had been betrothed for half a year and planned to be married when she was seventeen. The death of Mrs. Drake when Miranda was barely five years old left the child clinging to her for comfort and the nurse begged her fiancé to give her more time to allow Miranda to adjust to her motherless state.

This request was repeated at intervals during the years as Sammy progressed from nurse to governess to companion. The death of Miranda's father just after her tenth birthday—complicated by the news that the estate was deeply in debt—had made Sammy's companionship more important to the young girl, for she had no other family except for her Owens cousins.

They could scarcely have taken her in at that time, for Professor Owens was far too involved in his travels to spend more than a few weeks of each year at home and leaving Laura to care for the children. Lucy was only five years old and Diana a babe in arms. Sammy considered it impossible to burden them with another small child, so she stayed where she had been for so long.

At last, the young man had come to the conclusion that there was no future in waiting any longer for a marriage he had begun to doubt would ever take place. As a result, he had turned to a more willing female. During the seventeen years that she alone had cared for Miranda, the other servants having to be dismissed for lack of funds to pay them, Sammy— growing a bit plumper, a bit shorter of sight, and adding several gray hairs—had become reconciled to her own loss. Now, except for an occasional faint regret, she forgot that she had ever planned another life.

When her charge had first shown a talent for writing the tales she had been inventing since childhood, Sammy was delighted and encouraged her, often advising her as to the changes she ought to make in her earlier tales. At times, she took money intended for her own needs to provide paper and ink for Miranda's efforts. Fortunately, most of these earlier mistakes had long since been consigned to the fire, but Miranda had learned from them and the later stories had caught the interest of a London publisher and then of the *ton.* By this time, Madam V's books were in great demand throughout the city.

Sammy was as happy over Miranda's success as the young authoress herself. There was only one point regarding the stories on which they did not always agree: although the former governess, who had managed to educate herself along with the young girl, had helped to contrive a great many of the earlier adventures, there were times during these past years when she regretted that Miranda's taste had run to tales that were so wild. Any suggestion, however, that she should write more romantic stories was laughed to scorn.

"I wouldn't know how to go about it, and would only make myself and everyone else laugh if I attempted to write in such a vein as you are suggesting," Miranda declared. "What little I have seen of what everyone speaks of as romance doesn't make me yearn for a similar experience—so how can I write of it?"

23

"That's the most foolish reason I've ever heard for not attempting them! And what experience have you had with ghosts and mad monks?" Sammy asked, but Miranda only laughed again.

"If I err in such tales, no one will be able to point out that I am wrong, so I am safe in continuing as I'm now doing. Besides, I do have to put a small measure of romance into my stories. Some of my readers are demanding it, Mr. Warrington tells me. I don't agree, but he knows what will sell, so I listen to him."

Sammy was determined now that her young charge must make a good showing when she visited her London relatives, and Miranda, although she regretted the time she had to spend away from her desk, finally agreed that something would have to be done about her scanty wardrobe. A perusal of *La Belle Assemblée* and the most recent issues of *Ackerman's Repository* showed them one or two gowns which were simple enough that the two could make them up in a short time.

"Isn't it fortunate," she said to Miranda, "that fashions have changed so greatly from what they were in my youth?"

"Sammy, you make yourself sound quite ancient," Miranda told her with a laugh.

"Well, not precisely the styles of *my* youth, perhaps—but I can recall seeing many ladies in gowns which must have taken more than twice the material one needs today—and so elaborately made that I wouldn't have dared put scissors or needle to the cloth."

A quick journey to Harrowgate to find materials for the new gowns was almost their undoing—or at least Sammy's—as it was difficult to decide between sprigged and barred muslins, brocades, crepes, and a great variety of beautiful fabrics which were either of one color or a variegation of shades. There were fabrics, too, with threads of silver or gold running through them.

Sammy longed to see Miranda garbed in gowns made from some of these finer materials, although Miranda protested that she'd have no opportunity to wear such expensive gowns. Despite what Sammy had said about the necessity of meeting Lucy's friends, she had no intention of going into society, even if her cousin asked her to do so. "Remember," she said, "I'm going to London only so I can be nearer to my publisher."

The cost of many of these grand materials was enough to limit their choice to the two gowns they had originally planned. A single pair of slippers to be worn with either choice completed their shopping. Any other gowns, hats, slippers, and similar items had to wait until they were settled in London.

"It may develop that I'll need several more gowns later, if we stay long," Miranda conceded.

"I think it more than likely that you'll do so," Sammy agreed. She hadn't entirely given up her hope that Miranda might have an opportunity to enjoy a taste of London life.

"But not at once. Undoubtedly these identical materials will be much more expensive there, and we may have to have them made up—for you cannot do everything for me, Sammy. But by that time, I should be receiving the money from these first chapters, rather than having to take it from what I've saved, so I won't mind having to spend it as much."

When these decisions were reached and the gowns were completed—with most of the sewing done by Sammy while Miranda continued to work on her book—word was sent ahead to Lucy Owens, announcing the time of their arrival. Some packing which had been left to the last minute was hurriedly done, and the pair set off, using a hired chaise, as they didn't want the problem of stabling Miranda's horse and the gig. That homely vehicle served them well enough in the country, but, as even they could realize, it would scarcely be the thing for London use.

Even Miranda had roused herself momentarily from her preoccupation with her story to examine the chaise they would use. She knew that the journey would be a long one and they would wish to be as comfortable as they might be.

Sammy had been most enthusiastic about the younger lady's having a taste of London life, but now she glanced back for a last look at their home and said, "I hope that we haven't made a mistake in deciding upon this visit. After all, you scarcely know your cousins and don't know if we'll be comfortable there."

"Oh, Sammy, you mustn't go into the dismals," Miranda told her, "or you'll make me think we have made a mistake to leave home. You know that everything will be wonderful once we arrive. I'll be able to see the girls and little Giles—only I don't suppose he's so little now—and we'll probably see more of the sights of London while we're there. My only fear is that I might not have packed my ink carefully enough that it won't leak onto my clothing."

She was ready to unpack the case which held her writing materials, but Sammy stopped her from doing so, saying, "I'm certain everything will be all right, but you'd have been wiser to have waited until you arrived in London and purchased ink there."

"I know. It *would* have been the wiser thing to do— but I want to begin writing as soon as I can do so, and there might not be an opportunity for me to purchase ink secretly. We don't want my cousins to know anything about my writing."

"We certainly don't!" Miss Sampson was aware that the polite world would look askance at a young female who was known to write books. Even the author of such popular works as *Pride and Prejudice* and *Sense and Sensibility,* books praised by everyone from the Prince Regent to the ladies of the *ton,* did not put her name to her work. It was titillating enough to know they were written "by a lady," as their covers declared.

How much worse, in the eyes of the *ton,* would it be for her charge to be disclosed as "Madame V," writer of such wild Gothic tales as *The Mad Monk of Harwich Abbey,* popular as that second volume had become? "It's a pity that you can't talk about your work to anyone but me, but it's the wisest way."

Miranda nodded, but continued to frown as she wondered if she truly *had* packed her writing materials properly.

Not at all worried, for she knew Miranda would have taken the best of care of her things, Sammy gathered up the few garments they had decided against including in their luggage and hung them back in the armoire while moving onto other topics of conversation.

Chapter Three

Although they knew the journey would be a long one, having traveled to London several times in the past two years, so Miranda might consult with her publisher about matters which couldn't be arranged by letters, their knowledge did nothing to make the badly rutted roads more comfortable to travel, even in the better hung chaise they had chosen. Both ladies were greatly relieved when the afternoon of the fourth day found them arriving at their destination. Or in the approximate area.

King Street had become quite a popular name in the city, it appeared, for it turned out there were numerous streets in London bearing that name. Miranda wondered if they had all been named for one specific king or perhaps for various ones throughout the years. "Or," she said to Sammy, "whether they have any meaning at all or were merely named according to some caprice."

The street they sought was not in the most prosperous part of the city, nor was it in one of the poorer districts. Their driver grumbled at the inadequate instructions he was given, which resulted in their arriving in a number of King Streets they had not wanted. But by making a great many enquiries and receiving much conflicting advice, at last he was able to find the location they sought.

The two-story house, built of aged red brick with ivy growing upward between the windows, was neither large nor elaborate, but even from the carriage they could see that it appeared to be offering them a warm reception. It was shaded by a pair of myrtle trees which were surrounded by beds of beckoning spring blossoms. Sammy began to name the varieties beneath her breath, but Miranda, although she enjoyed the sight and the fragrance, was more interested in the people they were to visit.

As the driver began to set their bags roughly upon the walk—making Miranda shudder at the thought his treatment might cause her ink to spill—the door opened and several figures hurried to greet them. A boy, who, she was certain, could be no one but Giles, flung himself upon Miranda with a force which sent her staggering back against the carriage, while a silvery-haired girl whose coltishness gave little hint of beauty to come, ran after him, shouting at him not to behave with so little thought for the visitor.

"Oh, hide your teeth, Di," the boy exclaimed. "I guess I can say 'hello' to my cousin if I wish to. You *are* my cousin, ain't you?"

"If you are Giles, yes, I am indeed your cousin." The boy's grasp had pinned her arms tightly to her sides. With some difficulty, Miranda was able to free one hand from its constraint and to extend it toward the girl. "And you must be Diana."

The girl nodded shyly and allowed herself to be drawn to Miranda's side as a voice from the doorway called, "Now, children, you mustn't tease your cousin. Allow her to draw a breath, if you please."

At the top of the front steps stood a pretty, golden-haired young lady, a thin, elderly lady wearing what

29

Miranda was to learn was a permanently worried expression, and a plump motherly-looking middle-aged woman who could be no one except Mrs. Hemphill, the Owens' housekeeper. It was she who had called out, telling the younger children to behave themselves more circumspectly, while Lucy came quickly down the steps toward Miranda, both her hands outstretched in greeting.

"I hope you'll forgive my brother and sister for their wild behavior," she said. "We've all been looking forward to your arrival. And they quite forgot themselves when they saw you had truly come. They're not *always* this bad."

"Oh, they made me feel quite welcome," Miranda assured her, not at all concerned about possible damage the young people were doing to her already travel-stained gown. Their enthusiasm actually made her feel less travel-weary.

Then she became aware that the driver, having at last unloaded all their bags, was waiting with an expectant look and his hand not quite outthrust for payment. "Oh yes, I haven't forgot about you," she told him, fumbling in her reticule to find the money she had put aside for the journey.

"No," Giles exclaimed, beginning to tug a number of coins from his pockets. "I'm the man of the family, so I shall pay your fare."

"Oh no—that's most kind of you, but it's too much to ask."

"No, it ain't," he protested, as stubborn as one could expect a ten-year-old boy to be, especially when he had bright red hair and a liberal scattering of freckles. "I've been saving *all* my allowance since I first heard that you were coming so that I could pay your fare as a man ought to do." He drew miscellaneous coins, mixed with oddments of chalk, broken twigs,

30

and other mysterious items, from both pockets and poured all of them together into the driver's outstretched hand.

Seeing from the man's scowl that the mound of small coins he was carefully separating from the miscellany was far from enough to pay her fare, Miranda shook her head to caution him not to give voice to his objection, then turned to Giles, asking, "As you are the man of the family, do you think you will be able to carry this case of mine into the house?"

"Certainly I can do it," the boy stated. However, instead of the small case Miranda had indicated, he picked up one of the larger ones, which had to weigh nearly as much as he did, and struggled up the steps with it.

Smiling at his efforts, Miranda added several coins to the handful Giles had given the driver. This additional stipend was enough to turn his scowl to a gap-toothed grin, and he called after Giles, "Thank you, young sir," at which Miranda recklessly added a third coin to his hoard, without looking at its size.

The man had noticed it, however, and realized that the total of what she had given him was now nearly what she had agreed to pay for the entire journey, in addition to what the boy had already paid. He departed quickly, fearing that she might become aware of how much she had given him and demand a return of some of the money. Miranda, however, didn't mind that he had been overpaid, nor did his earlier churlishness about their mistaken directions overset her. Giles's determination to play the man of the house had been satisfied.

With the help of Lucy and Diana, Miranda and Miss Sampson carried the remaining bags to the door, where, at Mrs. Hemphill's orders, several maids hastened to relieve the four of their load and take them

31

upstairs. This task required several trips on their part, as Miranda's repeated offer to carry a part of the cases kept being denied. Giles, however, refused to relinquish the case he held, although Miranda feared that carrying it up the stairs would be too great a task for him. Still, she wouldn't damage his self-esteem by protesting against what he was doing.

Mrs. Hemphill's welcome to the newcomers was almost as effusive as that of the children, while the other lady, whom Miranda now recognized as the "Cousin Augusta" she had once met, murmured a greeting in so low a tone that she could barely be heard. Between the two women, with Lucy and Diana leading the way, the newcomers were ushered into what Lucy laughingly described as "our drawing room, morning room, whatever we wish to call it, since we don't have enough space for all these rooms. Or need for them, either." It was a cozy room, but one which showed the effects of being lived in daily by a trio of active young people, one of them a boy.

Beyond a glimpse of a fireplace in the far wall and several scuffed chairs, they had little time to inspect it now, however. As they entered the room, a gentleman rose from an easy chair near the window and came toward them, his approach slowed by a severe limp.

"Oh my," Miranda said beneath her breath to Sammy, "he is the most handsome man I have ever seen. Not everyone would agree about that, perhaps, but I think so. His face is so strong, and I do admire the smooth way his black hair is arranged. Rather short, but I like the way he has allowed it to grow down in front of his ears. And such green eyes; I don't recall ever having seen any to rival them. It's a pity about his limp—not that it detracts in any way from his appearance. In fact, it makes him more intriguing, I think."

Sammy prodded her and Miranda closed her mouth quickly, embarrassed at her rudeness and hoping none of the others had been aware of her whispered comments. In that first moment, she had decided that this gentleman definitely must be the model for the hero of her new book. Those green eyes—if only she could describe them properly. Despite his limp—or, she thought, perhaps because of it—he seemed to be the sort on whom anyone might depend.

Of course, she couldn't use the limp in her story. Aside from thinking it was cruel to call attention to a disability, someone *might* recognize this gentleman as her hero, and she wouldn't wish to do anything which would draw the slightest attention to her cousins or their friends.

She had always made it a rule not to write about people she knew—but intended to make an exception in the matter of this handsome gentleman. He *must* be her new hero, for certainly no one she could imagine would fit the part as well. As well, in fact, as his dark blue coat molded itself to his broad shoulders.

Fortunately, there was still time for her to write a better description into the chapters she had finished before leaving home. Fortunately, too, no one except Sammy had noticed her preoccupation with the gentleman, and she hoped that Sammy would understand. It was unlike her to gawk at strangers.

"This is our cousin Jon," Lucy was saying proudly, as if she had brought him especially for the visitor's benefit.

"Captain—or I suppose I should say former captain, for I fear it will be a time before I can truly claim the right to use that title again—Jonathan Murray at your service, ladies," he said with a slight bow.

"Cousin?" Miranda said with a puzzled look. "I

know you spoke of another cousin in your letter, Lucy, but I didn't know—"

"Well, Jon's not really a cousin," Lucy owned. "He was Charles's best friend; they were in the army together in the Peninsula. When Jon was wounded at Bussaco—"

"I'm certain the ladies aren't interested in tales of the war," Captain Murray interrupted.

"Oh, but in this case, they must be. After all, Jon, you *were* a hero."

"My dear Lucy, I've told you often that's not the truth. There was nothing heroic about my actions. I merely happened not to be able to get out of the way of a charging Frenchman."

"Whom you defeated, of course, despite being wounded. Jon can say whatever he will about the matter, but *we* know better. So do the powers that be, for they gave him a medal for what he did, which proves my tale."

For that and some other things as well, Captain Murray thought, but merely shrugged and raised his eyebrows, as if to belittle what Lucy was saying.

She paid him no heed. "What I started to tell you was that, when Jon was invalided home, Charles asked him to look in on us from time to time to see that everything was well until he—Charles, I mean—came home. Not that Charles ever paid us much attention when he was home, but he does—Jon does—beautifully."

"Stop and draw a breath," the gentleman advised.

Lucy laughed but obeyed, then continued, "But we cannot call him brother—I don't know why, for he was almost a brother to Charles—but we began to call him Cousin Jon. And, Jon, these are our new house guests, my cousin Miranda—truly a cousin—and her companion, Miss Sampson. They're to spend several weeks with us."

Miranda was aware of the gentleman's sharp scrutiny, which seemed to rake her from head to toe, and of the equally sharp change of expression in those green eyes. They appeared almost icy as he said, "I don't think that would be a good idea."

"And why shouldn't they visit, pray?" Lucy demanded indignantly. "Charles had asked Miranda several times to come to us if she visited London. And we've all wished for her to come, but she'd never do so until now. We're all so happy to have her here. Why should you wish to spoil it for us?"

Jonathan Murray had indeed been studying the younger of the newcomers. For himself, he approved of everything he saw. She was a bit taller than the average female, would almost reach his chin, and was full-figured without being plump, what he would describe—but not before the children, of course—as a proper armful. From beneath the edge of her bonnet, several wisps of curly hair had escaped, brown hair with merely a hint of red. And her eyes—such a deep blue, almost violet. A man could drown himself in them . . .

He swung away from their spell and limped to the window, staring blindly out at the street. When he felt he had somewhat recovered his wits, he turned back to face the group.

Chapter Four

That was the trouble; she was too beautiful . . . far too beautiful to be true. By true, his mind did not mean a lack of artifice, for she appeared to be completely free of any such deception, but one who secretly used her wiles to attract men.

She reminded him too strongly of the dishonestly named Constance, to whom he had been betrothed just before he'd left London to join the army . . . Constance, who had decided while he was gone that she wanted to have a wealthier husband, but who indicated upon his return home that she would welcome a *liaison* with him. And since his return to England, he had met several other ladies who were equally welcoming, equally beautiful, equally false. He had had his share of loves, but had never knowingly taken one bespoken by another man. Beautiful women, such as this one, he thought, cared nothing for such rules; each of them apparently wanted to display as many scalps as possible. It was only a contest to them.

He could scarcely say anything about *that* to the girls, however. They would certainly be shocked at the thought of his having *affaires*. Ladies were not supposed to know these things, especially very young ladies. He was certain that Lucy was entirely innocent of such knowledge and hoped she would never change.

Not that he would mention Constance's name to them, nor permit them to know the full extent of his disillusionment. Nothing could be said to give the children a hint that, in his experience, a female as beautiful as the one standing before him would certainly cause trouble wherever she might be. A female who could raise such thoughts even in one as experienced as he would be a disturbance this household did not need. Not when her pretty, but definitely paler cousin was preparing for her comeout.

A moment's thought enabled him to say rather weakly, "I merely thought that, with so small a household staff as you have, now that Charles is away—only two maids, I believe, beside the cook, and no male servants—two visitors would make too much additional work for them."

"Oh, what nonsense!" Diana cried.

"Di is correct," her sister said, as Mrs. Hemphill led the visitors to the sofa and bade them be seated, while she rang for tea, apologizing for having made them wait while this discussion had been taking place. "It's foolish for you to think that Miranda and her dear Sammy—you do not mind that we call you Sammy, as Miranda does?"

"Certainly not—I should like that," Miss Sampson assured her. She had approved of all three children at once, although she could tell they were ill-accustomed to discipline, despite Mrs. Hemphill's attempts to see that they did what they should. She strongly approved of Mrs. Hemphill, as well, feeling that the woman had too great a task.

However, she had some severe reservations about the gentleman. Why should he think it his affair to decide whether or not they should make this visit? It had been kind of him to think of the amount of additional work the visitors would cause for the servants, but that should be a matter for the family to decide.

"To think that Miranda and Sammy should cause us any trouble at all," Lucy finished triumphantly.

"You'll find we're quite willing to do our share while we're here," Miranda said, while Lucy shook her head at the offer.

"Oh no—there'll be no need for you to do anything at all. We'll manage things very well. We always have."

"I can tell you, Captain Murray," Mrs. Hemphill crossed her plump arms and appeared to be defying the gentleman to disagree with her, "that no two *ladies* could begin to make one-half as much work for my girls as that useless tutor we just sent packing." Augusta murmured what Miranda supposed was an agreement, although she doubted anyone could hear what the lady had said.

"That is exactly it," Jonathan insisted, happy that she had mentioned the dismissed tutor, which gave him the chance to prove that he had been correct in his earlier objection to bringing more people into the house. "Now that Rogers has left—"

"Has been dismissed, you mean—and good riddance," Mrs. Hemphill stated, wishing to make it certain that the unreliable fellow had not gone of his own accord.

"That may be—but no matter why he left, his going means that we shall have to find a new tutor for Giles as soon as possible, for none of us—and especially Charles, I am quite certain—wishes for the boy's education to be neglected. Then you will have the new tutor to care for, as well as your visitors, which *will* make more work. You must think of such matters, unless you plan to employ additional maids as well."

"That won't be necessary," Miss Sampson said, almost as much to her own surprise as to that of the others in the room, but realizing that something must be done to resolve this discussion. "As long as we remain in London, I can quite easily serve as the young man's tutor. In that way, you can postpone attempting to find a new one until we go home. That will mean *less* work for you, not more."

"But your holiday—" Mrs. Hemphill began to protest, happy as she might be at the thought of having no more male tutors in the house for a time. As welcome as the offer of Miss Sampson's assistance might sound, she could scarcely agree to permit a visitor to take over such an exacting duty as that.

"I don't need a holiday. As I don't intend to spend much of my time in sightseeing, I shall doubtless be pining for something to occupy my hours." *While Miranda is hard at work,* she thought. "Tutoring Giles will give me a feeling of being useful."

There was a chorus of protests from the others, which Sammy fended off, but before any agreement had been reached, the sound of breaking china and a thud of colliding figures caused them to hurry into the hall. The youngest housemaid, almost in tears, sprawled on the floor near the foot of the stairway, the wreckage of the tea tray around her. Giles was picking himself up from the tiles, wiping his hands upon his breeches, an act which served only to rub the tea and the crumbs upon which he had fallen more deeply into the cloth.

"I—I couldn't help it, mum, truly I couldn't," the girl said, as Mrs. Hemphill picked her up and began to wipe her face and hands.

"Of course you couldn't," Lucy said, half angry, but almost laughing. "It was Giles, sliding down the bannister again. Is that what happened?"

"You know it is the quickest way down, Lucy," the boy said defensively. "And if you ever tried it you would see it is the handiest—most of the time. I never saw Sukey with the tray."

"I believe that, for you never see anyone who is in your way," the housekeeper told him severely. "This is the third time this week, young man, that you have managed to break something with your carelessness. You know you've been ordered to stay away from that banister before you break something more valuable than a tea tray."

"But it is—"

"Perhaps it will be your leg that is broken next time," Lucy said with the sternness that only an older sister could display to an erring sibling. *"Why* will you not learn to behave?"

Brushing crumbs from the maid, who was attempting to pick up the broken china, Mrs. Hemphill said, "Now, do stop crying, Sukey. I don't believe you're really hurt, and no one blames you for what happened to the tea tray. We all know where the true blame lies. Just run along, change your skirt, and bring us fresh tea. Then you may clean up the hall."

As the girl completed gathering up the broken china and hurried to the kitchen, still sniffling, Jonathan Murray saw this as an opportunity to make the point he had been trying to make.

"You see, Miss—I do not think I recall your name—"

"Sampson."

"Miss Sampson, I know you will agree with me that the lad is at an age where he needs someone with a strong hand to keep him in line. He takes too many liberties in an all-female household. So it is important that we find him a new tutor without delay."

"I doubt a young boy will be harder to handle than

40

a lively young girl, and I was equal to that. I shall be happy to act as his tutor while we are here."

"Why should I have to have a tutor?" Giles demanded. Having scrubbed his hands as free of crumbs as possible, to the further detriment of his already badly mussed breeches, he followed the others into the drawing room, where he threw himself down on the sofa, transferring a large portion of the tea-tray debris to its worn velvet cushions.

"They can't teach me anything," he continued.

"They might be able to do so if you would give them a bit more of your attention, instead of sneaking away when he wasn't looking," Lucy stated.

"Why should I give them any attention, when they don't pay me any heed? That old Rogers spent all his time trying to flirt with the next door maids."

"What?" Mrs. Hemphill's exclamation was almost a shriek.

"He did, whenever one of them came out of the house. And they came out a lot, knowing he was here. Besides, he smoked cigarillos all the time that he was supposed to be hearing my lessons. And I didn't like the smell, so it was hard for me to study as I should." He didn't add what the others already knew or suspected, that Lucy's description of his behavior was accurate and that he would have managed to do little studying regardless of his tutor's predilection for tobacco and flirtation.

"It is a very good thing that you don't like it," Miss Sampson told him, seating herself on the far end of the sofa and critically eyeing the damage being done to the cushions, thinking that if she took over the boy's education she would have to teach him more than his daily lessons, "for smoking is a nasty habit. You know that no gentleman would indulge in it."

Surreptitiously, the captain adjusted his coat to hide

41

the pocket which held his own supply of cigarillos; smoking was a habit to which he had become addicted while serving in Spain. Somehow, he gained the feeling that, if she should catch sight of them, the redoubtable woman would take away his cigarillos, as if he were a child with forbidden sweets—or even take him by the ear and make him throw them out the door. Somehow, she reminded him of a nanny who had made his childhood miserable.

"I ain't a gentleman," Giles stated, "but I still don't like it, so I wouldn't do it."

"You ought not to say 'ain't,' " Sammy told him, ready to begin her lessons at once. "Although I realize the word is quite acceptable in some circles. But we can work toward improving your grammar while you're learning other subjects you need to know. And I can assure you that, during school hours—or at any other time, for that matter—I shall neither smoke cigarillos nor attempt to set up flirtations with anyone. Those appear to be your principal objections to a tutor."

"I was aware that the man smoked in his bedchamber," Mrs. Hemphill said in a censorious tone, while Giles went into a wild fit of laughter at the thought of the prim, bespectacled Miss Sampson indulging in scandalous behavior of any sort, "because the smell of the smoke was always in the hangings of the room, despite the fact that the maids aired them every week he was here. Had I known that he was indulging in such a filthy habit in Giles's presence, you may be certain he would have been out of the house much sooner. Not to mention what Giles says about his flirting with the next door maids. I didn't know of that, either, and I'm sorry that such a bad example was set for the boy. We have nothing of that in *this* house."

"Anyhow," Giles continued his protest, "any number of people do say 'ain't.' And I don't need to have a tutor. When I'm old enough, I plan to be a soldier like Charles, and I won't need to study for that."

"Not true." Jonathan was temporarily diverted from his objections to the newcomers by the need to see that the boy was properly informed about matters pertaining to the army. "You forget that your brother Charles had graduated from the university before he entered the army. Common soldiers need no schooling, of course, for the future holds nothing more for them. But if you wish to get into the Hussars, you could never do so if you were an ignoramus. Nor could you ever become an officer."

"Captain Murray is quite correct," Miss Sampson told the boy. "As much as I deplore the thought of any sort of fighting, I agree that you must have an education if you wish to succeed in the army, as well as in any other line of endeavor."

"I still do not—"

"Are you angry at the sofa, Giles?" Sammy enquired as she watched him kicking idly at the sofa leg nearest him while he argued against the need for education. "Or are you kicking it because you can't kick me for what I've been saying?"

"Oh, I couldn't kick a lady—but—"

"I'm happy to hear that. It might be uncomfortable to try to teach a young man who kicks."

"Besides," Miranda added, "you'll soon discover that Sammy knows how to make your lessons a time of fun. She always did so with mine."

"You mean that *you* had to take lessons?" The thought of any adult having had to study was apparently far beyond the boy's comprehension.

"Certainly I did. And your sisters must have done, as well, I'm certain."

43

"Oh, they had governesses, of course, loads and loads of them."

"You make it sound as if the house was full of them. There was never more than one—at a time, that is," Diana protested.

"Well, it seemed like the house was full of them, but they was—"

"Were," Miss Sampson corrected automatically. She might as well begin her lessons at once, she decided, wondering if she was truly taking on too great a task.

"Were—" He knew the right word, but had fallen into the habit of making as many mistakes as he could do, merely in order to bedevil the tutor, who paid little attention to what the boy was doing, "—all as stupid as Rogers, so I doubt if either of the girls learned anything."

"That's not so," Diana protested. "Merely because I have some trouble with mathematics—much good they will ever do me, anyhow."

"When you go shopping," Sammy asked, "how will you know whether a merchant is cheating you, if you are unable to compute the charge yourself?" She was aware that very few ladies *could* tell if they were being cheated, but it was an excellent argument in favor or more education.

"Why, I never—"

"Yah!" Giles chortled. "If I must take lessons, so must you."

Miranda and her companion exchanged amused glances. It appeared to both of them that, if Sammy truly wished to take on herself the task of supervising the children's education, she would find a plenty of things to do while Miranda was occupied with her writing.

* * *

Aware that he had been overruled—for the moment, at least—in the matter of preventing the visitors from remaining, Jonathan made his *adieux*, agreeing that he would return to share dinner with the family. Somehow, he was resolved, he would see that the beauty was routed before she could do any damage. She reminded him far too vividly of Constance—not in appearance, of course, for Constance was a golden-haired pocket Venus, while this young lady was at least four or five inches taller, had darker hair, and looked to be quite sturdy.

Still, her arrival had brought back unpleasant memories that he thought were safely buried. He could see Constance as she had been at their last meeting. He had answered her summons, for he expected an introduction to the man who had displaced him. That had not been what Constance had planned, however. She received him alone, clad only in a diaphanous negligee, and pouted when Jonathan told her he would not see her again.

"But Jon, dear," she protested, "there's no reason for such heroics. You can't blame me for not waiting, not knowing when—or if—you would return. You know you were badly injured; you might have been killed, and then where would I be—without you or anyone? Algy is rich, and I needed his money. You should be able to understand that. But I didn't realize he would be so dull! But he is, dreadfully so; we could enjoy each other without his knowing anything about it."

"Thank you, no; I have no desire to hang about, making love to a man's wife behind his back, even if she does think him a dullard. You may be right about that, however, if he hasn't seen through your wiles."

She had continued to argue and as he stalked out of the house he could hear her wailing. He was certain, however, that she wasn't actually weeping; she wouldn't have risked spoiling her eyes.

He told himself fiercely that he should have realized from the beginning of their relationship that she wasn't to be trusted. She was far too beautiful a creature—and much too aware of the power of her beauty.

Aside from the fact that he had been taught by this bitter experience—and others that were only a trifle less hurtful—that it was always a mistake to trust a beautiful female, there was another reason for his objection to having Miss Drake living in the household. One which had come into his mind the moment he saw her and Lucy side by side. Could not everyone see that Lucy's blond prettiness was completely eclipsed by the other's more vibrant appearance? What sort of a comeout could the girl expect to have, under the circumstances?

With the captain's departure, the family began to settle their visitors in their rooms. Disliking the stairs, Augusta had long ago taken a small back room on the lower floor that the professor used for his study and, with the help of Mrs. Hemphill and the girls, had transformed it into a bedchamber for herself.

Lucy had settled herself in the room that had belonged to her parents and had recently moved Diana in to share it with her. "Truly, it is too large for one person," she had explained. "I had thought, perhaps, that you might wish to share with me," she said to Miranda. "So that we might have more time to talk. If so, Diana will not mind changing with you."

Oh no, Miranda thought. *I must have privacy so that I can write. It is wonderful that I can have a room where no one can bother me.* Aloud, she said, "That's most kind of you to offer, Lucy, and I'd like having your company very much. Unfortunately, I've never been able to sleep unless I'm completely alone. Sammy can tell you I've been that way since I was a child. I'm extremely sorry, but I didn't think, when we asked if we might come now, that we might put you to such trouble."

"Oh, there's no trouble. Except for the fact that I'll often be late in coming home and Diana must be in bed long before that, she and I get along together very well. It's only that the other bedchamber is small. I fear you won't be comfortable in it."

"I won't mind that. My room at home is tiny. Oh!" she exclaimed, as they entered the room she was to occupy. "This has *much* more room than I expected. That armoire is so roomy that I fear my gowns will be lost in it."

"There's only one thing that you might not like—this desk. When we made up the downstairs room for Cousin Augusta, we were forced to move out Father's desk, so we put it here. Will you mind its being here? It doesn't fit the room, I know."

"Not at all." It was almost providential that she should be given a desk on which she could do her work. She had worried a bit that she might be forced to write upon the edge of a small bedside table or by holding her work in her lap. In either case, her writing would be harder to read. "The room is quite large enough that it may remain here."

"There is one thing." Lucy's tone was conspiratorial.

"What?" She wondered if Lucy was about to divulge some secret about the room, but the girl had quite another topic in mind.

"You mustn't tell Sammy." She lowered her voice

still further. "My sense of mathematics is as weak as Diana's—but with the Season getting under way, *I* can't spend my time on lessons."

"Very well, I promise not to tell," Miranda told her, laughing.

"Oh, I'm so happy that you could come." Lucy hugged her and Miranda returned the embrace.

"And I'm happy to be here."

With Miranda's agreement to keep the desk, Lucy was satisfied. And since Sammy was equally delighted with a small but neat room they had planned for her, the visitors felt quite at home.

Jonathan was not certain that he would be welcome if he returned to the Owens house for dinner, but he had said he could come, so he made his way there. He still believed he had been right in objecting to Miranda Drake's living in the house, if for no other reason than that she put Lucy's blond prettiness completely in the shade.

Perhaps he had been too hasty in thinking that because she was so lovely she would be equally untrustworthy. If he studied her more closely, he might be able to tell more about her. *If* he were given an opportunity to do so.

To his surprise, no one appeared to remember their earlier altercation. He could tell immediately, however, that there had already been an argument. Had Miss Drake overset the Owens family so soon?

Nothing of the sort, he soon discovered. Lucy and Miss Augusta, as well as Miranda, had expected that Miss Sampson would sit at the table with them. The companion, on the other hand, declared that she had already accepted Mrs. Hemphill's invitation to share her dinner, and intended to do so. How long this discussion had gone on he had no way of knowing, but it appeared to have been settled just before he arrived.

The family—without Miss Sampson—took their places about the table, with Jonathan given a spot at Miranda's left. Lucy sat at the head of the table, although Giles grumbled, as usual, that this should be his place in his brother's absence.

This was an ongoing argument, and Lucy said, as she had done before, "Be quiet, Giles, and eat your dinner, or you may have it in the nursery if you do not like your present location," which had the result of silencing the boy.

Miranda remembered Captain Murray's earlier objection to her presence, but he made no further reference to the matter. It might have been that he had truly been thinking that the addition of two people to the household would make too much work for the maids, and she wished she could tell him that they were quite in the habit of caring for their own needs. A gentleman would not understand these things.

"And is this your first time in London, Miss Drake?" he asked, interrupting her thoughts.

"Oh no—that is, I *have* been here on occasion. Some time ago, of course." This was a prevarication, but if she should own to having paid a visit to the metropolis a mere month ago, Lucy and the younger children would ask at once why she had not come to them at that time.

"And do you find that it has changed a great deal?"

"Captain," Miranda said with a laugh, "I arrived here only several hours ago. There's been no time for sightseeing."

"Of course. You must forgive me—I didn't mean to sound as if I was cross-questioning you."

"Oh Jon," Lucy exclaimed. "Permit Miranda to eat her dinner. You'll have plenty of time to talk later."

49

Obediently, Jonathan fell silent and continued with his meal. He wished he were seated across the table from the newcomer so that he could look at her without appearing to be staring. Sitting beside her as he was, he could only look in her direction when they were conversing. And she was certainly worth a number of looks. At least, as Lucy said, they could talk later.

When the dinner was finished, Jonathan rose as quickly as he could to draw back Miranda's chair. She smiled her thanks, but asked, "And is this, sir, where we leave you to enjoy your solitary port?"

"No—that is for formal gatherings only, not for the family. And I do not think that port would be particularly enjoyable if . . . if I were left alone with it." He had almost said, "If you are not here," but feared she might think him too bold.

He offered his arm and Miranda permitted him to lead her out of the dining room. How much nicer he was tonight, she thought, than he had seemed when he was attempting to prevent them from staying her. Almost as nice as she had imagined he would be when she first saw him coming toward her across the room. She caught her breath, remembering that she was making him the hero of her new book.

"Is something amiss?" he asked.

"Oh—oh, nothing at all, sir. I was only thinking how kind everyone is."

"Surely it is no surprise." How could one not be kind to her?

"Perhaps it is, in a way. I have no family of my own—no one except Sammy. I'm not accustomed to brothers and sisters—and make-believe cousins."

"Perhaps you would allow this cousin to show you around the garden? It is not large, but Lucy and Mrs. Hemphill have made it quite attractive, I think."

50

"Yes—I should enjoy that very much." Involuntarily, she glanced downward.

Jonathan gave her a reassuring smile. "The exercise is beneficial—or so I am told."

"Then I shall be happy to go."

As they went out the side door onto the tiny terrace, Giles looked after them and started to follow. Intercepting a glance from Lucy, Diana caught his arm. "Don't bother them," she ordered.

"But I wanted to ask Jon—"

"Whatever it is, you can ask him some other time. He is here almost every day. Let him talk to Miranda now."

"But he can talk to both of us."

"No," Lucy said decisively. "You're not to follow them about. There are times when people don't wish to hear what you have to say."

Giles sulked, but subsided. Unaware of this, Jonathan was handing Miranda down the shallow steps which led to the garden.

"Oh, what is that which smells so sweetly?" she asked, sniffing the air.

"Lily-of-the-valley." He bent down to the sheltered corner near the steps and broke off several stems. The touch of her hand as he placed the blossoms in it was galvanic. He almost dropped the stems as her hand closed over them.

Miranda caught her breath as Jonathan touched her. Then she bent her head and inhaled the fragrance of the flowers. "Like a bit of heaven," she said softly, not quite certain whether she meant the blossoms or his presence.

"You're quite right—although I doubt I could have said it so poetically."

She bit her lip, thinking she must be careful to say nothing which would reveal her profession as a writer.

The gentleman's presence was doing odd things to her senses. "Let's go on," she suggested. "I think I see a bench just ahead."

"Yes, in the arbor." He led her to it and seated himself at her side. There were many things he would like to say to her, but he reminded himself that he had met this lovely creature only today, and speaking too quickly might frighten her. Seeking a safe subject, he said, "You must allow me to show you some of London while you are here."

Anywhere, with you. She caught herself from saying the words aloud, and substituted, "Thank you. That would be very nice," forgetting for the moment that her reason for coming to London was to finish her novel.

Jonathan began listing a number of the showplaces in the city, not caring what she might wish to see. Anything she wished would please him, as long as he could be at her side. When Miranda owned that she had seen nothing of any great importance, he promised to take her about as often as she would agree to go.

A sharp breeze made Miranda shiver, despite the warmth she had felt in his presence, and she looked about her. "It—is quite dark," she remarked in surprise.

"Yes—so it is. I shouldn't have kept you here so long." He rose, taking her hand which did not hold the flowers, and drew her to her feet. He kept her hand in his as they walked the short distance to the door through which they had come out, both certain this must be the loveliest garden in the world.

As they closed the door behind them, he drew her fingers to his lips, then dropped her hand as they strolled into the drawing room where the others were awaiting them.

Chapter Five

"I had thought it would be much simpler for me to stay here in London while I wrote this new story to take to the Warringtons," Miranda said fretfully to herself. "But I was never more mistaken in my life."

The room to herself was not quite the boon she had imagined. It seemed that no sooner had she taken her pen and paper from the drawer where she had secreted them and begun to write than someone rapped upon her door, forcing her to hide them again quickly. The younger children seemed to be fascinated by the presence of a cousin they scarcely knew, and wanted her to play games or accompany them upon their walks.

Even when they were safely in the schoolroom, Sammy having bullocked Diana into a further study of mathematics, Lucy took their place. She was always eager either to ask questions of her older cousin—questions that frequently caused Miranda to think that the young lady was far more sophisticated than she—or to display the latest creations the *couturière* had sent home.

Praising Lucy and her new wardrobe offered no problem. There was no shortage of funds for her comeout, and Charles, as if attempting to make up for his neglect of the children during the past years, had written that she was to have everything new, from carriage dresses to ballgowns. Lucy had, of course, been prompt to avail herself of this offer on her brother's part.

Clad in one of the white gowns which were *de rigueur* for a young lady in her first Season, Lucy, with her pale golden hair and pink-and-white complexion, looked exactly like a Christmas angel, and Miranda was quick to tell her so. " 'Tis fortunate for you that this is Spring and not Christmastime, or you might find yourself hung over the mantelpiece rather than being invited to the best parties of the Season."

Lucy blushed at the compliment, but laughed and said, "What a deal of nonsense you talk at times, Miranda. Who ever heard of a brown-eyed angel?"

"Not being closely enough acquainted with angels to see the color of their eyes, I don't know of any reason why one couldn't have brown eyes," her cousin said warmly. "But I still mean what I say, and I'm certain, at least, that you will be the **belle** of every ball you attend this Season."

"Now that you're here in London, why don't you plan to have a Season as well?"

"I? Never," Miranda told her firmly, clutching at a reason for avoiding more of these calls and visits which were already robbing her of so much time that she had planned to spend at her writing. "I'm far too old."

"Two-and-twenty is not *old,*" Lucy said loyally, although the five-year span between her age and Miranda's seemed almost a lifetime to her. Still, it was not *too* old for her cousin to have a London Season— something she could remember when she returned home.

As it was, there was little for Miranda to do here; she didn't go to museums or to look at the famous places, such as the Tower, which customarily interested visitors, who were curious about its history and about the famous people who had either lived or been imprisoned here. Many of them sketched the forbidding buildings or the warders in their quaint uniforms. Miranda wasn't interested in doing that. Of course, Lucy told herself, *she* would not have been interested in such occupations, but so many people were that she had thought it might be something Miranda would like to do. When questioned, Miranda only shook her head.

Her attitude confused Lucy. Aside from her cousins, she had no other friends in the city with whom she might pay calls. Since Miranda had come so far to pay her cousins a visit, Lucy thought it quite unfair if Miranda were allowed to become bored merely sitting at home or fending off the children's questions while she went out to all those interesting parties and routs.

"I am quite certain that, if I were to ask her to do so, Lady Smallwood would be quite willing to sponsor you, as well," she continued her argument. "She likes you—you know that she does."

"I know she has been kind to me since I came here, but that's merely because I'm your cousin," Miranda replied. "And it's almost impossible for her to refuse whatever you ask of her, as I am certain it is with everyone. So she has permitted you to tease her into including me in some of your invitations and drives."

"No, I'm certain she likes you."

"Perhaps she does. I like her ladyship, as well. But there's no reason whatever that she should consider doing anything more than that; she doesn't know anything about me, after all."

"What is there to know? You're my cousin; your family was a good one."

"That's true enough, and as far as being kind to me

55

is concerned, doubtless our relationship would suffice. But sponsoring me, a complete stranger to her, for a London Season would be a far different matter than it is with you, and I doubt very much if Lady Smallwood would wish it—even if I did so. And I do not wish for it, Lucy, truly I do not."

Lucy continued to tease her to consider a Season, and Miranda to refuse to think of agreeing, telling the other young lady that she merely planned to be in London for a short time and, although she had found she must have several more gowns, she would hardly have the time now to plan a proper wardrobe for the demands of a Season.

"It is a pity, Lucy, that I am not one of those who can refuse you nothing. It is difficult for me, I own, but not impossible to say 'no.' In most cases, I should do as you wish, but a London Season is not what I wish from life. I am certain, too, that I could not manage to go to all the places you plan to attend. It would tire me, making calls for most of the day, then dancing all night."

"No, Miranda, you would soon find that you could manage quite well. All you must do is sleep a bit later in the mornings. I vow that you are about before the servants are awake. That isn't necessary."

"It is for me, Lucy. I'm in the habit of early rising; even if I tried to do so, I wouldn't be able to sleep till noon, as you often do. Which reminds me, you've been saying that you're expected to attend a Venetian breakfast tomorrow. How will you possibly be able to remain as late as you customarily do at a dance to-night and still rise in time for breakfast? Even you will be too tired before that is over."

"Miranda, you goose! A Venetian breakfast doesn't take place in the morning."

"Then when does it take place, for goodness sake?"

"The time can be different. It quite depends upon the hostess. The one Mrs. Franken is giving tomorrow will begin at three o'clock."

"In the *afternoon?*" Miranda turned to stare at Lucy, wondering if her cousin was serious or was making a game of the country bumpkin.

Lucy, of course, was completely serious. "Naturally—for Mrs. Franken wishes to give everyone time to arrive and enjoy her gardens. And it will doubtless continue until six or seven. Just in time for everyone to return home and dress for the evening. So you see, it won't be too late for you. Please say you'll come. I think you would enjoy it."

"No, my dear, it all sounds too much for me to think of doing. Merely allow me to enjoy being here with you." The reply, spoken in a tone which brooked no contradiction, sent a disappointed Lucy off to make her own preparations for going out.

"Nor do I have the time to waste on such fripperies, when I should be working," Miranda said to Sammy, when they were alone.

"No, I suppose you do not," Miss Sampson agreed slowly, "for I know how much your work means to you. But I wish you would at least take the time to have a part in some of the affairs to which your cousin wants to take you while we are in London."

Writing was all very well, and she had always been in whole-hearted support of her former student's plans to continue with her work. A mind as clever as Miranda's would never be satisfied with just the frivolities of London life, as she was certain that Lucy's would always be. Still, writing—as Miranda planned to do it—could be a lonely life indeed, and Sammy wanted something more than that for her.

Because of her friendship with the young girl—now a young lady, Sammy was forced to own—her own spinsterhood had not been an unpleasant one. But she feared that once she was gone, Miranda would have no one to help ease the loneliness of her later years. She showed no inclination toward falling in love, nor had she ever made any close friends. What sort of future would she have?

Sammy stifled a sigh as she heard Miranda say, "Oh, I've been going about from time to time, as you know, but the trouble with all that visiting is that it leaves me so little time for my work. And truthfully, Sammy, it is more boring than I can say to spend hours calling upon people I don't even know!"

As much as Sammy might have wished for Miranda to go about more, she could understand her friend's disinterest in affairs such as these. "Perhaps it is, for I doubt if the greater part of them have any conversation."

"Nothing interests them beyond the comparison of their beaux and new gowns. Those are the young girls. And, from time to time, I have caught snippets of the gossip of the older ladies, not meant for young ears, I am certain—but it is never more worth hearing—about babies or bits of scandal."

"I can understand that would bore you. But you do enjoy the dances, do you not?"

"Well, yes, I will own that they are interesting—at times. But I wish such things would begin and end earlier than they do. The balls are even worse than these so-called 'breakfasts' which take place in mid-afternoon, such as this one Lucy has been plaguing me to attend with her."

"Breakfast in the afternoon?" This was the first Sammy had heard of the event.

"Yes, Lucy says that is the custom. And I doubt if you could find anyone in London—at least, in the *ton*—who wished to attend a ball before ten o'clock. It

58

seems that people here spend their nights at such things and their days sleeping."

Sammy was forced to laugh with her at that, and went away, leaving Miranda to the work she preferred to such trivial affairs. After all, the girl had always known what she wanted. Even when she was a small child, she had wanted only to tell her stories, then to write them as she grew older. If Lucy could not interest her in the affairs of the *ton,* it would be useless for her to attempt to do so.

Miranda thought it fortunate that, having spent most of her life in the country, she was accustomed to early rising. Even when she had accompanied Lucy and Lady Smallwood to some rout or ball which had kept her up hours beyond her normal bedtime, she found she could still wake early enough to put in at least an hour at her writing before she had to descend to the breakfast table. However, she was able to accomplish so little in that time, it seemed to her, and sometimes that was the only freedom she was allowed for her work during the entire day.

When she had finished the fifth chapter of her new book, she decided it was time for her to call upon Herbert Warrington and give him what she had written. She was forced to own that she would look forward to seeing it in his newspaper. It would be different, in a way, than seeing the completed books, as she had in the past. Searching for a plausible reason for being away from the house, she had concocted a tale of having to make a call upon a man of business who had represented a distant relative of her mother's.

"He—I think of him as an uncle, though he was actually a great-uncle of Mama's—left me a bit of money, since I am the last of his family," she fabricated, "but, although it amounts to only a little, matters have been so arranged that it must be given out to me a bit at a time, lest I should waste it." With a laugh to prove how far wrong she considered this sentiment to be, she added, "He was quite old, you must understand, and he didn't think that a mere female would be capable of handling even so small a sum of money, I suppose."

She thought the story was quite good enough to permit her to make her exit unopposed, but when she spoke of going, she was disconcerted to have Giles declare, "Then I shall accompany you to his office, Cousin. A lady should not go about London without a man's protection."

While both his sisters stared at him, surprised at this unusual evidence of gentlemanly behavior on the part of their customarily heedless brother, Miranda said, "That—it is kind of you to offer, Giles, but I should not wish to take so much of your time."

"Oh, that is quite all right. It doesn't matter how long we're gone, for I have nothing better to do," he said airily.

"That's not true, young man, and you know it," Sammy told him firmly. "You have an engagement with a set of irregular Latin verbs. Doubtless that is your reason for wishing to accompany your cousin."

Sammy knew where Miranda was planning to go and knew she didn't wish to have any of the children get an inkling of her true destination. Also, she had offered her services in the house and took her work as seriously as Miranda did her writing. "And, if you feel that time is hanging too heavily on your hands," she continued, "you might consider putting some of your things where they belong. These, for example."

She plucked a pair of skates from the place behind a chair where their owner had tossed them on the last cold day of the previous winter and where the usually overworked housemaids had left them to gather dust, thinking he would take them when he needed them again. "I doubt if you will have a need for these before next winter, so I suggest you take them to your room at once, for you must own that they do not make pretty ornaments for this room. And do not leave them in the center of your bedroom for the maids to fall over."

"But if I put them away," Giles protested, "I won't be able to find them when I do need them." The objection seemed quite reasonable to him. He could see, however, that no words of his would serve to move the lady's heart—in fact, he often wondered if she even had such an object—so reluctantly he did as she had ordered. There were times, such as this one, when he could have welcomed the return of the unobservant Rogers, even if he brought back those smelly cigarillos. Rogers, at least, had never burdened him with *work*.

As Diana was about to offer her company to Miranda instead, she was told quite as severely, "And you, my girl, still have a full page of problems which must be solved. You will never conquer them unless you put your mind to the task. There is no time like the present for both of you to do your lessons. So if you have quite finished with your breakfasts, we may as well begin at once. When your work is done, I shall accompany you to the park, so that you may have your exercise for the day."

Bless you, Sammy, for thinking of that, Miranda said to herself. The promise of an outing in the park was enough to divert the children's minds from her so-called "business affairs."

"I should be happy to accompany you, Miranda," Lucy told her, "but, as you know, Lady Smallwood is calling for me in half an hour. I'm going with her to visit some old friends of Mama's and Papa's. Of

61

course, I could put off the visit—but I've already done so once, and you know how much they look forward to my coming. They're not truly fashionable, so I've been forced to put so many other visits ahead of theirs."

"I know that, Lucy, and there is no reason that you should worry about me. It's only a brief journey. I shall be quite all right."

"Could you not delay *your* call until I return? Then I could accompany you."

"No—Uncle Jervis's man has set aside this time for an appointment and wouldn't like it if I didn't arrive when he expects me. He's a somewhat elderly man himself," she explained. "So one must agree with his plans. I'm certain you understand."

Wrinkling her brow as she attempted to think of some way of helping Miranda, Lucy said, "Of course! I could send a message to Cousin Jon. Why did I not think at once of doing that? He really has little to occupy his time, so I'm certain he wouldn't mind going with you."

"You shall do nothing of the kind," Miranda said decisively. "After all, I'm not even a imaginary cousin of the captain, and I'm sure he has a number of better things to do than to squire me about on an errand I can easily manage on my own."

There was no way that she was going to permit the captain to accompany her. She was certain that his sharp—but oh, so handsome—green eyes would see through her story at once. Even young Giles could not have been fooled about her journey after he had seen her entering a newspaper office rather than that of a banker or a solicitor. How much more difficult it would be to foist such a farfetched tale off on an adult more wise in the ways of the world than on the three she was facing.

62

"I shall take a hackney and be home before you are, Lucy," she promised, "and before the others have had time to finish their lessons."

The children began again to protest that they ought to keep her company; both of them could go, they offered, then do the lessons when they returned. But when Sammy told them she was certain Miranda would be able to manage quite well without them, they said no more. They had learned that they could argue with Sammy's directions only to a point, but no further.

Miranda quickly escaped to her bedchamber to change to one of her new gowns, a Clarence blue India muslin, with a matching spencer, and a straw Pamela bonnet for her errand. Knowing that both the editor and his brother were not only aware of her lack of years, but approved of it, she made no more attempts to conceal her youth.

For a moment, she had feared that even Miss Augusta might offer to accompany her, rather than permitting her to go out alone. She had seen how the old lady had frowned and shaken her head at the idea of Miranda's daring to travel about London unaccompanied—preferring to see her leave with a stalwart male who'd see that she was unmolested.

However, Miss Augusta's realization that she herself would be of little protection, added to her dislike of going into the bustle of the city, had prevented her from making such an offer. Miranda sometimes wondered how the lady had thought her presence in the house would be of any help to the children, for she went nowhere with them. Nor did she appear to take much interest in what they were doing.

Was she being cynical, Miranda asked herself, to wonder if the lady had merely used this method of ensuring herself a comfortable old age? Still, it was evident that she was fond of the children; it was only that she was uncomfortable when she was forced to leave the house.

Now that Sammy had fully taken charge of the younger children, Augusta spent most of her time in an easy chair in a corner of the drawing room, beneath the stern gaze of the caryatids at either side of the fireplace. She tatted what seemed to be miles of intricate lace, which was intended for no particular purpose that anyone could discern. What the children described as "oceans" of this lace was packed away, doubtless never to be seen again.

Fearing that the elder lady might feel more than a bit neglected with everyone occupied elsewhere, Miranda spent several moments talking to her, a difficult task, as Miss Augusta had almost no conversation, and what she did say was in such a low tone that it was almost impossible to hear her. As soon as Lucy had departed with Lady Smallwood and Sammy had the others safely in the schoolroom, therefore, Miranda slipped out of the house.

The five chapters, written in her finest copperplate, made rather a large bundle, and she was happier not to have anyone see that she had it. They were certain to ask many questions about what she might be taking to the man to whom her late relative had entrusted his affairs—and she was not positive that she would be able to fob them off with another tale. "I should be able to make excuses very well," she told herself, "but unfortunately, all my wild tales are too Gothic to be believed—by anyone."

Herbert Warrington greeted her happily and took the manuscript from her at once, giving it to a young man and telling him to make haste with it to the typesetter who was waiting for it. "I'm so happy that you were able to bring so much copy," he told her.

"Yes—I'm sorry to be so long in coming to you, but I thought I should wait until I had a fair amount written before I brought you anything. This should be enough for several weeks, I hope—and I shall bring more as quickly as I can. I'm finding it more difficult, however, to be able to write while in London than I'd thought it would be. It would have been much simpler for me to have stayed at home, I think."

"Oh, but you must contrive to see something of London while you are here," he told her. "I realize, of course, that nothing about today's society could be used in the books you write; still, everything you see and hear may be of help to you in some way, and a young lady such as yourself ought to be attending balls and outings, rather than constantly losing herself in her writing. Although I can tell you that I am most happy that you *are* writing for us." He laughed. "I fear my feelings on this are most contradictory, are they not?"

"Perhaps they are—a bit—but you must understand that is exactly the trouble," Miranda said ruefully. "My cousin has been whisking me about to various functions and, although I make excuses whenever I can do so, I must go with her now and then. This leaves me with so little time to spend on my writing. She would take me about with her even more of the time if I did not refuse to go. I must plead weariness to be left alone, even for a short time. A few moments snatched now and then is scarcely enough—especially when I don't wish anyone to know what I'm doing."

"My brother Edward and I appreciate your efforts on our behalf, let me tell you, Miss Drake—or should I say, Madame V?"

"After all, the success of this venture is as much to

65

my advantage as it is to yours. And I should prefer that no one but you knows my true name, if you please. News of that sort spreads so rapidly. Not that I think anyone who works here will meet my friends."

"It's most improbable that they should do so. They don't travel in such exalted company. So you need not worry about their betraying you, even if they knew your name, which they don't. We've made it a point not to leave anything about which has your name on it."

"I'm happy about that," Miranda told him with a deep sigh. "Doubtless you think me inclined to worry overmuch about this matter, but I'm in constant fear that someone will stumble upon my secret."

"No one here, I assure you. For I'm the only one who knows you. Even if the others see, as they sometimes will, they have no idea who you are."

"As I say, I'm thankful for that."

"And as I said, you need not worry. But while you're here, would you like to see something of my shop? It doesn't compare, as my brother informed you, with the *Gazette,* or with my brother's publishing house, but I am happy to say that we're growing quite rapidly." It was clear to her that he was proud of his establishment and wished to have it admired. "And we expect your stories to help attract new readers."

"It's kind of you to say that, Mr. Warrington. I hope it proves to be true—and, yes, I should like very much to see what you're doing." She found it difficult to refuse his request, as it seemed important to him to show her what he had done. Also, she owned to being curious about how her story was translated from the written page into print.

She followed Mr. Warrington into the shop, careful to obey his warning not to brush against anything as she passed. "It is all covered with ink or grease," he said, pointing out several machines as they went by. Miranda wrinkled her nose a bit at the sharp scent of the printing ink being swabbed across a plate, but decided she didn't find it nearly as unpleasant as the odors she encountered in the street.

Chapter Six

In the back room of the little printing shop, Miranda
watched fascinated as a thin, white-haired man swiftly
picked up tiny bits of metal from a long case upon the
table at his side and placed them in a sort of rack
before him. He hardly seemed to look at what he was
doing as his hands flew back and forth, but read from
a page which had been pinned beside his rack.

"Marky is setting type for an article to appear in our
next issue," she was told. "In its way, setting type is an
art; not everyone can learn to do it. I was able to learn,
after a fashion, because I wished to learn how to do
everything connected with my newspaper, but I certainly cannot equal his speed or accuracy, especially
the latter. You see, the letters are made backward, so
that they will come out right when the page is printed.
And that makes them difficult to read."

"I can see that it would be. But—did you say his
name is Marky?—he does not even seem to read the—
and you did call what he is using type, did you not?—
the type he is choosing. Only that paper beside him. I
should think that would confuse him."

"No—that's the story for which he's setting copy.
Newsmen write it for him and bring it every day.
Sometimes several times a day, if the news warrants it.

68

Sometimes we have trouble finding enough news to fill the newspaper; at other times, there's so much that we have to choose which is the most important."

Miranda nodded, although it had never occurred to her that there were people who actually went about seeking the news which appeared in the newspapers.

"As for his looking at the type," he continued, "after so many years, he knows where to put his hands upon each letter, and I believe he can tell by the way a piece feels if he's placed it correctly. And woe be to anyone who upsets those trays of type. Usually, he's the mildest of men, but he goes into a black rage if something happens to his type."

Miranda nodded again, looking at the bits of type the man was choosing. "I think I can understand why he would be overset if anything went wrong."

"Yes indeed. It takes hours, as you can well imagine, to resort all those small pieces into their proper places. And Marky has learned that only he can sort it with any degree of accuracy. Others are too prone to make mistakes if they try to hurry. And if a bit of type is put into the wrong place, it will cause an error in the printed copy. So he won't allow anyone else to do it. And he doesn't wish to waste his time in doing that sort of work, rather than setting up the type. He's proud of what he does, and has a right to be so."

Noticing that the old man stood first on one foot and then on the other, as if his feet troubled him, Miranda said, "Would it not be much more comfortable for Mr.—Marky—I must try to remember his name—to sit down while he is working?"

"One would think so—but he's stood at that rack, or one exactly like it, day after day since he was fifteen years old—and any suggestion on my part that he should take things easier would be considered an insult. He would think I meant he was growing too old to work—that is his one fear. I've tried to make things easier for him from time to time, but he only glares at me and goes on as he's doing now."

"I suppose if he is accustomed—" She realized how difficult it would be for her to adapt herself to a way of writing which differed from what she was accustomed to doing, such as standing at a high desk or leaning over one that was too low.

"Oh, I assure you, he was well trained for that work—and that he wouldn't feel comfortable working in any other way. Now, here . . ." Her guide pointed to another man who was cranking a form which moved toward them across its base as he released the lever. This held the plate which had been swabbed with a ball soaked in ink. Mr. Warrington stepped to the side of the machine and picked up the page just printed, holding it so that Miranda could read it.

This would be the first page of the newspaper, and in large letters in the center column of the page, she read, *"Beginning this week, an exciting new novel by Madame V."*

"How quickly you've done that!" she exclaimed, barely restraining herself from clapping her hands in admiration. "To have it set and printed already. But if I hadn't been able to come today, what would you have done?"

Herbert Warrington shrugged. "That wouldn't have mattered, although I own that I've been most anxious to begin printing the story. The announcement would have been saved until it was needed, as we've been doing."

"Oh—I see." Accustomed as she was to the need to save the pages of her story as she wrote them, it hadn't occurred to her that printed bits of information could also be stored in that way, possibly to be used long after they had been set.

"Yes, it was set in type some time ago—as soon as you agreed to our plan of serializing your story, in fact. We've been awaiting your manuscript, and I sent word back to have the notice inserted when you came. It was merely a matter of taking out a less important story—which will appear elsewhere—and putting this in its place. We plan to run a chapter of your story each week."

Curiously, Miranda reached out to take the sheet, but Mr. Warrington swiftly drew it out of reach. "You must be careful," he warned, and she noticed how gingerly he was holding the paper by the corners, not touching the part which had been printed. "The ink on this page is still wet, and if you stain your gown or your gloves, it will be almost impossible to clean them." He pointed to the ink-stained apron which the press man wore.

"And it would be equally impossible for me to explain how I got such stains," Miranda told him with a laugh. "As you say, I must be careful."

"I could give it to you when the ink is dry, if you like," Mr. Warrington offered.

Miranda shook her head. "Thank you, but I believe I shouldn't take it." As much as she would have liked to be able to show this memento of her new book to Sammy, it would have been only one more thing she would have to hide away, so it was just as well that she couldn't have it.

The children had been well trained, probably by Mrs. Hemphill, she supposed, and would never look to see what was in her desk, but her constant fear was that she might forget to put everything safely away. They always knocked before entering her room, but instead of waiting for permission, they came so swiftly after knocking that she hardly had a chance to hide her work.

The editor would have spent more time in explaining to her the various items about the shop he loved so well, but at last, Miranda said, "This is all so very interesting, Mr. Warrington, and I wish I had more time to learn everything about what you're doing here. Discovering how a book or a newspaper is printed is quite educational."

"Yes—as we were saying recently, one can learn from everything in this life. You think now that this is nothing you will ever use, but you never know. Sometimes what we learn is good, sometimes it isn't—but it teaches us and therefore is helpful in making our decisions."

"You're quite correct. But I can't take the time to learn more today, I fear. I have to reach home before anyone begins to realize that I've been gone much too long and starts to search for me. And I wouldn't want them to find me—here."

"But my dear Miss—I mean, Madame V—you mustn't go about alone. It's not proper for you to do so—nor is it entirely safe, for that matter."

"That's what my cousins told me—not that anyone actually *said* it was improper for me to do so, but I suppose that was what was intended. Nor was safety mentioned. Of course, I had no choice but to come out alone, since I couldn't tell anyone where I was going. And, truly, it doesn't matter."

"You have a choice now. Or rather, you have none, for I shall see you safely home."

Although she disliked the idea of taking the gentleman from the work she knew must be important to him, Miranda understood that if she refused his escort, she would wound his feelings. He seemed to feel so strongly that she should be protected; what else could she do but agree to allow him to accompany her home? Like his brother, he was so good to her.

72

"Very well, sir, I shall accept your escort with pleasure. However, you must promise that you won't take me to my door, but put me down a block before we reach the house. I'll be quite safe there, and there won't be any chance of one of my cousins seeing you and wondering who you might be."

"You might tell them that I'm the businessman you came to see—that would be the truth, so your conscience would be clear."

"But they would then expect you to be able to answer questions about my inheritance. No, I can't involve you in my deceptions. I feel guilty enough about my own lies. It's best that they don't see you at all."

Mr. Warrington protested that she shouldn't walk even one block without an escort, but Miranda laughed and said, "I believe I can persuade you, sir, that there'll be no problem if you leave me there. I'll come to no harm in that short distance. My cousins live in quite a respectable neighborhood. If you don't agree to put me down where I ask, I'll return home alone."

"It shall be as you wish," he assented, and sent a boy to fetch a hackney. As he helped her into it, he apologized for not having a carriage of his own. "You see, I've been putting every penny I can spare into my newspaper. Once it has become successful, I intend to indulge myself in many ways."

"I assure you, Mr. Warrington, that I have no objection to riding in a hackney," Miranda told him. "After all, that's how I came here. You see that I could hardly borrow my cousin's carriage—now that I think of it, she probably doesn't have one, or she'd have insisted that I use it. Which would have created more problems, of course, for I could never have been able to fool a coachman about my destination."

The ride seemed quite a brief one, enlivened by some

of Herbert Warrington's tales of his troubles in beginning a newspaper. It felt as if it had been no time at all until the jarvey pulled his horses to a halt at the corner she had designated. Thanking the gentleman again for his company, Miranda sprang down to the kerb.

Jonathan Murray was following his morning practice of taking a walk to strengthen his wounded leg. The damage caused to it by the Frenchman's sabre had been so extensive that the surgeon at the battlefield had taken no more than a cursory look at it before declaring that the limb must be amputated.

Jonathan protested in vain, and it was only due to Charles Owens' intervention that the doctor had reluctantly agreed merely to staunch the bleeding, then place a simple dressing about the wounded leg, and permit the patient to be transferred to a hospital in London instead, although he protested hotly while he was doing this that it was a waste of time to do anything of the kind. "You may be able to save the limb," he said several times, "but it will be only at the expense of killing the patient."

After several months of painstaking—and agonizing—treatment, the limb had been saved, but the damaged muscles were still weak. The brisk pace he now essayed caused him a deal of pain. However, it was a pain he supposed he would always endure with the changes of the weather, or so he had been told by a number of others who had suffered similar wounds.

Difficult as it was, however, for him to keep up so brisk a pace for any length of time, he forced himself to do so at least once each day, increasing the distance covered at least once every sennight. He felt that it was most important for him to be able to walk well enough to convince the War Office that he was once more fit to return to active service. And that without more delay.

Of late, he had been hearing rumors that there might soon be a renewed outbreak of hostilities between England and her former Colonies in the Americas. There was no doubt in his mind of the result of any struggle with the upstart nation, if it did occur—but if it began before Napoleon had been fully conquered, England would certainly need every fighting man.

This week, he had made his third attempt to persuade the surgeon to say he was fit to return to his regiment—but in vain. Instead, he was once more told he should be patient, should allow his limb to regain its strength, "which it will in its own time," the man had said, and told him to return to him in a month for a further evaluation of his condition.

Patience was not one of the virtues with which Jonathan had been endowed, so he forced himself to this exercise in the hope that he could soon prove the doctor mistaken. He was intent upon the arguments he would use next time to prove that he had made himself fit for battle rather than giving his attention to the condition of the pathway he was walking, until a stone rolled beneath his foot, causing a wrench upon his wounded leg which made him pause, trying to maintain his balance.

He bit back an oath as he admitted to himself that the surgeon was correct and it was not healed as completely as he wished it to be. It was then that he became aware of the attractive young female who was alighting from a hackney coach not far ahead.

It was not—surely it could not be—Miss Miranda Drake, traveling about in a hackney without an escort? True, the young lady was a stranger to London ways, but even she should know such behavior was improper.

Then he discovered that she wasn't alone. The other occupant of the hackney leaned from the window of the vehicle and called, "Miss Drake!" She turned back and he laughed, saying, "My dear girl, do you know that you forgot to take your money?"

Had he truly said "money," Jonathan wondered. But he *had,* for when she retraced her steps toward the vehicle, the man leaned farther and pressed what looked like a small roll of notes into her hand.

"Oh, you're right, sir!" Miranda was laughing, too, as she tucked the money in her reticule. "I was enjoying your company so much that I would have gone off without it if you hadn't called me."

"That was a sweet thing for you to say to an old man. But then, you are sweet, my dear." He patted the hand she extended to him.

Jonathan ground his teeth. The fellow had been quite correct in referring to himself an old man; he was easily old enough to be her father. Why should Miss Drake be riding about London in such a cheap vehicle with a man of his sort and without the company either of her companion or one of her cousins? He doubted that the man could be a relative or even a close friend; otherwise, why had the fellow not had the courtesy to deliver her to her door? No one with a right to visit her would have allowed her to leave him where she might sneak unnoticed into the house. Why should they creep around in this fashion? The only reason which came to his mind was decidedly not pretty.

"When shall I see you again?" the man was saying now, signaling the impatient driver to wait till he received a reply.

"Just as soon as I can get safely away from everyone," Miranda told him, and turned to walk toward the house. The hackney pulled away in the other direction, neither its passenger nor the young lady aware of the man who had witnessed their leavetaking.

Jonathan stood staring in Miranda's direction until a basket-laden woman ordered him shrilly to "make way." He moved grudgingly aside, still busy with his thoughts. There was something decidedly havey-cavey about this affair, he was certain. In his experience, no nice young female would jaunter about with someone she did not wish her cousins to see.

Yet that was precisely what Miss Miranda Drake had been doing, meeting a man in secret. An old man, definitely not one who could be considered a suitor. But had she not said she would see him again "when she could get safely away"? And taking money from him, as well.

Jonathan had told himself from his first sight of her that anyone so beautiful as Lucy's cousin wasn't to be trusted. For a time, in her presence, he had put that thought aside. She had beguiled his senses until he had begun to think her the most wonderful being in the world. When he was at her side, he even forgot his wish to return to the army. Being near her was far more important—was the only thing that mattered.

Now he knew he had been right about her at first sight. She was another one like Constance—or worse, for Constance had at least been discreet about her *liaisons*. She never would have stooped to meeting men on street corners like a common bawd.

No longer walking quite so briskly as he had been doing before he had seen Miranda's leavetaking of the fellow, and unconsciously favoring his wounded leg, Jonathan made his way to Gentleman Jackson's boxing saloon. A good match with one of the bucks who frequented the place would do a great deal to take his mind off what he had witnessed.

His plan to distract himself in this way was a failure. Each time he went over the scene in his thoughts, the fellow seemed older than he had been before. By now, he could easily have passed as Miranda's grandfather—except that grandfathers didn't ordinarily tell their granddaughters that they were sweet, or pat their hands. And if they might do such things, they certainly didn't pay them off on street corners for their favors.

He was brought abruptly back to what he was doing when his opponent cannily slipped a fist past his lowered guard and fetched him a blow on the jaw that sent him staggering backward, throwing his full weight upon his injured leg with a force that made him gasp and cling to the other man for support.

"That will be quite enough for today," Jackson ordered, having seen the bout—such as it had been—and now wondering what the captain had on his mind; what would make one of his best pupils act in such an unusually careless manner? "At least, it will be enough for you, Captain Murray. I think it would be the best thing if you deferred your sparring until a day when you're able to give your full attention to what you're doing. I wouldn't want it said that one of the heroes of the Bussaco campaign had been slaughtered in my rooms."

"Perhaps you're right," Jonathan agreed, and limped off to dress, his wounded leg throbbing from his having thrown his weight upon it in that fashion. Clearly, today wasn't a good day for him to trade blows with anyone who knew how to use his fists—and his head. The fellow he truly wished to feel beneath his own fists was the old man in the hackney. But even if he knew where to find the fellow, one could scarcely go about punishing a man for taking favors which were so blatantly offered.

The person who truly deserved to be beaten, of

course, was the jade—but he couldn't do that, either. No matter what the provocation, a gentleman did not strike a female—any sort of female. And he was not, he reminded himself, even remotely related to her, so he had no right to object to her behavior.

Or did he?

Chapter Seven

He asked himself if there was any way he could have misunderstood the scene he had witnessed that afternoon. What other reason could Miranda Drake have for acting as she had done? It was—or at least, it had appeared to be—the behavior of a common bawd. What else could one call it; had he not seen her being paid off by a man with whom she had been riding around? Could a relative of Charles and Lucy truly be guilty of such unseemly behavior?

"Certainly," he muttered. "Merely because it happens that she is Lucy's cousin does not mean that she is anything like Lucy in the way she acts. And after all, the family scarcely knows her. I know Lucy leaped to her defense when I said she ought not to remain there—but Lucy could never see anything wrong in anyone. She would think everyone as pure of thought as she. May she never have any reason to change."

Telling himself that the wisest thing for him to do was to stay as far from her as he could until he had made up his mind as to the female's guilt or innocence, he nonetheless found himself at the door of the house on King Street. It was only fair to his friends to learn what he could about the stranger, to protect them from her if what he suspected was true.

Welcoming his arrival as an excellent excuse to escape the schoolroom, Giles and Diana ran downstairs to greet him, followed at a more sedate pace by Miss Sampson, who was congratulating herself on having imparted at least a small bit of knowledge to her new pupils. Lucy, who had gone to change her gown after paying calls with Lady Smallwood, came down with Miranda, who had returned home some time ago.

Regardless of what I may think of her, can everyone not see how unfair it is to poor Lucy to have that creature at her side, where everyone will necessarily compare them? the gentleman said to himself, as he watched the two forms descending the stairs.

Lucy was in a demure white muslin with ruffles at neck and hem, and was completely put in the shade by her cousin, whose jonquil-yellow crepe gown boasted slashed sleeves and no less than three vandyked flounces on the skirt. Jonathan was forced to admit, however, that even had their gowns been of the same style and color, Miranda's beauty was such that no one would have given the younger lady a second look.

"Oh, it's so good to see you again, Jon," Lucy told him.

"It's nice to receive such a warm welcome," he replied with a grin, reaching out to wrap one of her curls about his finger.

"You're always welcome here and you know it! But I think it's a pity that you didn't come a bit earlier. If you had been here, you could have escorted Miranda when she went to tend to some business."

He looked from Lucy to Miranda, eyebrows raised. What had she told her cousins about where she had been or what she had been doing?

"I told you, Lucy, that I could manage to do what there was to be done very well without having to bother Captain Murray for his help." Remembering

81

that the man had never wished her to remain here, Miranda could not keep a trace of bitterness from her tone.

That you could do, he said savagely to himself. And you were wise not to wish me about. Had I been with you, you wouldn't have been permitted to meet the fellow who paid you off so handsomely. What sort of tale *did* you spin to the family about this?

As if in answer to his thoughts, Lucy was explaining, "Miranda has an inheritance, you see—just a small one, from what she tells us."

"Very small," Miranda put in.

"But she can't get all the money at once. She must see her man of business at intervals and he gives her what he thinks she should have."

"I see." It was a logical explanation of what he had seen today.

Completely logical.

And Jonathan did not believe a word of it.

Had the meeting been an honorable business affair, as she was pretending, the man would certainly have escorted Miranda to her own door, instead of allowing her to descend from the hackney on the corner of the street, so that she could slip into the house without her companion having been seen by any member of the family. Doubtless, too, a genuine solicitor or banker— or whoever the fellow was supposed to be—would have been invited in to have tea and to be introduced to all her relatives, rather than accepting her promise to see him "when she could slip away." Why did she have to "slip away" to an honest business meeting?

In the future, he told himself, he would have to keep a closer guard upon the witch to be certain her behavior didn't reflect badly upon her innocent cousins. After all, he had promised Charles Owens to watch over the children and see that they didn't come to harm. And it would harm them—ruin them, in fact—if anyone were to learn just what their cousin was doing.

He wished that he might make an excuse to move into the house so that he could observe the creature's actions more closely. But after having made a complaint that the addition of the two females to the household would make too much work for the servants, he could scarcely invite himself to move in with them. He couldn't even offer to make a place for himself by tutoring Giles—even if he had felt competent to take on such a labor—because that Sampson woman had already taken over the task.

Although he called at the house at every opportunity, such calls would not be enough to permit him to see what it was she was doing. Naturally, Miranda would not go out openly to such clandestine meetings when she knew he was in the house or in the neighborhood where he could watch her and tell her cousins what she was about. Instead, she would creep out secretly, as she had slipped away before, while those in the house were occupied with other matters and unable to watch her.

Since he had unfortunately—or stupidly, he told himself—arranged matters so that he could not remain in the house and watch her every movement, he compromised by changing the time of his daily walks so that he could keep the house under closer observation. He was determined that he would follow the hussy the next time she left for an assignation.

Of course, attempting to keep an eye on her meant that Jonathan had to be careful to keep himself out of sight of the other members of the family, as well as of his quarry. It was important that he do so, for he couldn't explain to them his reasons for dawdling about on the street or permit them to know they had a lightskirt living in the house.

Or could he do so—could he hurt them so much?

No, he knew he could never do that. Not to Charles's family, not to those who had become his close friends.

However, allowing them to see him waiting about would mean either telling them the truth or giving the appearance of being a lovesick swain, and neither role appealed to him. The former would scandalize the family—and he had resolved he could not do that; the latter would make him appear more than slightly ridiculous.

Giles was especially keen to notice if he passed the house too many times in his walks and would doubtless come running out to keep him company and to ask why he didn't come into the house instead. This would prevent Miranda from having an opportunity to sneak out, of course, but he wanted more than merely to stop her roaming; he wanted to catch her with her companion. Also, he mustn't appear to be loitering in the area, or some of the neighbors might begin to complain about a man who was apparently peeping about their homes.

He dared not use his own carriage or one of his horses for the surveillance because either would be recognized. Since the sight of an occupied hackney or riderless horse standing idly about the area would certainly arouse suspicion, he was forced to cool his heels and hope that he would be able to find some sort of conveyance if Miranda should decide to leave the house. There was no way that he could hide his appearance, so he increased the hours spent in walking to "exercise his wounded leg"—wondering if there was any danger of laming it further by putting too much strain upon it, and frequently passing the corner where he could see the house without calling attention to himself.

Several days passed without any movement upon her part. When at last she did venture out, there was no other vehicle in sight except the one she had summoned. Jonathan told himself that he might have anticipated something of the sort. He was forced to watch her disappear from sight, and could only gnash his teeth while he waited to catch her when she returned home.

Although her hackney had stopped before the door this time for her to enter, he thought that was because she was alone when she went out and that it was most probable that she would once more be put down some distance from the house. At least, he could expect that if she was again accompanied by her elderly carpet-monger. Not, he told himself, that it was *her* boudoir the fellow frequented—rather, the opposite.

Sighing over the lost opportunity of following her to catch her with her paramour, he prepared to wait where he might see her returning, risking the chance of a complaint from the neighbors about someone who was skulking in the area. Today, he told himself, he would accost her while the fellow was still in sight and inform her that he was aware of her activities.

He doubted if the wench was capable of feeling shame, for she appeared to be unconcerned except for keeping her meetings secret from the family. She did appear to have some feeling for her cousin, however, and the thought of what a scandal would do to Lucy's chances might be enough to force her to leave the family in peace and take her sordid trade elsewhere.

Miranda had received a message from Edward Warrington, requesting her to meet him at his publishing house at her earliest convenience on a matter of some importance to both of them. He didn't explain his reason for asking her to do this, doubtless fearing such a message might fall into the wrong hands, but its wording caused her to wonder. If there had been anything amiss in what she had taken to be printed, she would have expected the message to have come from his brother instead.

Begging, on the grounds that she was unaccustomed to so much activity, to be excused from accompanying Lucy and Lady Smallwood on their shopping expedition, she had waited until they drove away, then sent a servant to summon a vehicle for her, careful not to give the publisher's direction until she was out of sight of the house, fearing that Sukey might hear it and be curious.

The first two chapters of her new novel had appeared in Herbert Warrington's newspaper in the past weeks, but his brother should realize that she was still far from being able to have the entire tale completed. She had brought the next two chapters with her today, so that Edward Warrington could give them to his brother, but she could see problems ahead.

Under the present circumstances, she could scarcely continue writing her new chapters as rapidly as the earlier ones were being printed. She would have to discover some way to give more time to her work and, as matters stood, she could see no way she could accomplish that.

I should have remained at home, she told herself again. Even if I have to depend upon the post to get my story to the printer, I could have sent much more of it at one time.

The publisher, however, had not summoned her to make any complaint. He greeted her smilingly, thanked her for the material she had brought him, and conducted her into his office, aware of the envious looks cast in their direction by his clerks. "I have some quite good news for you," he told her at once, "but thought it better to have you call here than to send the word to your home, where, as you have said, someone might overhear what was said."

"I'm happy that you were careful about what you said, but your message made me curious to know what was so important that you should send for me."

"It wasn't essential that I see you quite so soon, of course, but I wished you to know that I was right about the wisdom of having your story appear serially in my brother's publication. It's already aroused a great deal of interest in your earlier books—so great, in fact, that we can hardly keep them on hand. I've just been informed that we shall be going into another printing of the *Mad Monk* to fill all the requests we've received for it. So I wished to give you this."

He handed her a roll of notes nearly twice the size of the one his brother had given her when she'd taken him her copy. "This is your share of our new profits. And, of course, Herbert will pay you later for the two chapters you brought today."

"Oh, this is wonderful," she exclaimed, tucking the notes into her reticule.

"Yes, we're doing quite well. But I wish that I could persuade you to open an account at a bank," he told her seriously. "It's not a good thing for you to be carrying large sums of money about. Cutpurses seem to be able to smell money whenever it's about. You could be struck down in the street for much less than this. If you had a bank account, I could pay the money into it and you could draw it at your leisure."

"How could I do that?" Miranda asked. "Everyone would look at me askance if I went into a bank alone, for I know ladies don't do such things. Especially to a bank here in London, although I *might* be able to do that at home. I've never tried it. I shouldn't dare to risk the censure that would cause."

"I could go with you to set up the account. After all, I am well known, so no one would be surprised to see you with me."

"You're very kind to offer to take such trouble for me, Mr. Warrington, but that would certainly draw attention to me, which I don't wish. And if I had an account, there would also be the problem of withdrawing funds. I couldn't ask you to accompany me every time I needed some money. And I can't take one of my cousins with me. They'd be too curious, although I've told them that I've come into a small inheritance that's being paid to me in dribbles."

"That was a brilliant idea."

"Yes, so I thought, although I dislike having to tell so many lies. But you need not worry about my carrying the money."

"I fear I do worry—"

"I assure you, sir, that I shall carry this no longer than necessary. Sammy—Miss Sampson, my companion—has opened an account for us in a bank near our home, and when we return from London, the largest part of what I have earned will be deposited there. The people there are quite accustomed to her visits and think nothing of it now if she pays in or takes out money."

"Yes, that's wise, but to have it in hand for so long a time—"

"The account is in her name, of course, so that no one will suspect that I've earned it, but I know that Sammy is completely trustworthy. Besides, as far as *this* money is concerned, I'll probably spend a deal of it while I'm here. The greater portion of my gowns and fripperies are completely unsuited to London, I fear— and all I see here costs so much."

"True enough. Everything is much more expensive in the city. Well, if you won't agree to setting up an account at a bank, you won't. I know better than to argue with a lady who has made up her mind."

Miranda laughed. "Thank you, sir, for owning that I have a mind. Most gentlemen wouldn't believe it possible."

"Ah, but you must remember that I'm not a gentleman—merely a hard-working publisher. And I know you do have a mind—a good one—else you could not be one of my best-selling authoresses."

Like his brother, Edward Warrington thought Miranda ought to be escorted home, and had offered to accompany her. A crisis arising just then within his plant, however, and her explanation that she could wait no longer, caused him to assent to her going alone, but he insisted upon summoning a hackney himself and inspecting the driver most carefully before allowing her to leave. Since no one was with her, she instructed the jarvey to stop at her cousin's door, so that she could hasten into the house, hoping Lucy hadn't come home to discover that she had gone out after all.

As she had said to Mr. Warrington, she hadn't thought that there would be so many prevarications necessary when she decided to come to London. Although it might have been more troublesome for her to send her chapters by post as they were finished, she would have had more time to give to her writing. And her conscience would have been clear.

From his post a block from the house, where he had been whiling away the time by knocking the heads off a number of innocent daffodils with his cane, Jonathan saw her arrive. Had she persuaded the fellow to

89

leave her earlier today, he wondered, or was she becoming so bold that she had allowed him to accompany her home? He hadn't seen her companion, but there was no doubt in his mind that there had been one.

"The next thing," he muttered, "will doubtless be that she will invite him to tea and introduce him to Lucy. Or I should say 'them,' for I don't doubt that she's acquired several wealthy admirers by this time."

He strode to the house as rapidly as his injured leg would permit him to move.

Miranda had barely reached her bedchamber when Martha announced that Captain Murray was below, asking to see her. The girl smiled widely when she mentioned the name, and Miranda told herself that one could scarcely blame her for that. The man was quite attractive.

She revised her opinion several moments later when she faced Jonathan and heard him say without preamble, "I don't doubt it will come as a surprise to you, Madam, but I know what you've been doing."

How could he have learned about her writing? Miranda knew that she had been careful to secrete her work from the servants as well as from her cousins, although she wasn't certain either of the maids could read, and the children weren't given to snooping among her things. She doubted that Jonathan would have any acquaintances among the booksellers—and Mr. Warrington had promised that he would tell no one her name.

There had been nothing in her earlier books to give her away, and, although the first chapters of this new one did carry a description of the hero of her new story, she had disguised him well enough that she was certain no one could recognize Jonathan Murray as her model. Even if he had been recognized, no one would have known that it was she who was writing about him. *Any* writer who had encountered him on the street could have modeled her—or his—hero on this man.

It was more probable that a lady would be impressed by his looks, and novels such as hers were customarily written by females—or so she supposed, since they were as careful as she not to sign their work—but male writers also needed models for their heroes. She wondered if a man might have thought it wise to mention the limp, explaining it as an assault by unnamed bullies.

While she wondered about his knowledge of her work and struggled to find a proper reply to what appeared to be an accusation, he continued, "I should think that you would be ashamed to practice your—shall I say 'art'?—while you are living beneath your cousins' roof."

Who'd have thought the captain would be so strait-laced as to speak of her books in that manner? She knew the ladies of the *ton,* who were devouring her novels and asking for more of them, would despise her if they knew she was the one who was writing them, but surely a soldier who had seen something of the world would be expected to have a more liberal mind. Or was he the sort who seemed to think that a lady should put pen to nothing more serious than notes of acceptance to balls, or at the most, a fragment of insipid verse about some flowers?

Fired with the indignation of a writer who hears her work maligned, Miranda said angrily, "I have been earning my living by my art for several years and doing it quite well, thank you. I do not believe, Captain Murray, that what I am doing is harming my cousins in any way." Of course, she knew it would reflect badly upon them, especially upon Lucy, if word was spread about her writing—but if he was the only one who knew . . .

"It has been a simple way of earning some much-needed money, and I thoroughly enjoy what I am doing. Besides," she continued, "they know nothing whatsoever about it—and they will not, unless you tell them."

Would he do that? she wondered. He would know that the disclosure of her authorship might reflect badly upon Lucy, might even ruin her Season. He called himself a friend of he family and, whatever his opinion of *her* might be, Miranda hoped he would have too much consideration of the others to say anything.

She walked to one of the windows and pretended to align the curtain while she waited to hear what he might say.

Chapter Eight

Jonathan stared at her, hardly able to credit what he had heard. Had the creature no shame? Clearly, she didn't, from her answer to his charge. Saying that she enjoyed what she was doing! Still, he supposed that must be true, or she would seek a more genteel occupation. She didn't look as if she had been forced into her present way of life by poverty.

Of course, one could scarcely tell about such things. Her present state of comfort might be due to payment or presents from—he supposed they would be called her clients.

After a moment, he realized his mouth was agape, so he closed it with a snap. When he had recovered his voice, he replied stiffly, "Certainly I shall do nothing of the kind. I should not think of discussing anything of *that* sort with a young lady of Lucy's background. Or with any other lady. To say nothing of speaking of such things to the children. Tell me—does Charles Owens have any idea of what you are doing?"

It was Miranda's turn to stare at him. What a dreary-minded fellow he must be, to object so strongly as this to what she was doing. She wondered if he felt as strongly as that about all writers, or was it only her work that he disparaged?

It was true that she didn't wish her cousins to learn about her writing—but it was certainly not because she was ashamed of anything she had written. Nor had she any need to be ashamed. Some of her tales might be a bit wild, but there was nothing deleterious about them. Evil was always defeated by the end of the story, and the pure of heart were always vindicated.

She had never thought of her books as having a moral tone, but she supposed that they might be thought of in that way. And she recalled having told Mr. Warrington that she had no wish to moralize! The thought made her want to laugh until she looked at the angry face of the captain.

Her reason for keeping her work a secret was merely because she feared the reaction of the ladies of the *ton*. Not that she would mind what they might say about her, but although they clamored for such exciting reading matter, they might well blame Lucy for having a cousin who actually *wrote* such stories.

Miranda realized that most of these ladies pretended to be unaware of how those novels reached their hands, acting almost as if they thought the books sprang full-blown into being without any human aid. She would have thought that Captain Murray was a man of the world, the sort of man who could accept her work without acting as if it were something unmentionable. And asking if she had told Charles about it.

"No—that is, I have never spoken to him about it," she owned, "for we have seldom had many opportunities to speak to one another, and there was always so much to say. But from the little that I remember of Charles, I don't think he would object."

Miranda had to own that her recollection of Charles Owens was indeed a slight one. He had seldom been at home, and she hadn't visited the family often, so that their visits often didn't coincide. But she remembered him as a young man of great good humor, a gentleman who—except for this war—might have been found roaming the streets of the city at night with his comrades, seeking what mischief they could manufacture.

"I can tell you, Madam, that he *would* object, and most strongly, to the thought of such things going on beneath his roof."

He thought she might saucily retort that her activities were taking place elsewhere, not beneath her cousins' roof—but since the strumpet was living in this house at present, he considered the accusation most appropriate. However, she made no reference to that part of his remarks.

"Rather than what you say of him," she retorted, "I think my cousin is the sort of man who would consider that the entire thing is a rare jest on the members of society who play at being so puritanical. I doubt he's as prudish as you say."

"It would hardly be prudishness," Jonathan said in his stiffest manner, "for a man to be concerned about the danger of having his family involved in a scandal." Charles Owens was a good fellow, but Jonathan knew he was protective of his family's name.

"There will be no scandal," Miranda informed him in icy tones, "unless you plan to air what you know." Even if she became known as the author of the popular Gothic novels, she still thought that *scandal* was too strong a word to describe the effect it would have.

Jonathan's fists were clenched, as were his teeth. He had an almost unbearable urge to shake, even to strike, this hussy—certainly she deserved it. But of course, he was in no position to do anything of the kind. He was not her brother—thanks be to heaven— nor even a cousin. Not one who could enforce his strictures against her. His wish to protect his young friends was scarcely enough to allow him to treat her as she should be treated.

After a time, he was able to say, "Am I to understand, then, that you do not intend either to leave your cousins' home or to give up your way of life?"

This was outside of enough! What made the man think he had the right to order her out of the house? He had tried from the first moment they'd met to prevent her from coming here. After all, he wasn't even a member of the family; he was supposed to be merely a friend of Charles's. From the way he was describing Charles as something of a prudish fellow, however, she wondered if that claim might not be false, for it seemed to her that they were speaking of two different people. And even if this man was a friend of Charles's and of her London cousins, he was certainly not a friend of hers, she decided at once.

She was tempted to ask him if he had read any of her books, but thought he was doubtless the type to condemn them without a reason. "That is precisely what I mean," she said angrily.

"Then I warn you, Madam, I shall be keeping an eye upon you from this time on—and I plan to inform Charles as speedily as I can as to the manner in which you are abusing his hospitality."

Donning his hat with a force that spoiled the shape of its brim, he stormed out of the house, slamming the door behind him and nearly upsetting Lucy, who was just mounting the steps, her arms filled with parcels that she couldn't wait to have sent from the shops.

"What in the world can be the matter with Jon?" she demanded, placing her purchases upon the stairs while she removed her bonnet and fringed pelisse, tossing them upon a chair in a manner that was quite foreign to her, for Lucy was customarily neat in handling her belongings. This time, however, her curiosity to learn what had occurred overcame her usual care.

"I merely wished him a good day when I passed him on the steps, and he snapped at me. He's never behaved that way before! Do you know if he received bad news about his injury? I know he's been hoping to persuade the army to let him rejoin."

"I don't know what it is," Miranda prevaricated, then added truthfully, "The man is completely impossible!" She turned and fled up the stairs.

Lucy looked after her, then glanced through the window to see the captain stalking away as quickly as his injury permitted. "Oh, this is wonderful," she said with a smile. "They must care for each other very much to have quarreled so deeply. And in this short time, too. I *knew* they would be perfect for one another when I first saw them together. I just knew it!"

When Sammy released the younger children from the schoolroom, promising that she would take them to the park later for having done so well at their studies today, she tapped at the door of her friend's bedchamber. She was curious to see whether the news she had from Mr. Warrington was good, or if there had been some problem with the new story. She could scarcely recognize the voice which bade her come in.

Miranda was pacing the floor and, from her expression, the older woman felt that she had been striding about for some time. Past experience told her that she wouldn't have to wait long for an explanation of Miranda's temper.

"That man!" The words sounded as if Miranda had bitten them off.

"What man?" Sammy had never known Miranda to refer to her publisher in such scathing tones. They'd always dealt so well together in the past, and Miranda often spoke of how good he was to her. What in the world could the man have said that would drive her into such a rage that she would behave in this fashion?

Perhaps he didn't like the trend of her new book and had been attempting to make her change parts of it. Miranda had definite ideas about the way her stories should be told, of course, but normally she would listen to reason and any suggestions that she should make changes would scarcely call for this display of temper.

"Captain Murray, of course!"

Sammy nodded her head in agreement. It had been clear from their first meeting that the captain hadn't wanted them to be here. Hadn't he said as much, inventing all kinds of ridiculous reasons why the family shouldn't accept them? Whether he had wished them out of London or merely out of this house, she wasn't certain. And it didn't seem to matter; it was enough that he didn't like them.

She doubted his opinion of them—whatever had caused him to think as he did—had undergone any change since that first meeting. She and Miranda had agreed that, since they had to see him often, the best thing to do was to ignore his dislike, to treat him as they would treat anyone else. What had happened to bring about this sudden change in Miranda's opinion? She wasn't long in receiving an answer to her mental question.

"The insolence—I am so furious that I could scream! Sammy, if you could have heard the way that man spoke of my writing—"

"How did he learn of it?"

Miranda sank into a chair, still glowering. "I don't know. I wondered about that, for I don't know of anyone who could have told him." She caught up a quill pen, mangling it between her fingers until Sammy reached out and took it from her; she then began shredding bits of paper. "Somehow he learned about it; he told me as much. And he spoke as if there were something pernicious about what I was doing."

"How could he say that? I've read all your stories and—although they may be a bit wild at times—I've never found anything *wrong* in any of them. I certainly would have told you if that were so."

"Well, Captain Murray doesn't agree with you about that. He called it a scandal and has even threatened to write to Charles to tell him what I've been doing. As if it would matter so much to Charles; I haven't seen him for some time, of course, but unless he's changed greatly, I doubt that he would mind, even if my authorship became public knowledge. Except, of course, that he might feel as I do, that it might harm Lucy's chances."

Sammy shook her head, not in disagreement with Miranda's words—for she also thought that Charles would not care in the least that his cousin was an authoress—but rather as a sign of wonder that the captain should so strongly object to the writing in question.

"You're correct about Charles Owens, I believe. To him, all this would be a matter for great amusement. I recall that he was reported to be quite a prankster before he entered the army and, although he may be more mature now, I doubt he'd object to a thing like your writing. But I can't help thinking that a gentleman of Captain Murray's background ought to be equally broadminded about such matters; more so than his words to you would indicate."

"You might think so, but you would be quite mistaken in doing so. It would be wrong to label him as puritanical; it is far worse than that. And to think that

99

I used him as a model for my new hero merely because he is so handsome. He *is* a handsome man, no one can deny that. But knowing what I now know about him, how can I continue writing pleasantly about him?"

"Must you do so?"

"It's too late to make any changes in my description. Mr. Warrington has too much of the story, and the man has been described in several chapters which have already been printed."

Suddenly, she began to chuckle. "No—it is not too late! All I need to do is to make a few small changes in the chapter I'm now working on, to show how my Elizabeth learns that she has been mistaken when she looked to him for help."

"What do you intend to do?" Miranda seldom discussed her writing, but there were times when she liked Sammy's opinion of what she had done. This time, however, Sammy had doubts that any words of hers would change Miranda's mind about what she was going to do.

"It is still somewhat early for there to be a rescue scene, anyhow. I'll have to add several more scenes before that occurs. So, rather than having her saved from the monster at this early part of the story, she will discover that the man she thinks of as her hero has been deceiving her all this time, and that his handsome face disguises an evil soul."

Laughing at Miranda's method of revenging herself upon the gentleman—she still thought of him as a gentleman despite his words to Miranda—Sammy went downstairs. At least the temper storm had passed and Miranda would soon emerge from her room to take a part in the activities of the household.

* * *

Giles and Lucy were waiting impatiently for Sammy to keep her promise to take them out for a romp in the park. Martha, whose duty this had been before their coming, smiled gratefully at her as she donned her bonnet and pelisse for the outing. Although Martha was a number of years younger than Sammy, she had long ago come to consider herself too old to serve as a companion for such active children.

Too, now that Lucy's Season was under way, the maid was often pressed into additional service in helping with that young lady's clothing. She was thus left with very little time for what she thought of as normal household duties, not to mention what she called "running about after Giles and Diana."

"How kind you are to give so much time to the children, Miss Sampson," Miss Augusta said in a faint tone. "It gives you very little time, however, to do anything else. I feel I should offer to take them out when the maids are busy, but I fear . . ."

Well aware that the elder lady would never have taken the children farther than their front steps, if that far, Sammy replied, "Not at all, Miss Owens. I really feel that I need some air myself after our hours in the schoolroom, and it will be good for me to keep up with the young people for a time."

She hadn't planned to take the children to Hyde Park. It was far too crowded with people, even when it wasn't the hour of the promenade, and all the children would be allowed to do was to walk quietly along the paths, which would not appeal to them, especially to Giles. Also, Sammy thought they were in need of more exercise after the stint at their lessons.

A short walk took them to Green Park instead. In the morning, it was frequented by nannies with their charges in prams or rolling their hoops, the women visiting with one another, catching up on the gossip of the neighborhood. But at this time of day, most of these had already gone away and there would be room enough for the children to romp without disturbing any others who might come here.

Giles had brought along a ball and urged his sister to play with him. At first, Diana objected that she was too old for such children's sport, but soon forgot her criticism and raced about with him, chasing the ball and flinging it wildly back in his direction.

Grinning, Giles tossed the ball high in the air. Diana reached up to catch it, spun around, and fell face downward on the grass. Her brother and Miss Sampson hurried to help her to rise.

"I did not mean—" the boy began, but Sammy waved him to silence.

"Are you hurt, Diana?"

"N-no—but—" She stared down at the grass stains on the gown, and her eyes began to fill with tears. "But just look at me!"

"Don't worry," Sammy told her. "We can wash them out when we get home."

"Good. I hope it will come clean—and I hope no one we know sees me before we reach home, for I look like some ragamuffin."

Miss Sampson turned to tell Giles to find his ball so that they might leave, but something else had claimed his attention. He had seen a small herd of cows, one of the features of the park. Giles immediately demanded a cup of the milk offered by the attendant milkmaids.

Diana quickly refused this "treat," but Miss Sampson, deciding that Giles had not intended to cause his sister's accident, permitted him to have the milk he wanted. As soon as he tasted it, however, he began to complain that it was warm, not cold, as he preferred it.

"Of course it is, silly. It was fresh from the cow, so it would have to be warm," his sister told him, still a bit cross at the damage to her gown. "That's why people like it."

"Well, I don't," Giles declared. "Next time, I don't mean to drink it. You'll bring us here again, won't you?"

"Certainly," Sammy promised recklessly. "But only when you've done your lessons as you should."

"That's good—old Rogers never would have thought of bringing us here. But then, he never cared if my lessons were done or not."

"It would be best," Sammy said, "if you forgot about your former tutor. But if you *do* speak of him, refer to him as 'Mr. Rogers.' "

"Why should I say that, when we can call you 'Sammy'?"

"That," she told him, "is because we're friends."

She sent Giles off to retrieve the ball he had dropped when taking the milk. Then, with her handkerchief, she brushed as much of the dirt as possible from Diana's dress. There was not much she could do about the grass stains until they reached home but, to save the girl more embarrassment, she chose a less traveled route back to the house.

Chapter Nine

When the door closed behind her companion, Miranda quickly brought out her story, hoping that Lucy wouldn't come to her room to exchange confidences, as frequently happened. But it seemed that Lucy was too occupied at the moment in opening all her parcels and admiring them herself. She would doubtless come and display them later, expecting that Miranda would be as enthusiastic over her purchases as she was. And Miranda was certain that she would be equally so—later. But not now.

Just now, she looked through her pages, making the changes she had planned, changes which would show that her "hero" was someone quite different than he had seemed. For a time, she debated whether she should also make a change in the man's appearance—perhaps make him as twisted as Shakespeare's Richard III.

She scribbled some more lines, then crossed them out. No, she could scarcely make such drastic alterations in the villain's looks at this stage in the story; some astute reader was certain to wonder why such a hump had not been mentioned before this.

Readers were willing to accept all manner of wild tales, as long as one didn't deviate from the original plot. The gentleman's face and form would still be as perfect as she had described them (and the original was still as perfect in face and form as she had thought). These pages would reveal that it was only his inner self that was deformed.

As she penned the scathing words which would change her erstwhile hero into a deep-dyed villain, the greater part of her bad humor vanished. Not that she was ready to forgive Jonathan Murray for what he had said about her work . . . he had implied—no, he had actually stated—that the mere fact that she was writing was scandalous.

Miranda doubted that he had read a single word she had written, which only made matters worse. For him to make such an accusation as he had done was despicable; to overlook his hateful remarks was too much for anyone to expect.

Since she could say nothing before anyone but Sammy, however, about the change in her opinion of the captain without giving a reason for feeling as she did, she could pretend that he hadn't so grossly insulted her. She could hug to herself the knowledge that, in return, she had heaped more insults upon him.

"There you are, Captain Jonathan Murray," she said, as she replaced the altered pages in her desk. "Insult my work, will you? Now all the world can read that you are indeed a villain. You may not know I have done it, and no one else will know it is you—but I shall know, and every time someone reads this, I shall be getting back some of my own at your expense."

So pleased was she by her success in transforming her hero into a villain, Miranda was only mildly irritated when Lucy rapped at her door. Thankful for the commodious desk drawers, she slipped her writing out of sight and called for the other to come in.

Lucy, however, was not bringing her purchases for her cousin's perusal. Already clad for her afternoon's outing and carrying her new bonnet by its ribands of her favorite pink, she cried, "Miranda dear, you *must* come out with us today. Some friends are driving out for an afternoon at Hampton Court—and if you would not feel insulted by our asking you to play chaperon, we want you to come along. Come anyhow, of course, but since all my friends are about my age, Cousin Augusta thinks we should have someone to play propriety. Do say you will come."

"What about Lady Smallwood?"

"She'll be unable to accompany us today," Lucy fibbed. She had particularly asked her ladyship not to come with them today, although she did not tell her true reason—an attempt to give Jonathan and Miranda some time together.

Having already decided that she would give up some time to the enjoyment of her cousin's new purchases, Miranda thought it would do her no harm to waste a few hours with her. Lucy would begin to wonder why she had come to London if she shut herself away too often.

Lucy had been so certain of Miranda's acceptance that all arrangements had been made. An old-fashioned barouche was standing before the door, and three young people were waiting impatiently for her to come down. Lucy presented them as Melissa and Laurence Phillips—clearly brother and sister, possibly even twins, Miranda thought, viewing their identically red hair—and Bryan Haver, whose reckless mood belied his glum expression.

"Are we all here?" Melissa asked. "I thought—"

Lucy had been glancing from the window, but now turned to the others and smiled. "Yes. Let's go."

As they left the house, they encountered Jonathan at

the foot of the steps. "I thought I had been asked to call," he commented.

"Not to call, exactly," Lucy told him. "But to help Miranda play propriety on our drive out to Hampton Court."

Jonathan's eyebrows rose at the thought of Miranda being chosen to add propriety to any gathering. Still, he was forced to own that some hours spent in the company of one so beautiful would be anything but a hardship. And since he was there to keep an eye on her, the wench would not be able to do anything scandalous. Unless, he added silently, the two of us can find a spot away from the others. I should not object to enjoying her charms. But I fear we can do nothing—with this crowd.

"I'm happy to be able to join you," he said.

How could Lucy do this to her, Miranda wondered. But of course, Lucy knew nothing of the captain's hateful words to her. Had she known he was to be one of the party, she would certainly have pleaded the beginning of a severe migraine, but she could scarcely do so now.

Then she smiled, remembering how she had vilified the man in her novel. He could say nothing among these friends of Lucy's; he would be forced to be polite to her and would never know how she had taken her revenge.

Jonathan caught the full force of her smile and almost gasped. She had been so angry with him when they had last met . . . but then, he had been angry with her as well. If she was willing to call a halt to their quarrel, so was he. He grinned down at her, as he handed her into the barouche, then assisted the two young ladies, leaving the boys—as he would call them—to find their own places as he seated himself directly across from Miranda.

"I'm so happy, Jon," Lucy was saying, "that you and Miranda could help us out today. Else we should not have been able to have this nice drive."

"But I thought—" Melissa began, then shut her mouth suddenly as Lucy drove an elbow into her ribs.

Seated on Lucy's other side, Miranda hadn't been aware of her action, but Jonathan saw it and chuckled. The girl was a minx; doubtless she thought he would enjoy this afternoon in the company of her beautiful cousin. Well, he would do so—and he didn't doubt that Miranda would as quickly forget his angry words as he would do.

The sextet lunched at a rustic inn not far from their destination, the driver stomping off to seek his own meal. By the time they were again on their way, there was a deal of hilarity. They alit near the gardens adjoining the historic palace.

"I wager you won't be able to find us," Bryan shouted, catching the protesting Lucy by the hand and almost dragging her with him through the entrance to the maze. Melissa and Laurence whooped with laughter and dashed after them.

"Oh, they ought not," Miranda protested. "They're certain to become lost."

"There are watchmen who will find them," Jonathan assured her. "Or do you think we should go after them—and perhaps lose ourselves, as well?"

There was something in his tone which made Miranda feel that being "lost" with this handsome man in one of the many passageways which went nowhere might not be a good idea. "If there are watchmen to care for them, I think I should prefer to enjoy the flowers. There's too much of a sameness about the walls of the maze. The blooms here are magnificent."

"You're right about that," he agreed, offering his arm, although he was somewhat surprised that she had so quickly refused his invitation to "lose themselves" away from the young people.

Miranda placed her hand upon his arm and permitted him to guide her along the carefully tended walks, with stops now and then so that she could sniff at a particularly enticing blossom. Even here, where they were in sight of others, she felt almost overwhelmed by his presence. If they had gone into the maze, she didn't think she could have borne the feeling. He had done or said nothing that a gentleman should not, so what was it? She felt almost as if her fingers were tingling where they lay along his arm.

She wasn't certain what she would have done if Lucy hadn't suddenly appeared in the opening to the maze, crying, "Jon—hurry! We need you."

"Wait here," he ordered, and ran after Lucy. Moments later, the group returned, Jonathan and Bryan supporting Laurence, who clung to them and dragged one foot.

"I don't think the ankle is broken," Jonathan said. "Merely a bad sprain. But we must get him home as soon as possible."

"I don't want to spoil the afternoon for the rest of you," Laurence told them, his paleness showing his pain.

"Nonsense," Jonathan said brusquely. "We can't have you sitting about like this while we just go our way. Too, it's almost time we should be leaving."

A jerk of his head had sent the two girls running off in search of their driver and a moment later the barouche was at hand. Jonathan lifted the young man into the seat with his injured foot propped upon the seat opposite him. His sister and Lucy took their places beside him.

"No," Laurence protested again. "I can't take one of the ladies' places."

"Don't concern yourself," Miranda assured him. "We'll manage."

"I can sit with the driver," Bryan offered. "Then you can have my place, ma'am."

She thanked him and allowed herself to be helped to the seat facing Lucy, who immediately offered to change with her. "No," Miranda said. "You know you'll feel out of curl if you must ride backward. It won't bother me."

She realized that she had spoken too soon when Jonathan entered the coach and seated himself at her side, using one hand to make certain that Laurence's injured foot was held firmly on the seat. His other hand lay between him and Miranda, and she was suddenly conscious of his hand touching her knee, although she didn't think it had been done purposely.

Her attempt to move farther to her side of the seat brought Jonathan to a realization of his position, and he withdrew his hand quickly, thrusting it into his pocket. Her withdrawal surprised him, but he thought the presence of the others might be responsible for this. Certainly, she was not being coy. As far as he was concerned, he liked sitting beside her, inhaling her perfume, feeling their shoulders touching whenever the barouche struck a rough place in the road.

I don't know what's the matter with me, Miranda told herself. Where her shoulder touched his, she felt almost as if she were being burned. It was the same feeling that her fingers had experienced when she had laid them on his arm. As the journey went on, the feeling spread through her entire being, a sensation quite unknown to her. Odd, but not exactly unpleasant. Still, she wished that it would stop.

When the barouche was halted before the Phillips home, the driver came to help Laurence out of the vehicle and into the house, then returned to drive the others to their homes. Miranda had thought of taking this opportunity to move to the opposite seat, but felt it would be impolite. To her relief, Jonathan took his place farther from her, as if he had realized his presence made her uneasy.

As she made her way to her room, she agreed with Lucy's statement that it was too bad that Laurence had to fall and injure himself. To herself, however, she was profoundly relieved that the experience was ended. It had been much too unsettling.

After a day that Miranda considered wasted as far as her work was concerned, she hoped to be allowed to remain at home next day. Lucy, however, had other ideas.

"Lady Smallwood is calling again this afternoon to take me for a drive in the park," she announced, "and you haven't come with us one day this week."

"I was with you almost all of yesterday."

"Yes, but that was different. I'm talking about your coming with Lady Smallwood. She'll think you've taken her in dislike, and don't wish to be seen in her company. It's not polite of you to be this way."

Miranda would have preferred to remain at home and continue with her writing. She was already far behind the schedule she had set for herself and now had to compensate for the time lost by the changes she had recently made in the story. She considered that the time it had taken her to change Jonathan Murray from her hero into a villain was well spent, but it did add to the amount of unfinished work ahead of her. But— although she was not nearly as certain as Lucy appeared to be of Lady Smallwood's wish for her company—Lucy *might* be correct in her opinion, and

Miranda knew she ought not to displease her cousin's sponsor.

Lady Smallwood had always been pleasant to her and it might be that her company was wanted, although she couldn't see any reason why her ladyship should particularly wish her to come. Still, one could never know what people might think and such a small thing as her refusing to accompany them at times might endanger Lucy's chances this Season, and that wasn't to be thought of.

Pretending a delight at the invitation that she was far from feeling, Miranda quickly donned a new walking dress of a soft rose color, and a matching bonnet which had a medium poke. This, she thought, would not be quite such a contrast to the white Lucy had to wear as would some of her more vivid gowns.

Lady Smallwood, who was far too polite to express her true feelings about having two young ladies instead of one in her charge, greeted her pleasantly. "I hope," she said, "that you've been able to enjoy a few hours of rest, so that you'll be able to join our outing this afternoon."

"Oh yes, thank you, I've rested quite well, Lady Smallwood, and it's made me feel like quite a new person," Miranda prevaricated, remembering in time that when she had refused the last invitation to go riding, she was supposed to have been lying upon her bed, recovering from some of the late nights she had spent with Lucy, rather than calling upon her publisher, and quarreling with the hateful captain—not quite so hateful any longer, but certainly disturbing in a way she could not understand.

Of course, Lucy knew something about her quarrel with Jonathan Murray, but not the reason for it, so she doubtless thought that Miranda had merely been told the gentleman had arrived and had come downstairs to receive him. Expecting that Lucy would wish to learn what had occurred, Miranda knew that, as soon as they were alone, she would have to think up a tale that would explain their quarrel. Of course, they had not quarreled yesterday—but *something* had happened. Something that she could not have explained to her cousin, as she did not understand it herself.

Despite her wish that she could have remained at her work, Miranda soon found that she was enjoying the customary afternoon drive. She hadn't realized how deeply she had missed her country life these past weeks until she gazed about her at the budding trees and the many flowers which were blooming beside the roadway. Of course, these flowers were carefully tended, as had been the ones they'd seen yesterday, and they were not allowed to bloom in rioting profusion as were the ones at home, but the color and the scent of them was the same, and she was able to enjoy them thoroughly.

Riding through the park, no matter how sedately they might be forced to travel, was a far different thing from the rather stultifying morning visits that every young lady was expected to make during the Season. This was an orderly procession along the carriageway, of course, rather than an outing, but it was pleasant to be outdoors. She told herself she should be able to write much better after a few hours of complete laziness. It wasn't the relaxation she would have found by staring out her window at home, but it should work more rapidly after this.

People stopped their carriages from time to time to exchange a greeting or a bit of gossip with a friend, then went their way, doubtless to gossip about those they had just left. Sometimes a gentleman leaned down from horseback to pay a compliment to the ladies he knew—or at other times, to pretend acquaintance with those whom he only hoped to know.

Not only the members of the *ton* but a number of people of lesser importance might also be found in the park at this hour, many of them merely walking about so they could gaze upon the riders. The comments they shouted many times were extremely uncomplimentary, but attractive young ladies such as Miranda and Lucy had no need to fear that any unkind remarks would be made about them. Occasionally, an "oh-er" of deep appreciation could be heard from the watching crowd.

Lady Smallwood merely ignored all of these persons as if they did not exist. A great many of those riding about her whom she thought unsuitable for Lucy to notice received the same treatment, but she poked her driver sharply with her parasol to halt him as an ornate carriage drew up to a stop alongside hers. The plump, pretty passenger of the newly arrived vehicle— was the lady actually wearing paint on her face? Miranda wondered—greeted Lady Smallwood and Lucy pleasantly, and Miranda was presented to Princess Esterhazy.

"Tiens, but you are a beauty," the princess said, as she critically observed Miranda. She was well known for speaking whatever was on her mind, whether complimentary or not, so it was to Miranda's advantage that she found favor in the princess's eyes. "Why haven't we seen you before this? That's not right. You must bring her to Almack's," she told Lady Smallwood. "I absolutely insist. No one will notice Lieven's protégée, once they see her, I'll see she receives a voucher; you have yours, don't you?"

While Lady Smallwood replied in the affirmative and Miranda struggled to express her thanks for the unexpected—if unwanted—kindness, the princess, scarcely listening to what the others were saying, uttered several more pleasant remarks and bade her driver to move on.

"How wonderful for you, Miranda," Lucy exclaimed. "Not many young ladies are fortunate enough to receive vouchers from Princess Esterhazy. She's said to be extremely particular about her choices."

"Nonsense, Lucy—you shouldn't say things of that sort." Lady Smallwood wouldn't have owned that there might be even a tiny fault in so august a lady. She ignored that frankness of speech for which Esterhazy was so well known. In someone so exalted, much could be forgiven. "The princess is politeness itself . . . except when she suspects someone of trying to move above their station. That is when she seems stiff. After all, you must remember, my dear, that she is closely related to the queen, besides being the wife of the Austrian ambassador."

"Oh, I know that she is someone of importance; that's the reason I think it's so wonderful that she's offered a voucher to Miranda. It's a mark of signal favor upon her part."

"Yes . . . I'm grateful to her for taking such notice of me," Miranda said.

If she had told the truth, she'd have preferred to remain home on Wednesday night and add several more pages to her story. But she already knew enough of the ways of the *ton* to realize that to refuse to go to Almack's when she had been presented with a voucher would be to cause a scandal—and especially when the offer had come from one who was so well connected. Not only would it ruin Lucy's chances for a successful Season; such a direct snub to Princess Esterhazy would doubtless reflect badly upon Lady Smallwood, as well for having dared to present the culprit to Her Highness.

Her Ladyship had been kindness itself to an unknown from the country, and Miranda would certainly do nothing to cause her any trouble, nor did she wish to bring any harm to Lucy. Of course she would attend, and pretend that she was doing so happily, when Lucy made her first appearance.

There was only one problem.

"What am I to wear?" she asked. "I have nothing grand enough for such an occasion."

"Miranda, you haven't forgotten?" her cousin asked in surprise. She couldn't understand how Miranda could give so little thought to matters of such importance as beautiful clothing. Especially now, during the London Season, when every lady of the *ton* attempted to make her finest display. "Your new blue gown with the satin slip needs only another fitting."

"Yes, but—"

"There's no reason why Emilie can't finish it in time. You must simply tell her she'll have to have it for you without delay."

Miranda managed a cheerful smile, more for her cousin's benefit than for any delight on her part. "You're correct, Lucy, as usual. Princess Esterhazy's offering me a voucher was such a wonderful surprise to me that I wasn't thinking of anything else."

"I can understand your surprise at the offer. Despite what Lady Smallwood has been saying about her, the princess *is* quite haughty—the greater part of the time. I don't think I've heard of anyone who's received a voucher from her."

Lady Smallwood began to protest once more about Lucy's description of Princess Esterhazy. "She's not precisely haughty, my dear. It's only that she expects to have her position recognized."

"Oh, even with my lack of experience among the members of the *ton,* I was able to recognize that she is

116

someone quite out of the common way," Miranda agreed.

"Well, then," Lucy said, as if no more explanation was needed.

"And you are correct, as I've already owned. I *do* have a proper gown for the occasion—or I shall have it before the ball. The gown you argued with me that I ought to have made, Lucy, although I was certain I would never have need for anything so grand."

"Would it be impolite of me to say 'I told you'?" Lucy asked, smiling, but wrinkling her nose impishly.

Miranda ignored the nose-wrinkling, but returned the smile. "Perhaps it would. But it would also be correct. You did tell me that the time would come when I should want an exceptional gown, but I fear I didn't believe you—then. Now I do."

"Perhaps in the future you'll pay more attention to what I tell you."

"I will," Miranda told her, although still privately determined not to allow Lucy to usurp too much of her time for affairs such as these. Time was far too precious to be wasted on nonessentials. "I promise. That gown *would* be the perfect choice for such a grand affair as a ball at Almack's, and I thank you now for insisting that I purchase it. You must forgive me, Lady Smallwood, if I sometimes behave too much like a country bumpkin. I fear I'm not yet accustomed to London ways."

"You manage very well, my dear," Lady Smallwood said kindly. "If you would only plan to go about more, you would soon have the necessary polish."

This was a polite prevarication, for more polish was actually unnecessary, in Lady Smallwood's private opinion. There was certainly not the least sign of gaucheness in the young lady, despite her choice to remain at home more often than her cousin desired. If only she weren't so beautiful that Lucy paled beside her.

"It's only that I haven't become adjusted to city hours yet. I'm still in the habit of rising and retiring at early hours." This was true enough, but it also gave her an excellent excuse for not accepting some invitations, when she wished to remain at home and write.

"Oh, I'm certain you'll soon overcome that, if you'll only try a bit harder to do so," her ladyship said with a laugh, having no idea whether or not this was so. She'd never known a different sort of life than this; it didn't seem natural to her that anyone would wish to retire before three or four o'clock in the morning, or to rise before twelve.

If the truth were known, although she thought Lucy's cousin to be an agreeable young lady, and could not fault her manners, her ladyship owned to herself that, selfish of her or not, she was as well pleased that the other didn't wish to accompany them every time they went out. She hoped to make a good match for Lucy before the Season had ended; it was her principal reason for sponsoring the girl. It didn't help her to do so when Lucy was accompanied by her more attractive cousin, who—without meaning to do so—often drew away the intended suitors.

Still, Lady Smallwood was also forced to own that Miranda could scarcely help her great beauty, and she certainly didn't put on airs about her appearance. And to have come to the attention of Princess Esterhazy—even if it had only happened because the princess wished to outdo Countess Lieven in the matter of bringing a new young lady to these affairs—was not a small accomplishment.

Two gentlemen were riding toward them, stopping now and then to speak to acquaintances, as many of the others were also doing. They came at once to the side of the carriage in response to Lucy's excited waving of her handkerchief. Lady Smallwood whispered a light reproof at the display of such gauche manners, but for once, Lucy was far too excited to pay her any heed.

"Is it not wonderful, Jon?" she cried, quite ignoring the younger gentleman, who was doing whatever he could do, short of falling off his mount, to attract her attention, but without the least success. "Princess Esterhazy stopped her carriage to speak to us a moment or two ago and has just promised that she will provide Miranda with a voucher for Almack's."

"Indeed?" The captain's brows went almost to the edge of his hair at this news. If it had been the prince who had noticed the jade, he wouldn't have been surprised, for the prince was well known to be a connoiseur of the Fashionable Impure—but Jonathan would have thought that a lady as experienced in the ways of the world as the princess would have seen through her at once.

And while she might condescend to take notice of such a person in the park when she was accompanied by someone as influential as Lady Smallwood, it was quite unlike Esterhazy to extend the offer of an entry to Almack's to the creature. As one of the Patronesses, she made certain that the rules of proper conduct were strictly enforced. How had the jade managed to conceal her true nature from one who was so well informed as the princess?

"Yes, indeed—so now the two of us can go together. I'm so happy, for I've been wishing something of this kind for Miranda. No matter how much I urge her, she goes about so little that I fear she won't truly enjoy her visit to London."

Little you know about the manner in which your cousin goes about, Jonathan said to himself. He

119

grimaced, but Lucy noticed the expression at once, jumping to the wrong conclusion.

"What is it?" she wanted to know. "Is it your injury? I haven't seen you riding until today. Should you be doing so?"

"Oh, certainly—it should be a good thing for me," he told her, although he found that riding a horse was almost as painful to him as walking. He refused, however, to be driven about in a carriage during the hour of the promenade, as if he were ninety years old. Exercise of any sort, he thought, should be good to bring his wounded leg back to normal use, and if it was painful, he wouldn't mind it—overly much—for he expected nothing else. The expression Lucy had noticed was caused not by the pain, however, but by his suspicion of the activities which took Miranda Drake abroad at odd hours.

A quick glance at Lady Smallwood's expression told him that the lady didn't share Lucy's enthusiasm for Miranda's presence. He doubted that she had a true reason for her reserve, save that Miranda would certainly outshine Lucy and would perhaps take away some of her admirers. Certainly, if she had suspected the truth, she wouldn't have permitted Lucy to be seen in her cousin's company.

Jonathan was happy to note, however, that young Colin Matthews, a neighbor who was accompanying him today, had spent the entire interval ogling the completely oblivious Lucy and apparently hadn't noticed that Miranda Drake was present. Of course, it was doubtful that Miranda would be greatly interested in one who was little more than a puppy, but one could never be certain about her type of female. She might consider it amusing to lure the young man into her net—especially if she knew her doing so would displease *him*.

120

Before his young friend could fall prey to the lures of the jade—he must own that she was making no attempt to attract him, but he feared she might do so at any moment—Jonathan pled the necessity of making a call elsewhere, and removed his companion from danger. He fervently hoped the wench would do nothing at Almack's to bring censure upon herself, and upon Lucy, as well, for being her cousin.

He was forced to own that, for the present, Miranda had been most cautious about her assignations, not risking being seen by anyone who knew her. How she managed to meet these fellows when she was new to London he could only guess, but supposed that one of them would mention her to another. He didn't think anyone in the family would have the least suspicion of what she was doing when she slipped away "to meet her man of business."

Chapter Ten

Miranda was much happier when the gentlemen took their leave, for she had feared she could not remain pleasant to Captain Murray for many more moments when she recalled how hatefully he had referred to her writing. Later, she might be able to greet him in a civilized fashion, but—despite what she had done to the hero of her story, who embodied his good looks—and despite yesterday—it was too soon for her to be calm about the way he had treated her. She knew that she was particularly sensitive on this point, but until now, she had heard only compliments about her work.

If the man had criticized what she wrote, it would have been understandable, although unpleasant. She was almost certain, however, that the captain had never read one of her books or that he had the slightest idea of what she had been writing about. He was only condemning her for having written them. This was complete fanaticism on his part and not to be accepted.

Her relief at his going caused her to be unusually pleasant to the others who stopped to greet them along the drive, with the result that a number of beaux were begging her to save them dances tomorrow night at Almack's. Lucy, of course, had not been able to keep the wonderful news about Miranda's having received an offer of a voucher from Princess Esterhazy to herself, and all the young gentlemen were suitably impressed.

Almost any lady of good birth and good manners might receive a voucher from the soft-hearted Lady Sefton. Like Lucy, they knew that only a few were so favored by the princess, which made the recipient a person to be noted—and her favor to be courted.

"I fear you will be greatly disappointed," Miranda told each of the supplicants, "for I've had little opportunity for dancing, and I don't doubt I shall tread upon your toes."

All of them assured her extravagantly that they were certain nothing of the sort would happen, and many of them would have ridden alongside the carriage, were it not that Lady Smallwood, well aware that it wasn't her own charge but the other young lady who was attracting the greater part of the male attention, announced that they must return home, since she and Lucy had been invited to a ball that evening and must rest until then.

"I'm certain, my dear, that Mrs. Westing would be more than happy for you to accompany us, if you'd like to do so," she assured Miranda pleasantly, hiding her hope that Miranda would refuse. "Then perhaps you might practice your dancing with some of these young gentlemen."

"Yes, do, Miranda," Lucy begged. "You may practice now so that you'll do well at Almack's."

Those who heard her promptly began begging Miranda to agree to be present that evening, although many of them knew they would have to make changes in their own plans and go to Mrs. Westing's if she said that she would go. But it would be worth the trouble to be able to boast that they had been among the first to enjoy the favor of one who had been so honored by Princess Esterhazy's notice.

"I thank you for offering to take me with you tonight, Lady Smallwood, although I'm not so certain Mrs. Westing would appreciate having an unexpected addition to her affair at this late date."

"Mrs. Westing always enjoys a crush at her parties. She would be gravely disappointed with anything less," Lucy said.

"That may be, Lucy, but you must remember that she doesn't know me. Her crushes are made up of her friends. It's quite another thing to welcome a stranger, even one who is brought by Lady Smallwood."

Lucy started to protest, but Lady Smallwood nodded. The young lady was displaying good sense in declining an offer which she had made only out of politeness.

"Then, too," Miranda continued, "I think it the best thing that I retire early this evening, Lady Smallwood, so that I won't completely disgrace myself— and you—tomorrow night by falling sound asleep between dances at Almack's. Or even in the midst of a dance, which would be much worse." She laughed and assured all the disappointed gentlemen that she would see them on some other occasion.

Would the few hours she might put in at her writing while Lucy was at the ball be enough time to finish the present chapter? She hoped they would be, for she was certain that Herbert Warrington would soon be expecting more of the story from her. If only she was able to devote her full time to her work!

Lady Smallwood smiled at her refusal and said, "Very well, my dear, we shall excuse you for this evening, for we wouldn't wish anything so terrible to occur. But you must learn to keep city hours."

In truth, she had made the offer only because she

knew it would please Lucy, of whom she was quite fond. She was well pleased, however, that Miranda had declined to come, for Mrs. Westing had a handsome young son, and her ladyship thought that there might be an opportunity to make a match between him and Lucy. She would count the Season a loss if none of the young gentlemen were to make an offer for her fair charge.

When Lucy had gone to her ball and the children were in their beds, Miranda found that she was able to complete her chapter and to write several pages on the next one before the need for sleep truly overcame her.

As she put away her work, she smiled, wondering what the studious Professor Owens would have said if he had known that the desk at which he had worked would one day be used for the writing of Gothic tales. Doubtless he would have been as shocked as everyone else would be if they learned what she was doing.

The desk was the only masculine item in a room which was otherwise completely feminine in decor. The hangings about the bed were richly embroidered in a pattern of birds in variegated colors and matched the window curtains, while the dressing table mirror was surrounded by a delicate frieze of roses and cupids, and the table itself boasted a frilled skirt of white tulle.

The thick carpet was a mass of pink roses. Miranda was certain that this must once have been Lucy's bedchamber and wondered if it had been vacated especially for the visitor, or if Lucy truly preferred to use the larger bedchamber and share it with her sister.

Despite the late night spent at her desk, she was still able to be out of bed early enough that she could slip out of the house before any of her cousins were awake.

Herbert Warrington greeted her happily when she arrived at his office, as he had done before, but was disappointed when he learned that she had brought him no more than two chapters this time.

"I'll be ready to print one of these next week," he told her, "which means I'll need more copy soon if we aren't to leave our readers disappointed. We've heard that a number look forward each week to the perils of Elizabeth and Roger, and are wondering what will befall them in the next installment."

Miranda sighed. "It's wonderful to know that people are truly interested in my characters—and I had fully intended to be able to bring you the remainder of the story before this time. But it's been so difficult for me to find time to write in such a busy household. I think I should have done better to have remained at home, after all, and sent you my material by post."

"But think how much you would have missed had you not come to London."

"That's true. I would have missed several pleasant rides in the park, a number of rather boring calls, and a ball or two."

"Haven't you found them enjoyable?" Mr. Warrington asked. He couldn't believe that such a beautiful young lady as Miss Drake wouldn't wish to take advantage of all the pleasures a London Season could offer. She ought to be enjoying flirtations and breaking hearts, even if that would leave her less time for writing.

"I must own that I have liked the rides and the balls," Miranda agreed. "The morning visits, however, are usually too much alike, and most of them have been spent with people I hardly know, who gossip about others I don't know, so I cannot truthfully say I enjoy *them.*"

"My dear young lady, I fear you are much too critical of society."

"That may be, for many of its members appear to have no other interests than those I mentioned. And had I remained at home, I should have had time to complete my work without losing my sleep."

"Young people like yourself can frequently go for some time without a great deal of sleep, unlike us oldsters, who must have our rest at regular hours."

"That may also be true, sir, but even we must sleep now and then, which it seems I hardly have any opportunity to do. And I am living in constant fear that I shall soon let my cousins discover what I'm doing. A gentleman who is a friend of the family has already learned my secret—how he did so, I haven't been able to discover."

"Not from anyone in my shop, I assure you. None of my workers know your name."

"No, I didn't think that. And I doubt if it matters how he learned about me. I haven't thought it important enough to ask him the name of his informant. At present, he has agreed not to say anything to my cousins about what I am doing—except that he has threatened to write about me to Charles, who is in the Peninsula. Charles wouldn't mind, I am certain, except that he would agree with me that nothing should be allowed to mar Lucy's comeout. But how long I can depend upon the other man to remain silent about me, I don't know. For some reason, he dislikes the idea of my writing, almost to the point of violence."

"The man must be a boor, not to appreciate your work." Mr. Warrington's tone was indignant. How dare the young man insult the work that was so enjoyed by the *ton!*

"Between us, I doubt he's read a line of it."

"Then he shouldn't condemn it. But would it be

such a dreadful thing if others were to learn the truth about you?" the editor asked in a teasing tone. "After all, you know that Madame V's books are very popular."

"I'm thankful that they're well liked; your brother has told me that he'll be able to go to another printing of my last one—and I'm certain it's all because of your printing these chapters."

"Not all, of course. Most of it is due to your writing—which is excellent. But I like to think that it has been of help—as printing it has helped my newspaper."

"That's good to hear—that means we're good for each other. But the fact that I'm writing Gothic novels would be enough to cause any number of people of the *ton* to avoid me—and perhaps to condemn my cousin, as well, merely because of her relationship to me."

"I wonder if the result would truly be as fatal as you fear."

"I'm certain that it would be. I've been promised a voucher to Almack's—not that I truly care about attending—but if the truth about me were known, neither Lucy nor I should be permitted to enter its doors."

"Would it be such a terrible thing if you were barred?" Mr. Warrington asked again, with a grin which showed he was merely jesting. He knew how important Almack's was to the members of the *ton,* and doubtless to Miss Drake as well, despite her denials. "You've just told me you don't care about such places, so being barred from its doors would merely give you more time to write."

"For myself, I don't care, for I hadn't sought it in the first place, nor would I go now, if I could avoid it. And soon I shall be going home, so it doesn't matter what the *ton* thinks of me. But if the disclosure were to

TO GET YOUR 3 FREE BOOKS
FILL OUT AND MAIL THE COUPON BELOW

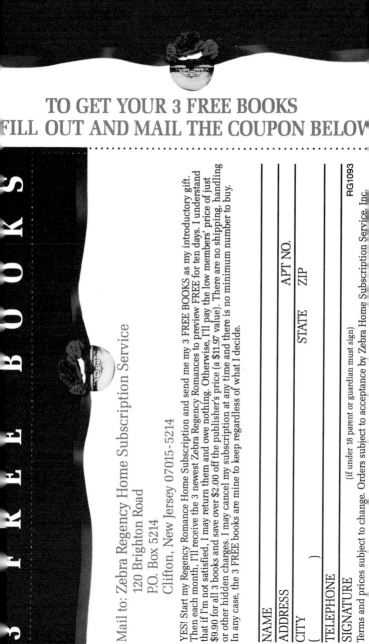

3 FREE BOOKS

Mail to: Zebra Regency Home Subscription Service
120 Brighton Road
P.O. Box 5214
Clifton, New Jersey 07015-5214

YES! Start my Regency Romance Home Subscription and send me my 3 FREE BOOKS as my introductory gift. Then each month, I'll receive the 3 newest Zebra Regency Romances to preview FREE for ten days. I understand that if I'm not satisfied, I may return them and owe nothing. Otherwise, I'll pay the low members' price of just $9.90 for all 3 books and save over $2.00 off the publisher's price (a $11.97 value). There are no shipping, handling or other hidden charges. I may cancel my subscription at any time and there is no minimum number to buy. In any case, the 3 FREE books are mine to keep regardless of what I decide.

NAME

ADDRESS _____ APT NO.

CITY _____ STATE ____ ZIP

TELEPHONE ( )

SIGNATURE _____
(if under 18 parent or guardian must sign)

RG1093

Terms and prices subject to change. Orders subject to acceptance by Zebra Home Subscription Service, Inc.

GET
3 FREE
REGENCY
ROMANCE
NOVELS—
A $11.97
VALUE!

ZEBRA HOME SUBSCRIPTION SERVICE, INC.
120 BRIGHTON ROAD
P.O. BOX 5214
CLIFTON, NEW JERSEY 07015-5214

spoil my cousin's Season, one that means so much to her, I'd never forgive myself!"

"Then we must hope the one who knows your secret may be depended upon to keep it quiet. Although I think you'd find yourself more popular, rather than being scorned when people learned how well you have been entertaining them."

"It's evident that you don't know how rigid the *ton* can be," Miranda said with a laugh. "At any rate, we shall say no more about it. And I shall do my best to have my next chapters to you on time."

Although he was still as reluctant as before to allow her to travel alone, Mr. Warrington had learned it would do no good for him to argue about it, so he summoned a hackney and saw her into it, waving her out of sight.

Her next stop was at the *couturière's*. "You must send my new blue ball gown home today without fail," she told the reluctant Emilie.

"Mademoiselle, how can I make such a promise as that? You know how busy my girls are at this Season. Every lady wishes to have *her* work completed first." *Many of whom are much more important than you,* she thought, but did not say. Even a minor customer shouldn't be insulted—as long as she was willing to accept Emilie's advice about her gowns, as this lady had done. Then, too, her gowns would look much better on this lady than on some she knew. However, they were people of importance, and this young lady wasn't.

"True—and ordinarily I'd hate to make more work for you." In Miranda's mind, a demand for special service was a sign of selfishness. But for this occasion, she would do so. "I know it's almost finished. And I have to wear it to Almack's tonight."

129

"Ah, I understand, but then there'll be so many who go there—"

"My voucher came from Princess Esterhazy." Miranda had learned the power that could be found in such a statement. "And I wouldn't wish to disgrace her by appearing in less than my best."

The words worked as she had known they would. "When you wear a creation known to come from Emilie, there is no danger of that," the *couturière* informed her grandly. "The gown will be sent this afternoon. Without fail. And should the princess comment upon it—"

"I shall be certain to mention your name and tell her I wouldn't *think* of having my gowns made by anyone else," Miranda promised—doubting that the question would ever arise—and hurried out of the shop, thankful that she had no more errands. She returned home just as Lucy was coming down to breakfast, rubbing her eyes.

"Don't tell me that you've been out so early," she exclaimed, seeing Miranda's cape and bonnet.

"Yes, I went to insist that Emilie send my gown for tonight." Miranda was happy that she could tell that much of the truth. "And it's good that I did so, for I could see how busy she was and I'm certain if I hadn't paid a visit to her shop, it wouldn't have been sent today. It didn't seem right to make demands on her time, but I did so. I even invoked the name of the princess to hurry her along."

"See, you are learning your way about the *ton*. But I don't know where you find so much energy," her cousin said. "I won't be worth a farthing until mid-afternoon and then I'll have to rest again before tonight. After all, this is a most important evening for us."

"Yes, I know it is, and I'll be able to rest, too, now

130

that I'm certain my gown will be here. I feel that I've already done a day's work." It was, of course, not the work Lucy thought she had done, but that didn't matter.

She shared Lucy's breakfast, then went to her room and lay down upon her bed, gazing up at the huge rosette in the center of the gathered tester and feeling that she should be at her desk, turning out more pages of her novel to give Mr. Warrington. Still, she couldn't fail Lucy by falling asleep this evening.

She had laughed when she'd said that to Lady Smallwood, but the danger of doing something of the kind was quite real if she went too long without rest. She'd simply lie here for several minutes, at least, then write until Lucy had roused from her afternoon nap.

She was still asleep when Lucy tiptoed into her room with the parcel from Emilie, and shook her shoulder. "Wake up, slugabed," she called, laughing. "I knew it would do you no good to go out so early. Your gown has arrived and I can't wait to see you in it!"

"You have to be the belle of tonight's ball, Lucy. But I'm happy that I'll have this beautiful gown, so that I won't disgrace my city cousin this evening." She had told Emilie that it was the princess she didn't wish to disgrace, but Lucy was far more important to her than was Princess Esterhazy.

Since Lucy was so excited about the upcoming evening that she couldn't keep quiet, her preparations required the combined assistance of both Martha and Sukey, with an occasional hand from Mrs. Hemphill, leaving Sammy free to go to Miranda's room to help her dress. The white satin slip had been skillfully cut so that it outlined her form, while the blue net overdress was made fuller than was customary, and trimmed with a deep flounce of matching lace.

"You don't think the décolletage is too extreme, do you?" Miranda asked anxiously, tugging at the top of the bodice while she craned her neck to see that not too much of her bosom was uncovered. Looking downward from that angle, it seemed to her that she was bare almost to her waist, although a touch told her that wasn't so.

"Well, I'll have to say it's more so than you're in the habit of wearing," Sammy owned. "But it's quite the fashion, and you can wear it well."

"Well, if you think it will be . . ." Still somewhat doubtful, Miranda fastened a slim necklace about her throat and marveled that anything so slight as that could give her the feeling that she was not quite so undressed. She drew on her long white gloves and went down the stairs to wait for Lucy. To her surprise, Jonathan Murray rose and came to meet her.

Lord, he thought, the creature has no right to look so lovely. Tonight, in a gown which displayed her figure so magnificently, with her curls piled high on the back of her head, she was stunning. The beaux would be falling over one another to vie for her attention.

Yet it was her beauty, plus the air of innocence about her despite her behavior, that were her stock in trade. "I've been bidden to escort the pair of you this evening," he said, "as Lady Smallwood finds she's forced to be somewhat late in arriving. You need not worry; she assures me she will arrive before the doors close."

"I . . . see." She hadn't expected to see *him,* and wasn't sure what she should do, after their scene of the day before. She could scarcely refuse to accept his escort when Lady Smallwood had sent him, but his presence made her uneasy. Could she truly depend upon him not to spread the word of her writing, and so ruin Lucy's important evening?

How could the man look so handsome, she wondered, when he was so mean-minded? One would have thought his shabby disposition would show in his face, but it didn't. At the moment, he wasn't even scowling at her, but that could change at any time.

His mulberry-red evening coat was molded to his broad shoulders and narrow waist. And she ought not even to think of how the buff satin breeches outlined muscular thighs. She caught herself wondering how he would look in a uniform. The appearance of most men was improved by regimental scarlet, but she didn't see how Jonathan *could* look better than he now did.

Gathering her thoughts quickly, she managed to say, "I trust there's nothing seriously amiss with her ladyship. I know how she has been looking forward to Lucy's success tonight."

"I don't think it's a serious matter, for her message didn't hint at such a thing—but she merely sent to ask me if I would bring the two of you. I must confess, Miss Drake, that I was surprised when I learned that you actually planned to attend the Marriage Mart, even after hearing Lucy's boast of your important voucher."

"The . . . ?"

"That is what it has often been called, for the hopeful mamas parade their daughters there, hoping to make matches for them."

"I see. As if the young ladies were prize cattle being paraded before buyers, I suppose—"

"I doubt if many of the ladies would see the affair in that light."

Miranda shrugged. "You may be quite right. Well, I certainly hadn't planned upon going when I came to

London, but when the princess was so kind about allowing me a voucher, I could do nothing else."

"I see," he said in turn. "Then you don't plan upon making use of the occasion and attempting to make a match for yourself?"

"It is merely that I had given little thought to such a future. However, it might be that I would meet someone who pleased me. And whom I pleased, of course."

"Of course. Then I hope this will mean that you plan to give up your present . . . activities."

"Certainly not. Why should I do so?"

"But—" He stared at her, open-mouthed.

She knew what he was thinking, and some imp made her say, "After all, it's nothing so bad, is it?"

"So that is how *you* see it. And would you dare to tell a prospective suitor how you've been conducting yourself?"

"Certainly. And, whether I meet someone tonight or at any other time, I can assure you, Captain Murray, I wouldn't consider marriage to any gentleman, unless he agreed that he wouldn't interfere with my present career."

How *dare* this man speak so insultingly about her writing, as if it were something beneath contempt. For two groats, she would go upstairs, refusing to accept his escort to the ball.

Still, she could hardly do that without telling Lucy the reason for her change of mind. This was Lucy's big night, and she would be disappointed if Miranda didn't share it with her. So she would go to Almack's in the company of this—this clod. However, if he said anything more in that manner, she would—she did not know exactly what she would do.

She folded her arms and tapped one toe rapidly, almost daring him to speak.

Chapter Eleven

The vixen's audacity knew no bounds, Jonathan told himself, his jaw dropping as he stared at her. Did she truly think so highly of herself that she believed any husband would remain complaisant while his wife engaged in so sordid a trade as hers? She didn't know the world well if she thought that.

Perhaps she meant to keep what she was doing a secret from her victim—he would consider any man she snared as a victim—yet she had said, "He mustn't object," which meant that she would tell him what she had been doing, and would expect him to accept that.

There were a number of wives in the *ton* whose virtue was, to say the least, questionable. (He suddenly recalled Constance and her offer to continue in a *liaison* with him, as well as some of the others he had known.) But in these cases, the husbands were—or at least, they pretended to be—ignorant of what was taking place as long as the wives continued to be discreet about their *affaires*. No man would openly consent to his wife's being a *fille de joie*.

Before he could recover his wits to the point where he could make a suitably scathing reply to her insolence, he heard Lucy calling to him and looked up to see that she was descending the stairs. On no account must she learn what he knew about her cousin; Lucy wouldn't know such creatures existed, and he hoped she'd always be as innocent as she was now. If he'd been granted a sister, he would have wished her to be just like Lucy, sweet and untouched by the sordidness exemplified by her cousin.

He tried to force the suspicions—no, the certainties—about the Drake creature from his head and to smile. The smile became genuine as he watched Lucy coming toward him. Her white gown, made of Indian muslin—not that he would have been able to put a proper name to the material—was worn beneath a slim overdress of heavily embroidered tulle, trimmed with bows made of pale pink ribands scattered with apparent aimlessness around the skirt and decorated at waist and neckline with wreaths of pink rosebuds, which exactly matched the clear color of the bows and of her cheeks. Several buds were also placed skillfully among her golden curls.

Tips of her white satin slippers were visible beneath the hem of her gown as she moved toward him across the black and white tiles of the hallway. Her long gloves were also white, as was the fan which was his gift to her in honor of the occasion. He didn't know that Miranda had compared her to a Christmas angel in that white gown; if he had known, that would have been one time they agreed.

"So Lady Smallwood has given you the duty of escorting us tonight?" she said. "Poor Jon. I know how you dislike such affairs as these, without even an opportunity for some serious gambling. For I know you won't wish to dance tonight."

"Fortunate, rather," he told her, "to be able to squire two belles rather than one, as most others will be doing." *One belle and one trollop,* he said beneath

136

his breath. "I understand from Lady Smallwood that she'll be joining us later."

"Yes—she sent word to me. She's received several unexpected callers, whom she'll bring with her as soon as they've had a bit of time to refresh themselves from their journey. She says they'll be careful to arrive before the doors close at eleven, but she didn't want us to miss anything."

"And you won't," he answered. "You can depend upon me." *In more ways than you can imagine. That includes shielding you from any knowledge about your disreputable cousin.*

"Of course, Jon. We know that."

Lucy had always been a pretty child, far prettier than her sister would ever become. Now that she had outgrown her earlier tendency toward plumpness, he had to own that she had certainly become a most attractive young lady. Someone to be sheltered and protected.

Then his critical gaze went to the other female. She could have been wrapped in sailcloth, he thought, and she would still stand out against Lucy—or any of the others who would be at Almack's tonight—as the sun would stand out against the dimmest star. And gowned as she was this evening in that shimmery cloth covered with the brilliant blue which made her eyes appear larger and deeper in color than ever . . .

It was not honorable of her to do this to Lucy! The wench had no right to jeopardize her cousin's first truly important appearance before the *ton* by casting her entirely in the shade. Who would notice Lucy when they saw that gorgeous creature?

But how could he tell Lucy she should leave her cousin at home? Lucy was much too fond of her cousin, and too sweet to recognize that she was being overshadowed by the other. She would have thought that he had lost his wits had he made such a suggestion.

As he first draped Lucy's long black mantle with its swansdown trim about her shoulders, then did the same with Miranda's dark blue one, he could only hope that the jade would neither do nor say anything tonight to embarrass her cousin. What if she should make some remark in the vein of their last conversation, to people she met this evening? Still, she apparently had enough decency—or caution—not to wish for Lucy to know anything of her "career," as she called it, so he doubted she would do anything to make trouble.

It seemed she was able to hold her tongue well enough, except when she was with him. For some reason, she seemed determined to shock him, to dare him to unmask her. Of course, he had no way of knowing what she said when she was alone with others, but since he had heard no rumors about her, Jonathan felt that she had not divulged her guilty secret to anyone.

He ushered the pair ahead of him through the doors into Almack's unpretentious hall, saw both of them immediately surrounded by more than a dozen hopeful swains, and stopped for a moment to check his shirt points and the arrangement of his snowy cravat before seeking a place where he could keep a watch on what happened to the pair of them. Behind him, he heard a hearty voice, "Well, Murray, how is it that we see you here amongst the fledglings?" Turning, he found a fellow officer grinning at him.

"I might ask you the same, Hedge. I thought you were still in Spain."

"Caught a scratch so they sent me home." The grinning lieutenant indicated a lightly bandaged hand. "But not for much longer."

"Lucky fellow, to be going back so soon. They won't tell me when I can expect to receive a clean slate. But you aren't convalescing *here?*"

"No—merely doing my duty to my baby sister. You know how it is. But then, you have no sister to dragoon you to affairs such as these. So what's your excuse? Surely you're not in the market for one of tonight's belles? Best beware of them—*they* expect more than a quick flirtation, you know."

"I know—and heaven forbid that I should ever be so stupid as to step voluntarily into parson's mousetrap, which is what such an encounter would be. No, it's the sister of a friend who brings me tonight. You remember Charles Owens? Big, blustery fellow, always a good friend to everyone. And a friend who saved me from the butcher, for which I shall be forever grateful to him. His sister Lucy is making her comeout this Season."

"And you're playing watchdog? I know the two of you were friends, but isn't that asking *too* much in the name of friendship?"

"Not after what Charles did for me. Nothing would be too much to ask in return. But fortunately, he never asked anything of the sort. I've managed to escape that task; I'm escorting her tonight only because her sponsor has been slightly delayed in coming and Lucy didn't wish to miss a moment of her first appearance here. For some reason I can't understand, these things mean a great deal to the females."

"I see." Hedge blew through the bushy mustache he had managed to keep despite orders from his direct superior, who despised a hirsute growth he could not match. "So you *were* dragooned into service?"

"I suppose you might say it's something of the kind. But only for tonight, however—not for the Season, as it seems you must be."

"Nothing so bad as that, I'm happy to be able to say. It's only for a few days more. They've already told me I could leave. Just waiting for the necessary paperwork to be completed—it's late, as one might expect. The war will be over before half the papers from the last one have been handled by these fellows. And what of the other beauty in your party?"

"Miss Miranda Drake." The sharpness in his tone caused Lieutenant Hedge to stare at him.

"Oh, like that, is it? Keep away—private property. You should erect a sign—but what were you saying about mousetraps? It sounds to me as if your foot is about to slip into this one."

"Nothing of the sort," Jonathan said, so stiffly that the lieutenant was certain his guess had been the correct one. His friend must be fairly trapped at last. He would hardly have expected it of Murray—but the best fell at some time or other. He thanked his fates he was above that.

As if he suspected what the lieutenant was thinking, Jonathan continued, swallowing his wrath and attempting to sound less severe, "It is only that I don't think you would have good fortune with her. But you certainly have my leave to try what you can do."

He could make no guess as to what Miranda's price might be, but he would wager that Hedge's pockets weren't deep enough to be of more than momentary interest to her. She might be willing to set up a mild flirtation with him, as she would doubtless do with some of the others who were clustering about her, but those would only help to hide her true ambitions. The oldsters, the sort who would be willing to part with their blunt for her favors, wouldn't be found in the Marriage Mart.

"I should have told her she would have better fortune tonight in Haymarket," he said beneath his breath. He hadn't believed her for an instant when she'd implied she might be seeking a permanent alliance. Not among the gentlemen she would meet tonight. Men didn't come to Almack's when they were in the market for a mistress, and it was doubtful that she would find any other kind.

If she *did* plan to trap a husband, this wasn't the way to do it. That speech, he told himself, was mere bluster on her part. She had wanted to see if she could shock him—and she had indeed succeeded. Not that he would ever permit her to know it.

Lucy had already been led to the floor by a very young neighbor, and Miranda was attempting to make up her mind among several other importunate young gentlemen, all of whom seemed to her to be far too coltish to be allowed to attend dances, when Princess Esterhazy came to greet her, briskly shooing all of them out of her path as she said, "Welcome to Almack's, *ma chère*. I knew I was doing the right thing when I gave you a voucher. See?—that is Lieven's newest find over there—the one who looks exactly like a frightened sheep."

Miranda stifled a giggle at the description, which was much too near the mark to be flattering to the young lady, and curtsied as she said, "It was most kind of Your Highness to include me."

She had been right in her suspicions, she told herself. The princess *was* wearing paint on her face. A great deal of it. But she had to admit it was cleverly done. Miranda hadn't suspected that a respectable lady would do so.

Still, as she looked about her, she could see several other ladies, most of them no longer in the first bloom of youth, who had either made a valiant attempt to recapture that lost—or perhaps never-existing—bloom by diligent applications of paint, or were suffering from the heat. Even some of the younger ladies' faces showed traces of rouge.

Not all of them had been able to apply their cosmetics as skillfully as the princess had done. Doubtless that was an art which took a great deal of practice. It was an art in which she had no personal experience, and she knew that Lucy, too, eschewed paint. Somehow, the practice seemed rather decadent.

"Nonsense," the princess was saying to her words of thanks. "You've brightened my entire evening by coming. And not only mine, I was surprised to see. How did you persuade the so-handsome captain to escort you?"

"I beg—oh, you're referring to Captain Murray? He's a friend of Lucy's brother Charles, so she's known him for some time. Or so I've been given to understand. Lady Smallwood asked him to accompany us tonight, as she's been delayed."

Miranda didn't add that to escort her anywhere in the world—unless it was to a homeward-bound stagecoach—was the last thing Captain Murray would have wished. The only reason he was here tonight was that he didn't wish Lucy to be disappointed. She would have to grant that he had some consideration for her cousin, at least. It was the only thing she could say in his favor.

"But you didn't mind that it was he in the lady's place tonight, did you?" The princess's voice seemed to hint at things Miranda couldn't quite understand. "Believe me, it does a *jeune fille* no harm to be seen in his company."

Miranda laughed. "Lucy, you mean? He would do a great deal for her, I'm certain."

"Certainly I mean nothing of the kind. *She* is much

too young for him to give her serious thought. I was speaking of you, of course."

Barely able to contain a laugh at the idea that Captain Murray would give her a thought—or at least, a pleasant one, Miranda replied, "I must thank you for the compliment, but I can scarcely be called a *jeune fille*, madame. I'm practically on the shelf."

"On the . . . ?"

"An old spinster."

"What nonsense you talk!" The princess emphasized her words with a painfully sharp stroke of her fan, leaving a rather vivid red mark above the top of Miranda's glove, one which Miranda hoped would soon disappear. If it didn't, people would be wondering what she had done to herself. "You're little more than a child. Besides, one is never too old for romance. And you must admit that the captain is *très beau*—very handsome."

"Oh, yes, one can't deny that he's quite handsome." *I was aware of that the moment I first looked at him,* she said to herself. *But that was before I learned just how hateful the man can be, that he doesn't have manners to match his looks.* "One can only wish that he weren't so—so straitlaced."

Princess Esterhazy laughed so hard that Miranda feared for a moment that she would choke. "Straitlaced? *Jonathan Murray?* I doubt if one could begin to count the number of high-flyers he has . . . but then, of course, it's evident that you haven't heard reports of his *affaires*. Not that *le cher* Jonathan is the sort of gentleman who would boast of his many conquests. And certainly never in your presence. We females are never supposed to know how these gentlemen amuse themselves, are we? But we learn of all such things, don't we? And it does no harm to know that a man is a practiced lover."

143

Miranda wished for an instant that her cheeks were painted to hide the blood she could feel rushing to her face. How could the princess say what she had just done? About—about *lovers?* But then, one had to remember that she wasn't English—and Miranda had heard that both manners and speech were much freer on the Continent than the ones with which she had been raised. Or it could be merely that Esterhazy wasn't familiar enough with the language and had meant something quite different? It was possible to give an innocent remark quite a double meaning without intending to do so.

Seeing the blush, the princess laughed again. "Now I see that I've shocked you. You're probably thinking, 'Shame,' but I say nothing more than the truth. Sometimes I forget—you poor, cold English. How such backward people can ever contrive to attain any sort of satisfactory romance surprises me, when they continue to pretend that such things don't exist."

This was going too far, even for a princess. "Your Highness—"

"But you'll see that I'm right. I'm never mistaken about love. Now, I must leave you to these eager young men or I'll be blamed for spoiling your romance." She tapped Miranda's arm once more with her fan, a bit more gently this time, and hurried away.

Miranda allowed herself to be led into the dance which was now forming and hoped that she was making the proper responses to her partner's compliments. Her mind was awhirl with thoughts of what the princess had said. When she spoke of "high-flyers," had she meant . . . ?

She had said that Jonathan Murray was a practiced lover, and she had also spoken of his *affaires*. Princess Esterhazy might have used the wrong term *once*—but she certainly wouldn't have done so three times. She'd been saying that the captain had a reputation as a rake.

Even as sheltered as she'd been, Miranda knew that such things happened. Were even expected, it seemed, among the people about her just now. No one in the *ton* appeared to care if it was a gentleman who was indiscreet. But if he was such a man of the world—and she realized that she didn't doubt the princess was telling the truth about that—why should he be so censorious of her writing? She was determined that the next time they were alone, she would ask him.

Then she realized that the music had stopped and that her partner was asking if he might bring her an orgeat. She nodded and he dashed away, leaving her wishing that she had asked for lemonade instead. But at least the gentleman was happy to think he was of service to her—so she would drink the orgeat he brought, even though she thought the taste insipid.

Fortunately, she had taken only a sip of her drink when two gentlemen came to her side, each asking for the next dance. She gave the glass back to the young man who'd brought it, thanked him for his kindness to her, then turned to the others, telling one he might have this dance and the second that she would dance with him later.

Chapter Twelve

Jonathan eased himself carefully onto one of the gilt chairs which lined the walls, almost holding his breath as it creaked beneath him, hoping it would be strong enough to support him. He wished the management of the hall had been thoughtful enough of their patrons to provide them with sturdier furniture for the benefit of those people who were not intending to dance. Was the oversight intentional—an effort to see that *everyone* danced, even those who didn't wish to do so?

If the chair quivered so much under his weight, he wouldn't have been surprised to learn that one or more of them had collapsed entirely beneath the bulk of some of the matrons who were here tonight. And why it should be that merely standing about always made his leg so much more painful than exercising it he did not know, but was glad of the opportunity to rest, even on a chair whose strength he doubted.

"You can't be tired, Jon," Lucy said, surprising him by seating herself in the chair beside him. "You haven't *done* anything!"

"I must confess to being a slight bit weary," he confessed, smiling down at her, thinking again how sweet she was. Not at all like . . .

He brought his thoughts back quickly to the subject

146

at hand. "But you must remember, my dear, that I'm no longer as young as you. And I will own to you—but you musn't breathe a word of this to the War Office, or they'll keep me tied here even longer than they now plan to do—that my leg, and thanks to your brother for saving it, still tires more easily than it ought to do. But surely, my dear, *you* can't already be weary of this affair?" He would have thought she could dance until dawn without a pause, and wondered at her downcast expression.

"Oh no, but—" She looked enviously at Miranda, who was circling past in the arms of a partner who seemed to be much too busy counting his steps to think of carrying on any sort of conversation. The brilliance of Miranda's gown was enough to tell anyone that she wasn't in her first Season, so no permission except Miranda's was needed to waltz with her. "It is only that—"

"Then why aren't you dancing? Surely you're not lacking partners."

"Oh Jon, you know the rule—"

"The rule? Oh, this is a waltz, is it not? Sorry, my dear. I wasn't paying enough attention, I suppose. But I think your worries are almost over." He was aware that Princess Esterhazy was heading in their direction with his young friend Colin Matthews in tow.

Colin was beaming, but he was also blushing; doubtless it was the result of having to ask one of the Patronesses for permission to waltz with the young lady of his choice. At least he had chosen to approach one of the more amiable ladies. Mrs. Drummond-Burrell would have scowled at his request, and Sally Jersey would have expected at least five minutes of compliments from the young man, so that he could scarcely have reached Lucy's side before the dance was over.

"Miss Owens," the princess said, "I bring Mr. Matthews, who has asked permission to waltz with you. You may do so if you wish."

"Oh yes, indeed," Lucy exclaimed, leaping at once to her feet, forgetting that she shouldn't appear too eager to have a partner, forgetting even that she should curtsy to the princess. She started away, then turned back, blushing as she realized her error.

The young man, however, was equally eager for the dance and, although he was still blushing furiously, gave her no opportunity to say more, but swept her out among the dancers without delay. Colin doubted if she recognized him from their meeting in the park, for she had been far too excited as she told Jonathan about her friend's voucher.

Whether or not she remembered that encounter didn't matter now, however, for she appeared more than willing to dance with him. He had practiced the steps of the dance, unlike so many of his friends, who could only look on enviously as he waltzed away with Lucy. He could, at least, persuade himself that she would remember him as the one who made her first waltz possible.

Lady Smallwood was in the midst of a group who had come into the hall just as the music for the waltz had begun. She had looked anxiously about the room for Lucy, hoping the girl wouldn't forget the ruling of the Patronesses. Seeing that the princess had the matter well in hand, however, she returned to the conversation she had been enjoying with the friends who had accompanied her.

As Lucy danced away, feeling that she was in seventh heaven to be waltzing at her very first appearance at Almack's, Princess Esterhazy slipped into the chair she had vacated. "Well, now I have done my one good deed for the evening," she said, rolling her eyes upward.

"One hardly associates the term with you." Jonathan's smile took the sting from the words.

"Oh, I can be good at times," she told him, pursing her lips in an attractive manner, "although I often find it's much too boring to do so. I might find it necessary to behave at the Russian or any of the German courts, but not here. But I must say, *mon cher,* that it is unusual to see you here. You don't often give us your company, but I suppose we elder ladies hold no charm for you."

"Fishing for compliments, Therese?" he asked with a smile, his tone as provocative as it had been before. He recognized the invitation, but this was neither the time nor the place to reply to it, a fact of which she was quite well aware, or she wouldn't have issued it. Therese Esterhazy was a good friend, nothing more. "It is quite unnecessary for you to take such drastic steps, my dear. Not with me, at least. You know that you'll be forever young."

While it was true that Esterhazy wasn't quite as avid for flattery from gentlemen as Sally Jersey and some of the others, Jonathan Murray was aware that, like all her fellow Patronesses—and like most other young or no-longer-young ladies—she adored being complimented upon being ever-youthful.

She *was* younger by several years than the rest of her fellow Patronesses, but that still meant she was older than many of the eager young ladies who were here tonight. Many years older in experience than most of them could ever be, he was certain.

Now she laughed and tapped his cheek lightly with her fan. "You're not dancing tonight?" she asked. "One remembers that Wellington's officers were all expected to be excellent dancers. Some, I have been told, could dance better than they could fight, but of course, Jonathan, you were never one of *those.* You excelled at whatever you tried, didn't you?"

149

Jonathan shook his head. "In the past, perhaps, but I fear it will be some time yet before I can take the risk of going onto the dance floor. Especially upon a floor as uneven as this one. Why don't some of you ladies make it your duty to see that it's smoothed? It would be only a little thing, but it would add much to the enjoyment of those who come here."

"Don't be foolish. As you're aware, we don't hold these affairs for the enjoyment of these young ones, but to give them a chance to display themselves to the admiring gentlemen. *They* don't mind that the floor is rough or the cake stale."

"I know that quite well, as does every member of the *ton*. Except perhaps for tonight's fledglings. Nowhere else in London can one find such a bad dance floor as you have here, nor such meager refreshments as you offer us. Yet everyone continues to haunt your doors."

"And they always will, since exclusion from Almack's would be the death of a young lady's—or gentleman's—hopes."

"Too right. I sometimes believe that you Patronesses really wield too much power. You know what they say about absolute power corrupting."

"Are you suggesting that *we* are corrupt?" The tone was arch, but he spied a glint in her eye. She would not have objected if he had called her "wicked," for that term had possibilities. But "corrupt" was another thing, and not so nice.

"Never!" he declared feelingly, for—no matter what their private lives might be, and Jonathan was certain some of them would not bear close scrutiny—the Patronesses of Almack's were publicly the arbiters of social behavior for the *ton,* and as such for all of London. Malign the place as he might, he had no desire to be forbidden to come here again.

"That was merely a comment on the present times,"

he explained, "and to its morals—not meant as a warning. Anyhow, to return to the subject we were previously discussing, that of your floor, such a stumble upon my part just now would not only serve to embarrass my partner, but it might well delay my recovery even longer—and I can assure you I'm most anxious to be permitted to return to my troops."

"Ah, but there are other ways of finding enjoyment, even in our little establishment. Don't you agree with me, *mon cher* Jonathan?"

Equally at home in any number of languages, Therese Esterhazy had often declared that German was the language of politics, English that of business, but French alone was the suitable language for romance. Even for mild flirtations such as this. "And viewing what you might have merely by putting out your hand, are you truly so anxious as that to leave London for the perils of war?"

"I can't think of anything that would keep me here for another day if I were considered healthy enough to leave. You'd find me on my way to Spain tomorrow."

His declaration had been a vehement one, and now the princess's fan became a weapon, poking him in the chest. "I think you protest much too strongly, *mon méchant* Jonathan. What about the little Drake?"

"You are speaking of Lucy's cousin, I suppose?" He pretended not to understand. "The one to whom you gave a voucher? I can tell you—" But he couldn't say what was in his mind.

If he said anything at all about Miranda's exploits, it would certainly put paid to Lucy's Season. And might well bring down the Princess Esterhazy's wrath on Lady Smallwood, as well, since she had been the one in whose company the princess had first seen Miranda.

Esterhazy would feel that they had imposed upon her goodwill to obtain Miranda's entree into Almack's, and

151

she would never forgive the thought that she had been used. For the sake of those who were innocent of wrongdoing, he must continue to pretend he knew nothing whatsoever about the jade's activities.

"Well, *I* can tell *you, mon cher,* that the lady is not nearly so indifferent to you as you seem to think. In fact, she clearly has a *tendresse* for you."

"Drake?" he exclaimed indignantly. "She hates my . . . that is, she dislikes me intensely."

The princess laughed merrily. "And I thought that you were a connoisseur of such matters. Believe me, if you play your cards properly, she will tumble into your arms. *Dîtes-moi,* have you not yet made your move in that direction? I thought it was your leg that had been wounded, not your . . . head."

She laughed again, patted his cheek, and strolled about the room to exchange *on-dits* with some of the other ladies. Jonathan wondered if she was telling them what she had just told him, whether they were laughing at him for having lost his touch with the fair sex. It would be exactly like her vixenish idea of humor to spread such a story, if only to see the ladies clamoring to disprove it.

As he watched Miranda being passed from one eager partner to another, however, his brow creased in thought. *Could* the princess have been right about the strumpet's having a feeling for him? A feeling other than the intense dislike of which he had spoken to the princess? *Could* he have brought her into his net long ago, if he had only thought to be sweet to her, rather than telling her how he truly felt about the way she misbehaved?

He had seen no signs of anything other than antipathy toward him, but he could be to blame for that. When he had criticized her for her activities, she had responded with the dislike a wrongdoer would have for one who points out her failings.

Jonathan swore beneath his breath. How stupid he had been! Since she had first arrived in London, he had been seeking some way to get Miranda away from Lucy before she did something to spoil the young girl's life. It wasn't until his talk with Esterhazy that he saw the solution to his problem.

The easiest way to *get* Miranda away was to *take* her away. It would have to be somewhere out of Lucy's circle, of course, but that wouldn't be too difficult to manage, for Lucy's circle didn't include the lightskirts. Why hadn't he seen at once how easily it could be done, if only he put his mind to it?

He would have at least another fortnight, perhaps a bit longer, before he was once more pronounced fit for active duty. That waiting time could be used to good advantage in persuading Miranda to accept his patronage, to set her up somewhere far away from her cousins, so that she would have no chance to ruin their lives.

There was not only Lucy to consider; in a very few years, Diana would be at the age to enter the *ton*. And the *ton* had a long memory for scandal. Even young Giles could be hurt, in his turn, by something that happened now.

Of course, he would have to move carefully at first. She was far too clever to believe an immediate *volte-face.* "But if I can't outwit her . . ." he said half-aloud, causing several persons nearby to turn and stare at him. To himself, he concluded, ". . . then I shall eat my medal!" Well satisfied with the plan which sprang into his mind, he leaned back as far as the uncomfortable chair would permit and folded his arms as he lazily watched the swirling dancers.

Chapter Thirteen

In Miranda's opinion, although she had enjoyed most of the dancing, the evening at Almack's had been time wasted which she might have spent more profitably in completing the present chapter of her novel. However, she was unable to prevent herself from smiling whenever she listened to Lucy's enthusiastic retelling of every dance, every flattering word which had been whispered in her ear, every bashful request for permission to call upon her or to take her riding within the next few days.

To Lucy, the evening had been perfect. Which, Miranda thought, was what it *should* be for the first important appearance for a pretty seventeen-year-old. The young lady's eagerness to give an exact account of her evening's exploits had brought her to the breakfast table before the others had arrived—an unheard-of event in this household, and one about which her brother and sister lost no time in gibing at their usually slugabed sister until Miranda, while she laughed at their remarks, ordered them to refrain from tormenting Lucy. To her surprise, they obeyed her.

"And what about you, Miranda?" Diana asked. "You've said nothing of your evening."

"Has Lucy given me a chance to do so?"

Lucy looked a trifle guilty at having monopolized the conversation—and surprised that her cousin had apparently joined her tormentors—until Miranda smiled at her to show that she had merely been jesting in her turn.

"No—truly, did you not find it as much fun as Lucy did?" Diana felt as if she could hardly wait until she, too, was old enough to have a Season, to be permitted to go to Almack's and have all the young bucks flirting with her. It wasn't fair that she couldn't do so for another three or four years—almost an eternity in her life.

To be sure, her completely straight silvery-pale fair hair was no match for Lucy's golden curls, and her eyes were, in her opinion, "just plain blue"—not brown like Lucy's, or even a vivid shade of blue, like Miranda's—so it was quite probable that she could never cut such a dash in the *ton* as Lucy was doing. But there would surely be *someone* at these affairs who could be dazzled by her. Maybe by the time she had reached Lucy's age, she would be better able to attract the beaux. And if someone who was as old as Miranda had been popular with the gentlemen, there was no way of telling what *she* might be able to do.

"Oh, yes indeed," Miranda assured her. "It was all quite fine—although I must admit I was surprised, after having heard so much about the wonders of Almack's, to find it so plain a place."

"Plain?"

"Quite plain. If I hadn't been told where I was, I would have thought I was in some warehouse or other. There were no ornaments about the place, simply a row of chairs about the walls for those who weren't dancing. Something was rumored about there being a low-stakes card room for some of the gentlemen, but of course we didn't see *that*. There was no such refuge for nondancing ladies."

"Miranda! How can you speak that way?" Lucy cried.

"I'm only telling what I saw. I thought, also, that something might have been done to the floor to make it a bit smoother. There were places where one might almost fall, especially during a spirited dance, because the boards were uneven. It's a wonder no one is hurt there. And I've never cared for stale bread and butter."

"Do you mean that's all they gave you to eat?" Giles wanted to know, while Lucy frowned at further disparagement of what was, to every young lady, the most important spot in London. Secretly, she felt she must agree with Miranda's description, but would never have dared to say anything of the kind. It would take only one wrong word to bring on an order of banishment from the Patronesses. That would mean the sudden end to her Season, or to any Season to come.

"Only that and some cake which was even older," Miranda continued her disrespectful account, sipping her chocolate.

Giles piled a scone high with several spoonfuls of jam, licking around the edges in a vain effort to prevent any of it from falling into his lap, then crammed the entire scone into his mouth, despite the frowns of his sisters and Miss Augusta Owens at such a display of piggishness. "Pah," he commented, as soon as he could speak through the mouthful, while attempting to lick off the crumbs and jam coming out the corners of his mouth as he spoke. Yet he succeeded only in spreading them farther over his cheeks. "I wouldn't have liked it at all."

"No, I don't think that you would have cared for

it," Miranda said, while smiling at the way the boy ignored his sisters' scowls. He was quite an unprincipled imp at times.

"You needn't worry about that," Diana told him. "If anyone learns how you misbehave, and especially about the swinish way you gobble your food, you can be sure you'll never be permitted to enter the doors."

"And if you want to drink," Miranda went on with her relentless description, "you would be given weak lemonade or barley water."

"Orgeat," her cousin corrected.

"Whatever it was called, it had almost no taste. And you know how I enjoy full-flavored drinks—such as this." She touched her half-empty cup. She was forced to own that she was quite as fond of sweets as was Giles, and vowed that she would have chocolate often when she returned home. Now that her books were selling so well, she could afford to be extravagant at times. Since coming to London she had acquired a taste for chocolate, which she had seldom enjoyed back home and much preferred to tea.

"Perhaps they don't serve good meals, but who cares about such things as the food and drink they might find there?" Lucy demanded with more heat than she customarily displayed. After all, it was *Almack's* that her cousin was disparaging. Almack's—the one place every young lady aspired to attend. "One can always have something to eat or drink at home before going. But one can't see such people as were there last evening. And even *you* must admit that everyone was there—everyone of any importance, that is."

"Did you see the king?" her brother wanted to know. He had finished eating his breakfast and had wiped as much of the jam from his clothing as he could with a serviette, which had removed the greater part of the jam's color, but left its stickiness. He now flung himself sidewise on his chair, kicking at the table legs, ignoring Miss Augusta's mild reproof until his sisters, as if at a signal to each other, rose, pulled his chair away from the table, and tipped it to let him fall to the floor.

"Well, did you?" he insisted, thrusting his head above the table and making faces at the girls. His face was so streaked with jam and bits of scone that Miranda laughed, reminded of some of the less successful applications of cosmetics last evening.

"N-no—nor the Prince Regent, either. But the room was so crowded that," Lucy lowered her voice and giggled as she went on, "I doubt if there would have been enough room for him."

"That doesn't sound like everyone," Giles said.

Coming into the room in time to hear the last comment, Miss Sampson remarked, "It is good manners, Giles, to allow your sister to complete her story without interruptions."

"She said everyone was there, but they weren't. So she's telling bouncers."

"And that is no way to speak of her. You shouldn't be impolite to your sisters; that is ungentlemanly. It may be that she exaggerates a trifle when telling a story, but one can't call that 'telling bouncers.' Also, you shouldn't lie about on the floor."

"Lucy and Di threw me down here."

"If they did so, they shouldn't have done it. But that doesn't mean you must stay there. Sit up at once. And don't make faces at them."

Giles sulked but obeyed, having learned that whenever Sammy gave him an order, noncompliance meant the loss of an exciting outing in the Green Park, where he was allowed to romp to his heart's content, without regard to how dirty he might become. Privately, however, he had decided to forgo any more fresh milk while he was there. It sounded exciting to be able to be served milk fresh from the cow, instead of having what the cook bought at the door. But, being warm, the fresh milk tasted more like medicine.

"Well, even if they're royal, they weren't nearly as important," Lucy went on, "as the people who *were* there. There were four of the Patronesses—I think, although I'm not too certain that the older lady who scowled at us was Mrs. Drummond-Burrell. But everyone else was so pleasant that I supposed it had to be her. And Princess Esterhazy—wasn't it nice of her to come and speak to you, Miranda? And to spend so much time with you! What was she saying?"

"Oh, some nonsense or other." Miranda hoped she wasn't blushing again as she recalled the princess's comments about Jonathan Murray. She had tried to make herself believe that the princess had made mistakes because her knowledge of English wasn't good, but without success. After all, she had labeled the man a rake!

It would never do to repeat any of those remarks about his rakishness to Lucy—or to Miss Augusta—and certainly not to the children. The charges—although she was certain the princess intended them to be compliments—might be true, but Miranda knew he would never behave in such a way before any of them. "You know how it is with foreigners—half the time what they're saying makes no sense at all to us. Even the princess. At times I wasn't certain what she meant." This was true enough, but she thought she had come to understand its meaning. "But it was very kind of her to give you permission to waltz."

"Yes—I think I would have died if I'd been forced to sit out every waltz like some wallflower."

159

"Speaking of flowers," Diana interrupted. "There are *tons* of them in the morning room."

"I didn't mean plants," her sister told her with a sniff for Diana's ignorance.

"I did."

"All for Lucy, of course. It's wonderful that she's so popular," Miranda said, attempting to bring peace between the sisters, but Diana shook her head violently.

"Oh no, there are almost as many for you. I counted them." She proudly led the way to the morning room, where a multitude of flowers were displayed, covering every table and the mantelpiece, with some sitting on the chairs and the floor.

Most were roses or camellias, although there were several small bouquets of violets—and it seemed that a number of family greenhouses must have been robbed of their carnations. In the midst of this floral splendor was a large bunch of untidily arranged daisies.

"What on earth . . . ?" Miranda asked, going to it and examining the card. Wordlessly, she held it up so that Lucy could see the one word scrawled across it in large letters, "Brummell."

Lucy collapsed on the sofa, overcome by giggles. "We should have known, I suppose. Who else would do so odd a thing? But he doesn't care a fig for convention. He was there last evening, you know."

"Was he? I didn't notice him."

"Oh, the poor Beau." She giggled again. "We must hope he never finds out that he was overlooked, or he'll see that you're quite ruined as far as the *ton* is concerned. He'd consider it the supreme insult, although anywhere else someone so small and plain would go quite unnoticed. But not the Beau, however."

"What makes him so noticeable?"

"Well—that's difficult to say; there's nothing in his appearance to make one notice him more than anyone you might see on the street. Yet one can't overlook him. The man is insufferably arrogant, of course, but it's true that he can make or unmake anyone's career with no more than a raised eyebrow. When I saw him aiming his quizzing glass at me, I was shivering in my shoes, and wanted to run away and hide. What if he had decided to snub me? But finally he smiled and nodded before he turned his glass on someone else. I almost swooned with relief when he did that; it meant I was acceptable."

"Just as well, then, that I'm not having a Season, for I wouldn't want to risk his censure." What would a high stickler such as that man say about the authoress of Gothic novels—even successful ones?

"What did he say?" Giles wanted to know, conveniently forgetting Miss Sampson's instructions, or feeling that since she hadn't definitely told him not to interrupt Miranda, it was all right for him to do so. No one reproved him, for all were eager for the answer.

They were disappointed. "Nothing that I heard," his sister replied. "He never spoke to me, never came near me, in fact. I would have been completely overcome had he done so."

"I would have liked to have been there the night he said, 'Who's your fat friend?'"

"Giles!" Miss Sampson said reprovingly. "I'm certain no gentleman would say anything of the kind. Certainly not in a public place."

"He did so," Giles insisted. "Rogers told me about it. And *he* said that Brummell isn't truly a gentleman."

"I fear Rogers told Giles the truth," Lucy agreed. "On both counts. Although it doesn't seem that it's the sort of thing a tutor should repeat. It was quite *the*

161

scandal of the city at the time. Mr. Brummell and the Regent were good friends for a number of years, although the Beau wasn't even a member of the nobility. Still, for a time, it seemed the two of them were almost inseparable."

"One would think the Regent would prefer to choose his friends from the nobility rather than to promote a plain 'Mister' to such prominence."

"Not at all. He doesn't care in the least about such things. They say the Beau even advised the Regent about his clothing—and the Regent was willing to be guided by what he said. No one knows precisely what happened, but the Beau must have said something one day that displeased Prinny, for the next time they met, the Regent gave him the cut direct. And the Beau retaliated by bellowing his remark across the room."

Sammy gasped. "He said that? Insulting the Prince Regent? And you say that such a man is still accepted by the *ton?*"

"Oh, yes—he carries on in quite the same manner as he had always done. Except, of course, that he's careful not to attend the same affairs as the Prince Regent. For it would be deplorable if he were to be cut again—as he certainly would be. And if it happened again, people might think twice about inviting him."

"I imagine that the Regent must be equally careful to avoid any meeting with him," Miranda said. "Prince George may be our ruler in all but name—but to have something of that sort happen must have been a terribly humiliating occasion for him."

"Oh, it must have been, but—"

"It shows that one must be careful about the friends one chooses." Sammy thought this a good opportunity to help turn the children's minds in the right direction. No one, however, appeared to be listening to her.

"Especially if no one in the room took exception to

the insult," Miranda was continuing. "But I can see that the man who would do anything so rude as to insult the Regent would quite easily have the insolence to send a bouquet of field flowers to a lady."

"But what might be insolence in another is considered to be great condescension on the part of the famous Beau," Lucy said stoutly. Miss Sampson's advice to the contrary, she would never utter a word against the man who had made himself arbiter of Society. The *on-dits* she repeated were considered complimentary by the *ton.*

"Then I'm quite as happy that the *gentleman* did not deign to notice me," her cousin retorted. To her mind, Beau Brummell apparently had manners which were far worse than Captain Murray's. At least, *he* did not utter his insults before others, but kept them strictly for moments when they were alone.

Lucy only laughed and assured her that, if she spent more time with the members of the *ton,* she wouldn't feel as she did. Miranda protested that she would always do so, and the two began to walk along the table which held the display of flowers, reading the cards on each, some containing sentimental remarks or bad verse in addition to the sender's name. The two young ladies couldn't help but laugh at some of the offerings, although they appreciated the flowers.

Miranda was surprised to find that Diana had been correct; there were a number which had been sent to her. She attempted to recall the gentlemen whose names were on the cards, but made little headway in doing so.

Although she had been loath to take the time she felt could have been better spent in writing, she would have to admit that she had enjoyed everything which had taken place the evening before—despite her remark about the uneven floor and the quality of the refreshments—but had great difficulty today in re-membering exactly which of her dancing partners was which. They came and went so rapidly that none of them had made a lasting impression; while she danced or chatted with them, her mind was on the unfinished pages of her book.

Diana joined them and looked over the flowers a second time. "This one is for you, too, Miranda," she called. "Oh, it's from Cousin Jon!"

"There must be a mistake there. He must have in-tended them for Lucy, I'm sure."

"No—the pink rosebuds are for Lucy. He sent one for each of you."

"Now, why would he do such a thing as to make me a gift of flowers?" When he makes it clear that he dislikes me so intensely, she thought.

"Why shouldn't he? After all, he did escort both of you to Almack's for Lady Smallwood."

"Oh, of course. And perhaps he thought it would be impolite to ignore me when he sent flowers to Lucy." She lifted the pale roses and inhaled their fragrance. "I must tell him how much I enjoyed receiving them." Even though I know he couldn't have meant it as anything more than a gesture, she thought. I mustn't permit him to add discourtesy to the list of whatever other faults he finds in me.

Jonathan could not recall ever having so great a problem as he faced in attempting to find the proper bouquet for Miranda. Of course, most females of his acquaintance would have been thrilled that he had paid them any such attention. Despite what Princess Esterhazy had said, he was not certain that Miranda *was* interested in him, and he went from one flower seller to another, seeking the right flowers. Rosebuds, of course, were the only flowers for Lucy; he had discovered some which were the exact shade of the ones she had worn last evening, and it would make her happy that he remembered them. But what color would be best for Miranda Drake?

Not white flowers, certainly—white was the color of innocence. And the vivid red, which he thought would be far more suitable, was considered to be a declaration of extreme fondness, perhaps even of passion. It would never have done to send those to her.

The wench was no fool. When he bade them goodnight the previous evening, he had complimented her upon her great success in her first appearance in the *ton,* and had been aware of her rather pleased surprise at his words. He knew, however, that he could not have convinced her that his feelings for her had taken such a turn overnight. He had to play his cards carefully if he was to win her trust and make her believe that he was beginning to regard her in a different light than before.

At last, he found exactly the blossoms he sought. It was a bouquet the flower seller had put aside, since it was not a popular shade. The buds were of an unusual color, too deep a tint to be called creamy, yet too pale to be a true yellow. Their color would have no special meaning, but the unexpected tribute of the flowers should be enough to make Miranda begin to wonder if he *might* not be more deeply interested in her than he had appeared. This offering, he thought, would be the opening move in his campaign to bring her into his net.

As soon as he had arranged for the flowers to be sent to Lucy and Miranda, he had called at headquarters with a request that he be returned to active service without further delay. The rumors had been correct; England was presently involved in her struggle with the United States, so he hoped that an allowance might be made in his case.

He told himself that he should be accustomed to disappointments by this time, but the refusal to accede to his request—almost a demand on his part—was as bitter as before.

"You know better than to make so foolish a request as that one, Murray," he was told with several embellishments implying that there was much more than mere foolishness on his part to expect special consideration. "Anyone with half an eye can see that you can't walk across the room without limping. How do you think you could stand up under a long march? You can scarcely expect your fellow soldiers to carry you into battle on a litter, and the doctor has already told you that it will be another month or more before he'll allow you to return."

Jonathan had hotly protested the decision, knowing that he risked further censure for so doing, but it was quite useless; he needed to wait for a better report from the doctor. He left the office muttering to himself about the stubbornness of official minds.

Remembering last evening's conversation with the princess, however, he thought that—if she were right—he might be able to put the time to good advantage. It would be a good thing if he could manage to captivate Miranda and get her away from her cousins before he was able to leave to rejoin the army.

Once he had her settled in a place of his choosing, he wasn't worried that she would return to them. In fact, he would be certain to make that a condition of their *liaison*. His ill humor vanished and he began to whistle as he imagined their future.

Chapter Fourteen

There was no time like the present for him to initiate his campaign to charm the witch, Jonathan decided. The roses had been only the first step; this would be the next one. That same afternoon, therefore, his new phaeton was pulled to a halt before the Owens home on King Street. He had found, at least, that driving was a far more comfortable sport for him than riding; he was happy that he would not be expected to squire the hussy around on horseback. Lucy had never been interested in riding in the park, and he doubted her cousin was in the habit of doing so.

Jonathan dismounted, still finding that he had to move a bit gingerly. Flicking a speck of dust from the phaeton's gleaming side, he hoped that the splendid equipage would serve to impress her. In preparation for the drive he hoped to make, the vehicle had been polished and the horses groomed until his disrespectful young tiger had remarked, "Blimey—you'd think we was gonna take the Queen, at least," which remark had earned him a box on the ear. Not a hard one, as he had been expecting something of the kind and had nearly managed to escape it.

Lady Smallwood's carriage and her driver were already waiting before the house, the driver nodding recognition as he arrived. Good, Jonathan told himself, that must mean that no one has yet gone out. Miranda wouldn't have dared to creep out during the day in order to meet some man; all her assignations had been late at night or very early in the morning. At least, the ones he knew about; but he thought that must be her usual practice.

There had always been the chance, of course, that she would have decided to accompany Lucy and Lady Smallwood on their calls upon various members of the *ton*. He was happy to see he had come in time to prevent that, and had little doubt that she would prefer riding—even with him—to making courtesy visits. Certainly with him, if Esterhazy was correct. He had great faith in the princess's remarks about Miranda's feelings toward him. Why had he never suspected them before?

As one who was considered a member of the family, he didn't bother to knock, but walked in without hesitation. Lucy was coming down the stairs as he entered, tying the pink ribands of her white chip cottage bonnet beneath her chin, looking—although he would never have hurt her by telling her so—about half her age.

"Oh, Miranda," she called over her shoulder, "I wish you would change your mind and decide to come with us." She noticed the newcomer and ran down the remaining steps, hands extended to greet him. "Jon, I'm so happy you're here! How can I thank you enough? Your roses are so lovely—and my favorite color, too. It was so thoughtful of you to send them."

"It was indeed," Miranda agreed, following her cousin down the stairs. Today, her hair was arranged in soft waves about the nape of her neck, except for several curls which had escaped the confining pins. She swallowed an impulse to ask why he had sent them, deciding to be gracious—little as he deserved such consideration—as she went on, "Most thoughtful. I wish to thank you, as well, Captain Murray, for being so kind."

"It was an honor, Miss Drake," Jonathan told her with a slight bow. "I'm happy that I could please you as well, puss," he added to Lucy, slipping his finger into one of the curls escaping from her bonnet.

"Oh—must you and Miranda go on saying 'Miss Drake' or 'Captain Murray'?" Lucy exclaimed, in tones of deep disgust. "It would make anyone think you had met at just this moment, and it's quite stupid. Certainly the two of you have known one another long enough to cease being so formal. Try it; I insist that you do."

Jonathan smiled. Although she could have no inkling of what he planned, for which he was thankful, Lucy was making his task easier. Once they were on first-name terms, the next step would be easier. "Of course. It would make me happy—if Miranda doesn't object."

"Certainly not—Jon. After all, Lucy says you're almost a cousin, so I suppose that must make us relatives as well. At least, relatives of a sort."

Miranda was completely confused by the change in his attitude. Until now, he had been, it had seemed, her sworn enemy, but all that appeared to have changed. First his gift of the beautiful roses, and today the courtesy he was displaying in pretending that he wished to use her name. He had always behaved with surface civility toward her when her cousins were near, of course, but the tone he was using today was almost enough to convince her that he wished to be her friend.

How different this was from his earlier attitude toward her. But perhaps when the man had thought more about the situation he had come to realize that— while she wished her writing to be kept a secret from

169

her cousins and from the members of the *ton* for Lucy's sake—she had never had another reason for that secrecy, and what she was doing had nothing evil in it, after all.

She still wondered how he might have learned about her writing, but had determined at last that it might be best if she didn't ask him for the source of his information. It could be that he had merely overheard her name mentioned in connection with her writing. Doubtless, he would have a wide circle of acquaintances, but she didn't see how he could know anyone in the publishing business.

She had thought of this more than once and had been told that no one except her publishers knew her name. Both gentlemen had assured her that not even the people working for them had been given that information. For the present, however, it was enough that he didn't speak of it before the others.

"You see, Jon," Lucy was saying, as she led the way into the morning room, where Lady Smallwood was attempting to make polite conversation with Miss Augusta while she waited for her protégée, "that wasn't such a difficult thing to do, after all."

"Not at all. I've only been waiting for permission to use Mi-Miranda's name."

"As if you needed to ask permission. You're part of the family, as is Miranda, so you should act as if you are. And," she thrust her nose in the air and spun about several times as if to show how important she felt after her success of last evening, only—he thought—managing to look more childish than ever, with her posturing, "if you look about, you will see that *you* were not the only one to send us flowers."

"I see that I wasn't." He walked at once to the field flower bouquet and snorted as he read the card. "Brummell, of course. I should have known as much

170

without having to refer to the card. Doubtless, he'd prefer to have you think that he had gathered these for you with his own hands, sending them to you before the dew had dried, but you mustn't believe anything of the kind, for the Beau would never risk soiling his white boot tops or getting a scratch on their vaunted shine."

"Oh dear," Lucy cried in a hollow tone, as she threw her hand to her forehead in a gesture of mock despair, "and I thought I had made a conquest. Do you mean to say that he doesn't *care?*"

"Lucy!" Lady Smallwood shrieked, scandalized by such behavior. Miss Augusta's reaction was fainter but equally censorious, and the young lady threw herself down on the sofa, dissolving into a deep spell of giggles, extremely pleased that her impersonation of a despairing follower of the Beau had been such a success.

"You know very well, my dear, he's never cared for anyone except himself." Not fooled for one moment by the girl's performance, Jonathan tweaked at the fair curl he had earlier teased and continued his inspection of the floral tributes.

He was happy to see that none had been sent to Miranda by his friend Lieutenant Hedge. None was in sight, which was proof enough for him. It was most unlikely that one bouquet out of the great number of flowers the young ladies had received would have been taken away to be smiled upon in private, for if Hedge had chosen flowers, his bouquet would have been nothing above the ordinary and undeserving of special attention.

He had watched carefully last night to see that there had never been an opportunity for the lieutenant to come near her. There had been some concern in his mind that the fellow was smitten at his first sight of

Miranda, and couldn't be steered away from her vicinity without being told the truth about her.

That would have been tantamount to taking space in the *Gazette* or the *Times* to broadcast the matter. Hedge could never keep his tongue between his teeth about anything except military matters, and would like nothing better than to be able to titillate the *ton* with the secret about one of their favorite members.

"I see you have as many admirers as Lucy," he commented to Miranda, discounting most of the offerings as being mere signs of politeness.

She laughed and shrugged. "It would seem that everyone with whom I danced felt he must send flowers. At least, I suppose they were the ones who sent these; if I must be truthful, I can't recall all the names, for I met so *many* people last evening. Or some of them might be from those who saw how kind Princess Esterhazy was to me, and who immediately leaped to the false conclusion that I'm now someone of importance."

"Or perhaps they're merely an expression of thanks for the pleasure of your company." Careful, Jon warned himself; I mustn't sound as if I've suddenly become too enamored of her. At this stage, she would never believe it. "It is customary to send flowers after a ball."

"Doubtless that would explain almost all of these. You understand that I'm not yet accustomed to London ways," Miranda said, as if in explanation, thinking she had solved one problem. *He* had sent her the roses only because it was the custom to do so. It meant nothing.

She was surprised that he had not sent weeds of some sort, something far worse than Brummell's bouquet to Lucy. She didn't think the Beau had meant any particular insult to Lucy; such an arrangement from

Jonathan, however, would have been much more in keeping with his earlier attitude. But of course, he wouldn't wish to have Lucy or the others ask inconvenient questions, which they certainly would have done after Lucy's talk about all being one family.

"You would become accustomed if you went about more," Lucy said, her tone so like her sponsor's that Miranda was forced to smile at her mimicry. Suddenly, her boasting of all her flowers was quelled as she became aware of their visitor's attire. "Jon—you have a new riding coat!

"And hat." Setting the pearl-gray curly-brimmed beaver at an angle, he caught the sides of his coat, spreading them as he turned about, ending with a curtsy in a burlesque of a young lady displaying her new ballgown. He felt rather foolish when he recalled that Lady Smallwood was also among those watching him. For a moment he had forgotten about her while displaying his new finery.

Courting clothes, he had thought when he donned them. No, hunting clothes would be more exact, for he had chosen his prey well, and she would have no chance to escape him.

He wouldn't say any such thing as that to Lucy, of course, for she wouldn't understand. He was happy to have it so. "I thought I must have something worthy of my new rig." He gestured toward the window through which his phaeton could be seen.

Lucy had collapsed once more on the sofa, hooting with laughter and clapping her hands at his performance, evoking further admonitions from Lady Smallwood. "But you're so handsome in your new finery," she exclaimed. "Don't you think so, Miranda?"

"Very handsome indeed," Miranda agreed. The man *was* handsome, no matter how he was dressed. Or no matter how hatefully he might behave. The fawn-colored coat with its single cape only added to his appearance. She was more than a bit surprised, however, to discover that he had a sense of the ridiculous.

Returning to the subject most often on her mind, Lucy asked, "Won't you change your mind now and come with Lady Smallwood and me, Miranda?"

"No—I thank you, but I think not."

"As a matter of fact," Jonathan told her, hoping he didn't appear *too* much like a bumbling suitor. At least not yet. "That's why I'm here today, complete with new driving clothes and new rig. I was hoping that I might prevail upon Miss—upon Miranda to drive with me."

Miranda looked at him with disbelief, surprised that he would want her company. Before she could think of an adequate excuse for refusing to go with him—she could not give her true reason before the others, which was the need to finish the last chapter of her book—Lucy cried, "Why don't you go, Miranda? Jon is an excellent whip."

"Thank you for the tribute, my child—but I've never aspired to join the Four-in-Hand Club."

"What nonsense!" Lucy protested. "You know that you drive better than any of them." Jonathan's only reply to that was a shrug.

Now, if she refused the invitation, he would doubtless think that she would be afraid to ride with him. "Th-thank you, Jon. I believe I should enjoy a drive. If you'll allow me to get my hat and gloves—"

"Certainly—although I've always thought it unfair that a lady could not be allowed to feel the wind in her hair while she drove."

"I would enjoy doing that if I were at home in the country," Miranda told him. "But here in the city, I wouldn't dare to be so bold." She hurried away while he told himself that it was odd, indeed, that the jade should be so particular about outward appearances, while she blithely ignored other rules of conduct.

Lucy and Lady Smallwood took their leave, both of them happy that Miranda would now be occupied for the afternoon. Lucy was quite pleased that Jon and Miranda were becoming such good friends—even if it wasn't the romance she thought it to be.

Whatever his reason for asking her, and hers for saying she would go, Lucy was certain the two would enjoy being in each other's company. For her part, Lady Smallwood was well pleased not to be forced to provide Lucy once again with unfair competition.

As Miranda came down, tying the ribands of a helmet-shaped bonnet whose feather was the same color of greenish-blue as the neat walking dress into which she had quickly changed, she found Jon had taken one of the rosebuds from her bouquet to wear in his buttonhole. "I hope you don't mind?" he asked.

"Certainly not. If I'd thought that you would like to have a flower, I would have offered it to you at once. Perhaps I ought to have thought of it. Remiss of me, is it not? I must thank you again for finding me such beautiful flowers."

"I wanted something out of the common run for you." He didn't explain why he would be doing anything of the sort, so she took it as a compliment, although she was uncertain as to his reason for complimenting her.

Surprisingly, it was Miss Augusta, putting her tatting aside for a moment, who now spoke up. "My dear child, you don't intend to go driving *alone* with a gentleman?"

"There's nothing wrong about my going with Jon, I'm certain, ma'am," Miranda told her. "Else Lady Smallwood would have advised against it."

"In my day, a lady wouldn't be so daring."

"Nor would I, with someone I didn't know—but after all, Captain Murray is such a good friend of the family."

"*You* know I can be trusted, Miss Augusta," Jonathan told her, although he meant nothing of the sort.

The old lady shook her head, but said nothing more. The manners and morals of today's young people were quite different than they had been in her time, she knew—but still, she couldn't quite approve of them.

"You need not worry, Miss Augusta," Miranda assured her. Then, touched by the old lady's solicitude, she bent and kissed a withered cheek before placing her hand on Jonathan's arm and permitting him to lead her from the house.

Chapter Fifteen

As they descended the front steps, the small tiger said impudently, "Took you long enough, it did. Thought maybe you'd decided to walk and slipped out the back, leavin' me here with the prads."

"You must forgive his lack of manners," Jonathan said as he flicked at the young rascal with his glove, a blow that the lad easily eluded. "He came with the phaeton when I took it off a friend's hands, along with a pair of broken-down hacks."

"Pure knacker bait, they was," the boy contributed.

"A good description of the beasts. I was able to rid myself of them, fortunately, I may say—for I never would have allowed myself to be seen driving such an outfit. I should have rid myself of this fellow as well, but so far, I've had no luck in persuading anyone to take him off my hands, which is not so surprising to anyone who has met him. His name, by the way, is Algernon."

" 'Tain't nuther—'s Mike!" the boy said, incensed at the use of the sissy name inflicted upon him by his last master, who had a taste for the exotic and little more sense about the proper name for a boy than for the handling of his cattle.

Jonathan grinned and winked at Miranda, but—

although she had been somewhat shocked by the wink, for she didn't think gentlemen ever winked at ladies— she ignored him and bent down to say, "Pay no attention to him. Mike is a much better name, you know," which earned her a grudging grin from the tiger.

"She's got some sense, anyhow. Not like some we've met," he observed in pleased tones to his master, as he handed over the lines and hopped to his place at the back of the vehicle.

"After so shrewd an observation as that, I can't bring myself to get rid of the imp," Jon said with a laugh. "It would imply a lack of sense on my part, would it not?"

"Hardly that, but it makes me wonder about some of the others you've met." Miranda echoed his laugh, which pleased him and brought a snicker from the lad behind them.

"Doubtless he is referring to his former master, whose choice of companions must have equaled his expertise in other fields."

"I see," Miranda said gravely, her tone implying that she believed nothing of what he was saying. Jonathan's grin told her she was correct.

"Well, you can see the problem I have with the brat, can you not? I can never depend on him to keep his mouth shut. Now, where would you like to drive? Through the park? Or shall we go out of the city for a short way, where the roads aren't so crowded?"

"Well, there's never the slightest danger of having the wind blow through your hair while driving in the park—especially at this hour. As you know, one is expected to stop almost every few feet of the way to exchange *on-dits* with someone. Of course, most of those we meet are Lucy's friends, not mine, so most of their *on-dits* go past me. But there would be a number of your friends there at this hour, as well—doubtless you would prefer to meet them."

"I can't think of anything that would please me less. I can visit with them any time. And most of them have no more conversation than the ladies you might meet. Which is to say, none at all."

"I didn't say that—precisely."

"No, but that was what you meant, wasn't it? Then the open, or at least half-open, road it shall be. We shouldn't have to stop at all, unless we see something out of the common way."

If she'd wished to show him off to acquaintances in the park as her newest conquest, Jonathan would have said nothing, but he was better pleased to keep her to himself. If he could manage to convince her that he preferred to receive her undivided attention, matters between them might be settled more quickly.

As they moved away from the heart of the city and the traffic upon the streets began to thin, he flicked his whip lazily above the backs of the grays, not touching them, for that wasn't necessary, but encouraging them to a trot. Miranda wished that she might remove her bonnet and permit the breeze to flow through her hair, carrying its mingled scent of many blossoms from the gardens and fields they passed. Even on this half-deserted road, however, she felt it wouldn't be proper.

She glanced at the driver, admiring the way he had set his hat at an attractive angle, but wondering if he, too, wouldn't have liked the feel of wind through his hair. Or maybe he was accustomed to wearing a hat. Or helmet—or whatever headpiece soldiers might wear with their uniforms. She smiled, remembering his comic display of his new riding coat.

Jonathan didn't fail to notice Miranda's smile and her long silence. Reaching into a pocket, he laid something in her hand. Miranda looked down at the copper coin, then at him.

"For your thoughts."

She could hardly tell him what she had been thinking—that he seemed a much nicer person today than he had been in the past. Looking down upon the shining coats of the team and choosing them for a topic of conversation, she said, "You have beautiful animals, Jon." She found that she was quite enjoying the right to use his nickname. "They're well matched, are they not?"

"Not quite perfect, I fear, but the best that I could do. My first pair—the wheelers—are brothers, and their markings are identical. But when I tried to match them, I found I couldn't precisely do so. However, I'm very well pleased with the ones I found."

"I'd think you would be, for as I said, they're quite handsome." Almost as handsome as their driver, she said to herself, wondering what would happen if she made her remark aloud. Doubtless he would laugh at her—and Mike would snicker, and perhaps make some remark about her good sense failing her.

"At least, I'm unable to see any difference in their looks. And you handle them so expertly. What is the Four-in-Hand Club?" she asked. "You mentioned it to Lucy before we started. And after all, *you* drive four horses, but you said you didn't aspire to become a member."

"You mean you haven't heard of them?" Miranda shook her head, so he explained. "They're a group of better-than-average whips, but instead of showing their skill by racing about the country, they celebrate the great importance of their group by getting together at intervals, wearing blue coats with blue-and-yellow–striped waistcoats and flaunting white cravats with large black dots."

"Goodness!"

"You may say so. Clad in that exotic fashion, they trot solemnly out to Salt Hill behind their expensive teams, eat, drink, and come home again."

"It sounds rather dull," Miranda commented. "Is that all they do?"

"No—they only do that for special days. Other times, they do race, place bets, attend sporting events, and behave themselves like any other members of the *ton*. But they don't do all these other things as a group, you must understand. Only those special members may join in their monthly outing."

"Well," she said, pursing her lips while giving the matter some thought, "it appears to me that there's little point in having been chosen to join that august body. But I suppose that's one of those things that's supposed to be beyond a mere female's comprehension."

They laughed together, while Jonathan wondered if she had purposely appeared to invite a kiss. He was tempted to ask her—then thought of his tiger's sharp ears and ready tongue. He would have to be careful of what he said, as long as Mike was present. After a time, he said, "I wonder—do you drive?"

"No. I know it seems odd. Most of my friends do so—my friends who live in the country, I mean. But I've never learned to handle the lines. We have a gig, but Sammy always manages the horse while I sit by lazily." Working out my plots, she was tempted to say, but thought it might be wiser not to mention her writing unless he broached the subject. He might say something disagreeable about her writing again and spoil so fine a moment. And she didn't wish to have it spoiled—by anything.

"I can teach you to do so, if you think you'd like to learn." As she cast a frightened glance at the now

181

swiftly moving team, he said, "Oh, not today. These would be much too difficult for you to handle. But sometime, we might start your lessons with a well-mannered pair."

Something she might like to have later, he thought. He would have to demonstrate enough generosity to make her forget all her present patrons. How much would he be expected to offer? It had been some time since he had found himself in the position of having to bid for a female's interest, and he wondered how quickly it could be accomplished.

"Well—perhaps I might wish to learn—sometime," she said slowly. "But at present I find it much nicer to be driven." She wondered if she would find it so enjoyable with another driver. It was pleasant to feel the country air and smell the flowers they were passing, but she felt that a number of the gentlemen she had met since coming to London would have spoiled the occasion by chattering about themselves or making compliments she felt undeserved.

"Thank you—I am enjoying the drive myself," Jonathan told her. He was enjoying it, quite aside from his plans to captivate the wench. She did not bibble-babble as did some females he knew. It would be pleasant to have a mistress with whom he could talk about something other than her charms.

"I've been wondering . . ." he ventured. "It's too long a journey to undertake this late in the day, of course—but what would you think of driving to Richmond Park one day, if the weather permits, for an *al fresco* picnic?"

"That would be very nice." But a picnic, alone with him—would that be a good idea? If Miss Augusta had been shocked at the idea of her driving alone with a gentleman, the though of a picnic *à deux* would scandalize her. And doubtless others as well.

"Perhaps we could take Diana and Giles. That is, if you have a carriage; for this would be too crowded for all of us. And if you wish to take them, of course. I don't wish to make any plans for you that you might not like, but I think they must often feel left out when Lucy and I go about so much."

"I hadn't thought of including them—but there's no reason why we couldn't make up a party one day." After all, he would be taking her away from her cousins soon enough, so if she wished to be exceptionally kind to them now, he could afford to do so.

Jonathan pointed out places he thought might be of interest to her as they passed, and as the sun moved lower in the west, swung his team smoothly about and drove her back to the house so they wouldn't be out alone together after dark. "Miss Augusta would certainly be shocked if that happened," he explained, laughing and expecting her to make some remark about the darkness being no barrier to some sports.

Instead, she merely said, "And doubtless many others as well. We may be friends, but the *ton* would think us far too adventuresome."

"And we wouldn't want that to happen, so here you are, well before the dangerous hour." He wasn't disappointed that she hadn't made a provocative response. Undoubtedly the presence of the tiger inhibited her from making suggestive remarks, as it would have prevented his making a suitable reply, and the time would come soon enough.

"Do you have other plans for this evening?" he asked, tossing the lines to Mike (it really was a better name for him than the one which had been bestowed by his former master) and dismounting to help her from the phaeton's high seat.

"No—it seems that one late night at a time is quite enough for me. I'm still unused to city ways, and find the pace much too tiring." Miranda wondered if he had planned to offer his escort to one of tonight's balls or routs—or whatever it might be that Lucy had planned to attend. It might have been nice to be in his company at such an affair without quarreling. But she had to think of her unwritten pages.

"Then I hope to see you tomorrow."

Miranda nodded, still surprised at his pleasantness, such a change from the manner in which he usually spoke to her. As she stepped downward, her foot slipped from the step of the vehicle and she lurched forward, to be caught in Jonathan's firm grasp.

He held her for a moment, while Miranda struggled for words to apologize for her clumsiness, and to regain the breath she had lost when he held her. The feel of his hands at her waist left her feeling more shattered than her near fall.

It was not possible—it could not be possible—that she was developing a *tendre* for this man. His attitude toward her work made such a thing impossible. Or did it? Why was it that his merest touch set her heart to pounding as if she had been racing, made her throat dry and her lungs feel as if her breath had been cut off?

Jonathan's fingers tingled as he clasped her, so that he wondered that Miranda had not felt the heat which seemed to run from them through every part of his system. He tried to tell himself that it was merely the force of her fall which had caused this feeling, but knew it was something far different. She had not thrown herself at him, he was quite certain. It had been an accident—a fortunate accident, he thought.

Then, aware of the unusual emotions being stirred in him by the feel of her lithe form between his hands, he said, releasing her quickly, "You *are* tired, are you not? That wasn't merely an excuse to avoid meeting me at some event this evening. It would be best to get some rest, so that you'll be able to enjoy another ride tomorrow."

"You're so certain I'll go with you again?" Miranda was finally able to get the words past the lump which had come up in her throat at his tone. If she hadn't known him better, she would have thought it was tenderness that had brought about that speech. She hoped he would not think she was merely being coy to question his invitation.

He grinned down at her. "Of course you'll go. You enjoyed today's ride, did you not—better than jauntering through the park with Lady Smallwood, or making calls with Lucy?"

She nodded. It had been most enjoyable, even if it had taken time she felt she could not spare. Somehow, when she was riding with him, that loss of time didn't seem to be important. It was only now that she had returned home, away from the spell he had somehow seemed to cast upon her, that she remembered what lay ahead of her.

"Then I shall see you tomorrow at the same time. Or—perhaps a bit earlier."

"Yes—and thank you, sir, for treating me to such a pleasant drive."

"It was my pleasure—and Mike's," he added, reaching down to tousle the hair of the young tiger, who stepped away and gave him an indignant look.

As Miranda went up the steps toward the door, Jonathan swung himself back to his perch, forgetting for an instant the pain that such action would cause him, and guided his team away from the house, whistling softly as he considered the success of today's outing. This conquest wasn't going to be difficult, he told himself. The wench already liked him. Within a sennight, he should have her consent to the arrangements he would make for her.

As his vehicle disappeared from sight, Miranda was saying to herself, "That was nice. But *how* am I to get my chapter finished on time?" She hurried into the house and up to her room, hoping that she would not meet Lucy, who would certainly wish to chat with her about her outing. She saw Sammy at the far end of the hall, but only waved at her before slipping into the haven of her room.

Chapter Sixteen

Miranda drew her night robe closer around her and felt about for the slippers she had kicked off while working. She yawned as she lighted a fresh candle and looked at the stack of closely written pages on the edge of her desk. Everyone else in the house—almost everyone in London, she told herself—had been asleep for hours. Some time ago, she had heard the church clock chime the hour of three.

"Whatever made me think it would be a simple matter to write my book here in London?" she muttered crossly. It was the same complaint she had made to herself so often since coming to London and learning how many ways she would be expected to spend her time. Ways that she had never wished nor intended to spend it. Time that could be much better spent here at her desk.

"There's nothing simple about it. Trying to keep up with what Mr. Warrington wants from me at the same time that I'm gadding about with Lucy—or riding with Jonathan, of course," her voice softened slightly as she thought of his kindness to her today, "is more than one should be prepared to do."

She wiped her hand once more over her face, as if that action would drive off the drowsiness which gripped her, and rubbed her gritty eyes, hardly able to see the paper on her desk. At times, the writing appeared to fade from view. She shook her head again, attempting to bring her work into focus.

After squinting for several moments at the last line she had written, one which appeared to dance about in the flickering candlelight, she furiously crossed it out. For the third time tonight, she had given her hero green eyes. Was it only because she was so tired that she continued making this mistake again and again— or was there another reason? One that brought to mind her enjoyment in this afternoon's outing?

It was the *villain* of her story who had green eyes— the handsome villain who, in the chapter before this, had finally declared his foul purpose to the cowering heroine, Elizabeth, while he dragged her, nearly fainting, away to his lair, where, he told her, no one would ever find her. She would be his forever. His eyes were green because they had been Jonathan Murray's eyes, and Miranda had changed the man from the hero of her story to the villain after the day Jonathan had first made such hateful remarks about her writing. He would never know it, but she had been avenged for his remarks to her by her treatment of him in her story.

She might no longer be so angry at Jonathan as she had been at that time; still, it was far too late now to make more changes in the story, to make her readers think he had only been misunderstood and was truly heroic after all. Any attempt to do that would be far too involved and would cause her to make glaring mistakes. And such errors were pounced upon at once by discerning readers.

"There are times," she muttered to herself, making the necessary corrections and rereading the previous page to be certain she hadn't made the same mistake before, "when I wonder if some of the people who read my books do so only to look for such mistakes."

What color had she finally decided that her hero's eyes ought to be, she asked herself. Brown? Blue? Gray? She could no longer remember, could scarcely remember anything about him. And she didn't remember how far back in her story she would have to go to find the page on which she had described them last. As tired as she was by this time, the search might last for hours, hours she could not afford to waste.

Did it matter now what color she had chosen? As long as she did not make another mistake and say again that they were *green*. When he looked down at the girl who had clung to him after he had saved her from the horrible fate which had threatened her, they could merely be described as "love-filled eyes."

That would be enough to satisfy her readers, the ones who insisted upon a touch—sometimes more than a touch—of romance after the villain had been vanquished. Miranda was much too tired to think coherently of anything at this moment, except the necessity of finishing this final chapter with no further delay, so that she could get it into Mr. Warrington's hands tomorrow morning.

This morning!

Knowing that Miranda was feeling desperately in need of more time to write, Sammy had supervised the bedtimes of the children. She overruled the more susceptible maidservants who—because it was easier than arguing with them—were inclined to listen when Diana and Giles protested that it was far too early for them to be asleep.

As soon as she felt that it was safe for her to do so without danger of being interrupted, Miranda had lighted her candle, drawn out the unfinished chapter, and begun writing. Intent as she was on finishing her story tonight, it seemed no time at all had passed until she heard the carriage stop before the house and the sound of Lucy's feet running up the steps.

Miranda had quickly put out her light and sat quite still, hoping the smell of hot candle wax would not be noticeable in the hallway. It was doubtful that Lucy, in her excitement over the night's events, would notice it, but one could never be certain. She didn't dare to move from her chair to the bed, lest she make a noise. Should Lucy suspect that her cousin was awake, she would want to come in and tell everything about her triumphs of the evening. As long as there were young gentlemen to smile at her and pay her compliments—and there would always be—Lucy counted every affair a triumph.

If that happened, there would be no time for Miranda to hide the pages from her. Naturally, Lucy would be curious and would have the secret out of her before Miranda could think of a good reason to be sitting up and writing at this hour, when she had claimed to be too weary to go out with her cousin.

As she customarily did upon coming home from a party, Lucy scratched softly at the door and Miranda held her breath until the other must have decided it was too late to expect anyone to be awake, especially her country cousin. For several moments after the sound of Lucy's footsteps died away, Miranda was afraid to stir, lest Lucy should change her mind and come back to wake her.

This had happened twice before, with nearly disastrous results, as Miranda had been writing on both occasions, and had barely slipped the pages from sight, along with the still smoking candle. She had been so frightened at her narrow escape that she had scarcely been able to rejoice with Lucy over her triumphs of the evening.

At last, certain that Lucy was safely in bed, she relit her candle and began to write once more. The last page was written over and crossed out in so many places that it was almost illegible. Angry for the time she had wasted, she crumpled it into a ball and threw it in the wastebasket, then reached quickly to retrieve it, muttering beneath her breath at having done anything so foolish.

After all, she must copy the parts of it which were still pertinent to her story—for not everything on the page was worthless. And even when she had finished with the copying, it would never do to leave such a page lying about where one of the servants might find it.

She doubted that either of them could read, but it never paid to be careless about such matters. Neither Martha nor Sukey appeared to be the sort to go through the papers in her wastebasket, but one of them might be curious enough to show it to someone to learn what it said.

"Let me see—where did I finish the page before this one?" She hunted for some time among the papers on her desk until she found the proper one, right where it ought to be. Deciding that it was not too badly over-written, she read the last line, then began to copy from the mutilated page.

Elizabeth screamed in terror as the madman drew her farther into the darkened cavern. No one else ever came this far from the entrance. How could anyone find her before the villain had his way with her, as he had boasted he would do?

As if in answer to her prayers, she could hear a beloved voice calling in the distance, "Elizabeth, I'm coming to save you. Answer me, my love. Where are you?"

"Somewhere in the cavern. I can't tell where we are. Farther from the entrance than we've ever been. We took so many turnings. This place is so terrible; he's so terrible. Oh, Roger—save me! Save me!"

"Be brave, my dear one, I will find you."

As Roger stumbled into the circle of light cast by the flickering candle, the villain quickly thrust Elizabeth to one side and fired point blank at the other man. Roger fell at her feet.

"No," she cried, "you mustn't—"

As she started toward him, the man fired another time and Elizabeth collapsed across the lifeless body of her beloved.

Miranda's head struck the desk with a force which made her open her eyes and wonder for an instant where he was and what had happened. Ink was spattered across the page where the quill had slipped from her unconscious fingers. It was lying beside the sputtering candle. Quickly she lighted a new candle and thrust it into the candlestick, then rubbed the bruise on her forehead.

If only she might sleep for an hour or two before she finished her story—the bed would feel so comfortable. Much too comfortable. She knew that once she lay down she would never wake in time to slip out of the house before the others rose. She must remain awake. She must finish this chapter!

"What on earth could I have been writing?" she asked herself. "I never could have allowed him to kill Roger and Elizabeth. The villain could never be victorious—such a thing would never be permitted. Readers wouldn't accept it! Even if he does look like Jon. Was that why I allowed him to win the fight? Whatever the reason, he can't do it. Besides, neither of the men had pistols; I don't even know if they'd been invented then."

Catching up her paper, she read the last lines she had scrawled before sleep overtook her. Not a word of that dreadful final scene had been written. She had dreamed it all! She drew the paper to her and began again.

Elizabeth screamed in terror as the madman drew her farther into the recesses of the darkened cavern. No one ever came into this part of the cave. Which way had they come? Who would ever find her here?

As if in answer to her prayer for help, she could hear Roger's voice, calling, "Elizabeth! I'm coming. Where are you?"

"Somewhere in the cavern. I don't know where we are. We took so many turnings that I can't tell you how to reach me. Oh, Roger—save me! Save me! I'm so afraid. He's not what we thought."

"I know—but you have to be brave, my dear one. I'll find you."

As Roger stepped from the tunnel into the light cast by the flickering candle, the villain thrust Elizabeth aside and sprang toward the other man, his knife drawn. Roger knocked it aside and landed a blow which sent the madman staggering. Clearly he wasn't too mad to know when he was beaten, for he dashed out into the darkness, his mocking laughter floating back to them, suddenly becoming a scream as he fell into nothingness.

Elizabeth clung to her rescuer. "I knew you would come," she told him.

Holding her tightly in the circle of his arms, as if he would never let her go, he looked down at her,

*his eyes finally reflecting his true feeling for her.
"Thank heaven, I arrived in time!"*

It was nearly dawn when she placed the final page with the others and rose to stretch, rubbing her stiff neck and clenching and unclenching her fingers, which felt as if they would never be straight again.

There was no time to reread what she had written; she could only hope that she had made no fatal flaws such as the one she had dreamed. After checking the numbers to see that all her pages were in order, she dressed quickly and made her way downstairs, happy that neither of the housemaids were stirring.

She could hear the cook building up the kitchen fire, but the woman was a bit hard of hearing and would be unable to hear her if she were very careful. She had heard Lucy shoot the bolt on the door when she'd come in and knew it would be too difficult for her to draw it without making a noise which would rouse the house, so she tiptoed through the library, opening the door which led to the terrace, closing it softly behind her, but leaving it unlocked, so that she could slip inside when she returned.

"Now, if only I can find a hackney—but will there be one at this hour?" She was prepared to walk several blocks if she had to, but she could scarcely walk all the way to the newspaper office. Walking on the streets was much more tiring than walking the country roads. And she was so very tired . . .

Hearing the clopping of hooves, she glanced around to see an early carter on his way to market to pick up his stock for the day. She waved him to a halt and asked if he would allow her to ride with him.

He was an old man, with a cart and horse which seemed almost as ancient as he. "Oh no—not with me, miss," he protested. "It wouldn' be fittin'. Not no way.

Me cart's too dirty for the likes of ye. 'Twould ruin all yer fine clothes."

"Oh please, sir, can you not take me—at least, until we reach a place where I might find a hackney? It's most important that I get to the city at once."

He nodded reluctantly, studying her and wondering that a young female should be wandering the streets at this hour. She didn't look the type one would expect upon the streets, nor was this the neighborhood for them. In fact, she reminded him of his own daughter— not that his Maria had ever been half so pretty as this—and he wouldn't have wished *her* to be alone on the street, prey to whatever ill-wishers might be about at this time. So how could he leave this one?

"Was there an accident?" he asked. "Can I send someone a message to come for ye?"

"No—no, no accident. Nothing like that. It's only that I must reach the city. To meet someone."

It sounded to the man very much as if he was being asked to assist in an elopement. But the lady was lovely and she looked to be of an age to know what she was doing—if any female ever did so. At least she was no runaway child. And she was clearly in a dreadful hurry to reach her destination. Why else would she be out upon the street when it was scarcely daylight—and walking alone?

She had told him there had been no accident, no need to call anyone. Still, at this hour and in so great a hurry to reach her destination, she could be on her way to someone's bedside, some dying person she have had to reach before it was too late.

He shook his head, but pulled a fairly clean bag from the back of the cart and spread it on the seat at his side. "I dunno, miss, as it is the right thing for me to take ye, but you ought not to wander about in this way. Come along, we should see a hackney soon."

Gratefully Miranda mounted to the seat, the carter swung his whip above his nag's back, careful not to touch it, but only as a signal for the animal to start, and they were off somewhat bumpily. The old man would have liked to know just where his passenger might be going and why no one had come to fetch her.

Someone—either a guardian or a sweetheart—was being much too careless of her safety. What if—instead of waving him down—she had met the wrong sort of fellow? This was hardly the neighborhood favored by dangerous prowlers, but one never knew what to expect.

Shortly they sighted an early hackney and the old man waved it to a halt for her. If the jarvey, who seemed to be almost as ancient as the carter, was surprised to see his passenger dismounting from a disreputable cart to take her place in his vehicle, he gave no sign, but only waited for her direction.

"Can I not give you something for bringing me here, for saving me so long a walk?" Miranda was asking of the carter, who shook his head violently.

" 'Twas no trouble, miss. I was glad to do for ye. But next time, 'twould be best to have someone call for ye, not chancing trouble as ye did. 'Twas lucky for ye I came along and not some other. The streets are no place for a lone female, even in broad daylight."

She thanked the man and watched him drive off, the wheels of his ancient cart wobbling with each turn as if they might fall off at any moment. She then gave her driver the address of Mr. Warrington's newspaper office and sank back in the seat, grateful to be able to rest her head for a moment against the squabs, despite the fact that they seemed none too clean. And they smelled. In fact, this was worse than the old carter's vehicle, but she realized she could scarcely have asked him to take her all the way. She could only hope that the odor of the squabs didn't cling to her clothing.

"Perhaps I *was* being foolish to slip out as I did at this hour," she said to herself. "But at home, I would have thought nothing of begging a ride." At home, however, the driver wouldn't have been a stranger, but a longtime acquaintance. "I suppose that he was right and I was taking a dreadful chance. But I'm just too tired to think of what I ought to do."

As was his custom, Mr. Warrington was already hard at work at the plant when Miranda alit from the hackney, still feeling more than half asleep, barely remembering to bring her important parcel with her, and, hardly looking at the coins in her reticule, over-paid the driver before stumbling into the office.

"Miss Drake—I didn't expect you at this hour," the newspaper man exclaimed, coming to meet her. " 'Tis hardly more than daybreak."

"I know it's early, but you don't know how difficult it is for me to get away from the house unseen. I was afraid that if I waited until later in the day, you would think I had forgotten that I was to bring you the rest of my material. *If* I could find an excuse to come without some of my cousins wishing to accompany me. And I knew you needed it without delay."

Miranda handed over the packet of sheets and sank into the chair he hurriedly provided. She knew that if she had tried to rest at home after finishing her story, she would have slept for hours. It was difficult even now for her to hold her eyes open while Mr. Warrington read what she had brought him.

"This is excellent," he exclaimed. "You've contrived a perfect finish to the tale. I must confess to being an enthusiast of Gothic tales. Especially yours. And you have brought it just in time, too, for the type is already

197

being set up for the remainder of the paper. We can fit it in with no trouble."

"I'm afraid some of the sheets aren't as neat as they should be," Miranda admitted, fighting to withhold a yawn. "But I was unable to take the time to make a fair copy of all of it if I was to bring it today."

"No trouble at all," he assured her. "If you could see some of the scribbles we receive from the men who go after news stories, you'd think this a veritable model of neatness. Marky can read this easily."

He excused himself and hurried away to give her pages to Marky. Miranda remembered that was the name of the man she had seen setting type on her first visit to the newspaper. She wished she had been able to see more of the newspaper plant. She wished . . .

This last wish was not completed. Despite her efforts to remain alert, Miranda's eyes closed, her head fell back awkwardly against the low back of the chair, and she gave herself up to the sleep which had been threatening to claim her senses most of the night.

Chapter Seventeen

Returning to his office after giving orders to have the story set at once, and discovering that Miranda had slumped sidewise in her chair, sound asleep, the editor touched her shoulder, then shook it more forcefully when the first touch wasn't enough to rouse her. "Come, Miss Drake," he said. "We can't have this. You'll slip off the chair and hurt yourself. It's clear that you need to rest. Would you like a cup of tea—or coffee, perhaps—before you return home?"

"Oh no—thank you," she cried, leaping to her feet, then holding tightly to the back of the chair until a slight dizziness, caused by the unexpected movement, had passed. "But I must go at once, so that I can get into the house before I'm missed."

"Another thing is quite clear—you certainly can't go home alone this morning in the state you're in. I don't care what you may say about not needing protection. This time you're wrong; you would doubtless fall asleep on the street and be run down by some careless driver. I can't have that happen, so it will be my task to see that you arrive home safely."

Miranda tried to protest that she knew he was far too busy a man to spare time for her, but was firmly overruled. When he said, "No, my brother would never forgive me, nor would I forgive myself, if I were to risk the life of our best authoress," she laughed, clutching at him so that she could stand upright, and admitted that she was in need of a helping hand.

" 'Tis only that I'm sleepy," she explained, the words almost cut off by a yawn. It was an effort to keep both eyes open, so she tried using only one. That was a bit better, but not much.

As he handed her into the vehicle he had summoned—a much cleaner one, she was able to note, even in her state of befuddlement, than she had found before—Mr. Warrington asked, "And may we expect another novel from you soon?" If he kept her talking, he thought, he might be able to keep her awake until he got her home. And an interest in a new book would do more than anything he knew to make her talk.

"Not until I'm home in Yorkshire," Miranda told him, trying to focus her gaze upon him. "I've found that it's much too difficult for me to attempt to work here in London without allowing anyone to know what I'm doing. There are just too many people about, and someone is forever wishing to speak to me or ask my company just when I've begun to write."

This was better, he thought. At least she was showing some signs of interest. "I can easily understand how such interruptions would make it difficult for you to do your work."

"It is indeed. As I told your brother when I saw him last, there's already one person who knows who I am. If I remain, I may find others who also know me, and the secret would be out."

"And you would be most unhappy if such a thing as that were to happen. I understand."

"It is only for my cousin's sake, as I have told you. For myself, I don't care. It wouldn't do me any harm."

"I would think it might do you a great amount of good."

She shook her head. "No, I don't think my neighbors in the country would care a great deal whether or not I write. Not many of them are readers. I was surprised to find that it is almost as bad here in London."

"We're both thankful for those who do care to read—either books or newspapers."

"As am I. After I've had some time to recover from my visit, I shall start another story. Your idea of having it appear in the newspaper has been a good one. But I won't have it ready for you for several months, I fear—even if you wish me to send you a few chapters at a time to be printed."

"I've been thinking of something else—my brother and I have discussed the idea of my running one of your earlier stories in serial form. He thinks it would be a good thing, and so do I."

"Will it hurt the sale of the books if you do so?" She hoped he wouldn't think she was being mercenary for asking such a question, but the money *was* important to her. With it, she and Sammy had been able to live more comfortably than before she began writing.

"On the contrary, we think it will help them, will keep up readers' interest in your novels until you have the next one ready. Then we can do the other one as well. In the meantime, of course, you'll be paid for the stories we print."

"That will be nice." The words were slurred. Her head slipped down against his shoulder and she knew nothing more until she felt him shaking her again.

"Miss Drake!" His voice seemed to come from a great distance. "Miss Drake, you are home."

"Oh!" She sat up, straightening her bonnet, wishing she dared rub her eyes, but thinking the gesture would be impolite, implying that he had bored her. "You must forgive me, sir, if I dozed off for a moment. It wasn't for lack of interest in what you were saying, I assure you. You were speaking of serializing my earlier books, and that is of great interest."

"Yes—but that was some time ago, soon after we started," the editor told her with a smile. "If I may say so, my dear young lady, you weren't dozing, but sleeping like the dead. You've been gadding about too much, I fear."

"Not at all. Still, you might say it could be blamed on that. Because of the 'gadding,' as you call it, I was forced to do, it was necessary for me to write all night to finish the book."

"That's deplorable. We must hope that nothing of the sort happens again. Neither my brother nor I would have wished you to deprive yourself of badly needed rest on our account."

"That's what was wrong about staying in London while I tried to write. There's so much happening that I don't have enough time for everything. Not if I wish to keep my work a secret from my cousins."

"I know that you told me once about the need to go about with your cousin, and that it robbed you of sleep. But I didn't know it was so serious as this. Had you only sent us word of your problem, we could have explained the delay to our readers."

"I had no doubt you would do so if necessary, but wouldn't have wished them to wait."

"I'm certain they would have understood. Now, we've reached your home."

"Oh, how dreadful of me, to fall asleep when you've been so kind." Even now, it was an effort for her to keep her eyes open. "I must go in at once."

"Of course." He opened her reticule, thrust in a roll of notes, and handed it to her. "Here's the payment for the last chapter. And I shall hope to hear before too long that you've started another book. But you must be certain of getting enough rest. This isn't good for your health, even as young as you are."

Miranda muttered a few words of thanks, stumbled from the hackney, shook her head fiercely in an attempt to waken further, returned the wave of Mr. Warrington's hand, and turned about—to face the angry glare of Jonathan Murray.

He had been for his customary early morning walk, still hoping to strengthen his wounded leg, and as had become his habit, had passed the house on King Street. He wondered if yesterday's drive had had the desired result of convincing Miranda of his interest in her. As the vehicle passed him and drew up before the house, he watched Miranda alight and bid farewell to the same old man with whom he had seen her once before.

"Have you no shame at all?" he demanded, catching her by the shoulders and shaking her, furious to see that his attempt to win her had made no difference in her behavior. "Bringing him right to your door, where your cousins might see?"

Miranda attempted to free herself from his grasp. "I—I hadn't meant to have him come so near—but I dozed off during the drive, and he thought it unsafe for me to walk even a short distance."

"After an unusually active night, I presume." And it had been quite a profitable one, as well, he thought, seeing the roll of notes which protruded from the open top of her reticule.

"Well, yes, it was," she said, ignoring the sarcasm in his tone, although she wondered at his attitude. Did he think he had the right to dictate how she should spend her time?

How could the man have guessed that she had spent the entire night finishing a chapter of her book—which need not have happened had she not taken the time from her work to go riding with him? Still, she ought not to blame him for the lost time, as she had enjoyed the drive. "It didn't matter this time, for no one saw him except you. But now you must forgive me. I must get back into the house before I'm seen."

"I should think you would wish to do so." He stepped aside, but as Miranda took several steps, almost staggering, he caught her arm once more, but less angrily this time. "Let me help you."

"Th-thank you—I fear I'm not so steady on my feet as I should be."

"Perhaps you should be more careful about what you're given to drink." The words were biting, for with all her sins, he had not considered drunkenness to be one of them. Men who overindulged were bad enough, but it was worse when a female did so. Or so it had always seemed to him.

She tried to draw away once more from his grasp upon her arm, but it tightened painfully at her attempt to free herself. "Don't be so foolish. I haven't been drinking. Not even a cup of tea, although I was offered one, because I didn't wish to delay my return home any longer than was necessary. Now, please, I must go in at once. But not by the front door," she said, as he was leading her in that direction. "It will still be locked, and I don't wish to arouse the servants. I came out through the library."

"Yes—that would have been less noticeable." He took her arm roughly once more and guided her around the side of the house to the library door, watching while she fumbled at the latch and leaned wearily against the door jamb while she tried to open the door. "In view of your present condition, perhaps it would be best if I were to see you to your room, rather than leave you here."

She was unaware of the bitterness which lay beneath his words, but even through her dazed condition, she realized the inappropriateness of his remark and said, "Of course you must do nothing of the kind—that would be most unwise of you. But I thank you for your help."

"Don't you think I deserve something more than a mere word of thanks?" Jonathan gripped her shoulders for a third time and roughly turned her about so that she was facing him. His mouth came down upon hers violently, angrily, then softened as he felt her lips move under his.

Almost against his wishes, it seemed, his hands slipped from their hold upon her shoulders to wrap themselves about her and draw her pliant form close against him. The kiss had been intended to be a punishment rather than a caress because he was disappointed to learn that he had impressed her so little that she would immediately go out in search of another man. Yet in that instant, something had changed. The feel of her softness in his arms, of her lips' response to his kiss, stirred a feeling within him that he could not understand.

He deepened the kiss, drawing her even more tightly to him, his fingers moving over her waist and shoulders. He inhaled the soft scent from her hair and marveled at the perfect way her lush form fitted itself to him. Then he realized that Miranda's lips were no longer responding to his, but had completely relaxed. When he raised his mouth from hers, her head drooped forward until she was leaning against his chest, sound asleep.

This was all his kisses meant to her, was it, that she could go to sleep in the midst of an embrace? Had he been boring her with his lovemaking? Could it be that she actually preferred the embraces of the old man—or men—she met upon the street corners? Furiously, he flung away from her and turned toward the street.

Dazed almost as much by the shock of Jonathan's kiss and by the warmth it sent spiraling through her as by her need for sleep, Miranda stumbled up the stairs and collapsed upon her bed. She didn't hear Lucy tapping at her door, and when Sammy, concerned at her absence, came to see why she hadn't come down to breakfast, she roused only enough to peer dimly at her friend and say, "Sammy, I was awake all night, finishing my story. I even fell fast asleep in the hackney after I had delivered it. Please give the others some excuse for my absence," then fell back upon her pillow, her eyes closed once more.

Sammy drew off Miranda's shoes and hat and made no attempt to undress her further, but covered her with a blanket and closed the door of her room. If Miranda had fallen asleep on the way home, how had she managed to reach her room as she had done? No hackney driver would have been so obliging as to help her inside the house, nor would he have been permitted to do so.

She shrugged, knowing that Miranda would tell her what had occurred. There was no need to question her now; the girl wouldn't be able to stay awake long enough to tell her what had taken place.

When Lucy, surprised to find her usually early rising cousin's face was absent from the breakfast table, asked the reason for it, she was told, "Miranda seems to be suffering from a severe migraine and has asked that no one disturb her."

"Migraines can be terrible things," Miss Augusta remarked, looking up from her tatting, which she apparently was unwilling to lay aside even while she ate her breakfast. Everyone looked at her in surprise, for she seldom ventured a comment. Seeing their faces, she added, "I've been a victim of them at times in the past—although happily, not since I came here. I always thought mine were due to the stress of wondering how I was to survive." It was the longest speech anyone had ever heard from the old woman.

"There can be many causes," Sammy said hastily, "or sometimes it seems there is no reason at all."

"Should we summon a physician for her?" Diana wanted to know. She would have liked to hurry to Miranda's bedside and care for her by plumping up her pillows when she had just managed to mold them to her head, laving her temples with lilac water—a scent which caused Miranda to sneeze violently—and rousing her from sleep every five or six minutes to ask if there was something more she could do to make her cousin comfortable.

With some suspicion of what was in the younger girl's mind, Miss Sampson said firmly, "No, indeed. It is quite useless to have anyone poking at her and dosing her. There is no medication one can take for a severe migraine. The only thing we can do for Miranda at this time is to leave her completely alone—and undisturbed—until the attack wears itself off."

"Poor Miranda," Lucy said penitently. "Perhaps, as she has said, we have been asking her to do too much. I know there have been times when she came out with us because I coaxed her, although she was reluctant to do so. We ought to have remembered that she's not accustomed to town hours. We must be more considerate of her so this won't happen again."

"That's thoughtful of you, Lucy. I know Miranda will be pleased that you have such care for her."

"And after all, we must remember, too, that she's not so young as we are," Diana commented.

"Oh Di, Miranda is not so old as all that!" her sister said scornfully. "You make her sound quite ancient. But—do you think that perhaps she might have caught a chill when she rode in Jon's phaeton yesterday? She isn't accustomed to *that.*"

Miss Sampson smiled to herself as she listened to the girls discussing various things which might have caused Miranda's indisposition, and willingly agreed with Lucy's suggestion that riding in an open vehicle might have been the reason for her present suffering. She was happy that neither of them had an inkling of the truth. There were some things about this affair that didn't appear to make sense to her, but although she was certain Miranda would soon tell her what had happened, they wouldn't be for her cousins' ears.

Upstairs, Miranda's slumber was deep for hours, then gradually disturbed by dreams—dreams that it had been Jonathan Murray, not Mr. Warrington, who had met her and brought her to the door, although Jonathan appeared to be angry with her for some reason. That he had held her in his arms, that he had kissed her . . .

She sat up suddenly. That had been no dream. Jonathan had been in front of the house when she returned from the newspaper office, had scolded her roundly for behaving in so reckless a fashion. Then he *had* actually held her and kissed her. She could still feel the strength, the wonder of his lips on hers, demanding her response to his kiss.

And receiving it.

It was true; she had clung to him, kissed him. What must he think of her? It was so shameless of her to return his kiss in that fashion. Was that why he turned away from her so suddenly . . . did he consider her behavior reckless, unbecoming?

Jonathan's anger faded as he strode away from the house. At first he had been furious that the hussy would dare to allow the man to come so near to her home. What if one of the children had seen him and had asked questions about their cousin's gadding about the city at that hour with a stranger? What sort of explanation could she have given?

Then he began to whistle softly, recalling the softness of her mouth under his, the way she had melted into his embrace. She had appeared to be suffering from lack of sleep. Perhaps it was not boredom, after all, which had caused her to fall asleep in his arms. She *had* responded to his kiss, had nestled against him in a manner to make him feel that he could win her.

Yes, this was the time. This very day, he would tell her of his plans, invite her to share them. Surely, she would prefer him to one of the old men she was meeting now, would be grateful to him for settling her in a nice, comfortable nest.

He returned home and wrote at once to the owner of the house he had in mind for her. Although he was certain that the house would appeal to Miranda as it had done to him, she should be the one to make the final choice. Rather than making a firm commitment to hire the house, he asked the man not to promise it to anyone else until he had brought his *chère amie* to view it.

Chapter Eighteen

Jonathan's next meeting with Miranda didn't take place that day as he had planned. When he called at the house to see her, having first waited to make certain that Lucy had gone out—and hoping that neither of the younger children would see him and begin to ask questions about his presence that he was unwilling to answer—Miss Sampson met him with the information that Miranda was abed with a severe migraine and could see no one. He expressed his sympathy and asked to have her told that he had called and that he would call upon her again on the morrow.

"Migraine, indeed," he said disgustedly to himself, as he swung back to the seat of his phaeton and dropped the lines on the grays' backs to give them the signal to start. "If she was larking about all night, it's no wonder to me that she is in need of rest today. She *said* she hadn't been drinking, but who knows what that old roué might have given her?"

Or could it be that she was not resting, but had merely remained in hiding, afraid of meeting him again so soon? He remembered how eagerly her lips had responded to his kiss—at the beginning. She had been half asleep at the time, of course. Had she realized who was holding her or would the reaction have been the same, no matter who had been kissing her? The thought made him cringe. It would be much better to be repulsed than to be accepted merely as one of a crowd of Miranda's men.

Then he smiled away his concern. No—that problem—was only of his own making. The wench had known well enough who was holding her. He remembered her softness as he had held her against him, the way she had clung, and knew that he could have carried her off at that moment with no protest on her part.

Perhaps he ought to have done so, but she had appeared to be half unconscious when he had first felt her lips responding to his, and she was wholly asleep a moment later, when she was resting against his chest. That was definitely not the time to press his claim to her. He wanted to be certain that when she decided to come to him, it would be with her eyes wide open.

He should resent the fact that she *could* fall asleep while he was kissing her. Nothing of the sort had ever happened to him before. She certainly hadn't been bored by his caresses, he assured himself, and remembered how she had stumbled about when he released her. There hadn't been a taste of liquor on her mouth, so he believed that she had been overcome only by weariness.

"I shall certainly make it plain to her when we come to our agreement," he vowed, "that there are to be no more meetings of this kind. And no more men—except for me."

Having no idea what had happened between the pair before Miranda had stumbled up to her bed, Sammy didn't trouble herself to deliver Jonathan's message to her friend. After all, the captain was a caller at the house almost every day, so she was certain to see him. It was thoughtful of him to wish to take her riding, and Sammy wondered if there was a deeper reason for his wishing her company, for he'd never done so until yesterday.

He was exactly the sort of man Sammy would have chosen for Miranda, so it was too bad that he felt as he did about her writing. Miranda might be able to overlook any number of shortcomings if she was fond of someone, but a slur upon her authorship would be something she could never forgive. Still, this unusual show of interest on his part might mean that they had reached an understanding. Sammy hoped that might be so.

Miranda's sleep for a day and a night was sound, except when it was disturbed by recurring memories of Jonathan's kissing her. Even in her dreams, there was something about that moment she couldn't understand, although she enjoyed the sensation.

Unlike the sleeping beauty who, the story ran, had been awakened by a kiss, she had gone fast asleep. Surely Jon's kiss could not have been responsible for *that;* she had been more than half asleep when she'd encountered him outside the house. She recalled, too, that the enchanted princess had been asleep for one hundred years when the kiss awakened her.

"Sleeping for one hundred years sounds so wonderful at this moment," she murmured dreamily, and turned over to sleep again. And to dream again.

No books in her library, her only source of information about such matters, had warned her that she would feel as she had done when Jonathan's lips caressed her, when he held her against him. Something deep within her had seemed to surge up wildly in response to his kiss, to the sensation of his arms about her. It was a feeling she had hoped would continue, but unfortunately, she had been unable to remain awake longer.

Did everyone feel this way at times? Were those times spent in the arms of only one special person? Was this the reason that her readers continued to insist upon her adding a touch of romance to her novels? It *had* been a pleasurable feeling, although she was certain that the caress had meant nothing to him.

Or had it?

Miranda came downstairs the next morning with a feeling deep inside her that was completely alien to her, but she was able to reassure two of her anxious cousins as to the state of her health. Lucy, however, still blamed herself for having urged Miranda to go about with her so much of the time; certainly she hadn't thought that her cousin's country backround wouldn't have fitted her for the busy whirl of a London Season.

It was difficult for Miranda to make her understand that it had only been a temporary indisposition she had suffered, one that would not recur. Not since I no longer have to write all night to finish my stories, she added to herself.

"Truly, my dear," she said at last, "I'm not in any danger of going into a decline. Nor do I think that it will recur. It's only that I'm accustomed to different hours than you and your friends, and I was forced to readjust to your way of life."

"I ought not to have insisted that you come with me so much of the time."

"You were trying to give me pleasure, Lucy. There's no reason to blame yourself if I felt a trifle down-pin one day."

Still not entirely convinced that her cousin was well again—and certainly feeling Miranda was not strong enough at this time to resume making social visits—

213

Lucy went off with Lady Smallwood, as they did almost daily, to pay calls upon other members of the *ton,* but without begging Miranda to accompany them—an omission pleasing to her ladyship, who had been growing anxious to have the young lady settled by the end of the Season and aware that Lucy would forever be overshadowed by her more attractive cousin.

Thinking it might be a good thing for Miranda and Jonathan to settle their differences, if the previous ride hadn't given them an opportunity to do so, Miss Sampson had herded the younger children upstairs after Lucy and her sponsor had left, so that if Jonathan should come, the two would not be disturbed. She put them to work for another hour at their books, telling them that she was disappointed that they hadn't made better progress with their work.

Once more she bribed them with a promise to take them to the park for an hour's enjoyment when their work was done. To herself, she owned that this, when added to the additional time she had promised them for their early bedtime two nights ago, would mean that she must give them almost an entire day to play. Well, she thought, they deserved it. Despite what she had told them, they had been working very hard at their lessons and she was proud of them.

When he arrived, Jonathan found Miranda alone in the drawing room, but aware that if they knew he was there the children might descend upon them at any moment, despite Sammy's watchful eye, he asked her to drive with him again. "Remember that we had planned this drive for yesterday; since you were unable to go then, you must come with me now."

Miranda was almost reluctant to accept the invitation. She was suffering an uneasy but unexplainable feeling at the sight of Jonathan, and was happy that he couldn't know he had occupied so much of her thoughts since she had left his arms and stumbled up the stairs yesterday. She wished again and again that she hadn't gone to sleep, but could have enjoyed the feeling for much longer.

Could she have read more into his caress than he had intended?

When they were not at drawn daggers, which occurred the greater part of the time, she found him to be a wonderful companion. Perhaps he thought the same about her. Perhaps they could be friends, after all. Or perhaps . . . perhaps there was something more.

Still, she thought, what can he say when we're in an open carriage, with the tiger perched behind us in hearing distance? They would have to speak of everyday matters, not of anything too personal to be shared with a servant. And now that Jonathan had come to accept the fact that she was writing, perhaps they could have a nice talk about books. Surely, he must read—although she had learned that there were a great many gentlemen who boasted of never having opened a book since they'd left the schoolroom.

She was surprised to see, as they descended the steps, that he had not brought his tiger today. Instead, there was a neighbor boy proudly holding the lines of the grays and reluctantly handing them over.

"Where's Mike?" she asked. Somehow, she had depended upon the lad's presence to see that this was nothing more than an ordinary drive. She was nearly certain that his presence would inhibit Jonathan's speech as much as it would her own.

"I ordered him to remain in bed today, although I doubt he'll do so. But I couldn't have him sneezing behind us all afternoon."

This was a deliberate untruth; nothing ailed the boy.

But Jonathan was all too well aware of his tiger's sharp ears and his tendency to take a part in the conversation. Later, he would have to learn about his master's plans for Miranda—but not until they were settled.

Despite Mike's comment about Miranda's good sense, Jonathan felt the boy would not approve of the idea of his master's taking the wench under his protection. And if he didn't approve, Mike would certainly say so. He might well ruin matters before they were begun.

"The poor lad—I do hope that he'll be well soon," Miranda said, in quick sympathy.

"I have no doubt he will be," Jonathan assured her, as he handed her up the phaeton's seat and took his place at her side.

Before today's visit, Jonathan had carefully rehearsed the upcoming scene, knowing exactly what he wished to say to Miranda, and equally certain what her response would be. He intended to tell her, among other things, that she must no longer see other men. This part had been rehearsed with extra emphasis. He wanted her full time for himself. Not, of course, that he could spend all his time with her—that wasn't the way these matters were arranged; that would be almost as bad as marriage—but she must be available when he wished her. It would be well to have her established away from temptation, as well as away from her cousins.

Now, for some reason he couldn't entirely understand, he found himself at a loss to begin, finally asking, "Have you ever visited Tunbridge Wells?"

"No—I don't even know where it is." Was he about to suggest that they drive in that direction? She didn't care where they might go, as long as their companionship remained so pleasant.

"Not too far from London, but far enough for one to be aware of the difference in the surroundings. It's another watering place, although not quite as popular in these days as Bath, I suppose. Still, a number of people go there. I was thinking of taking a place rather on the outskirts of the town, but near enough that you could take advantage of everything the place has to offer."

"It sounds to be a most interesting place, but I'll be returning home to Yorkshire soon, so I doubt I'll ever see it." She had told herself that she had seen enough new places and would be content to remain in her own home now.

"I'm hoping that I'll be able to change your mind about leaving," he said lamely. This dashed conversation wasn't going at all the way he had planned it. He thought she would understand at once what he meant by his talk of taking a house and would leap at the opportunity to have a settled connection, rather than being forced to sneak out of the house when everyone was asleep to meet old men on street corners.

"That's kind of you, sir, but I can't remain idle too long." After all, she had half-promised Mr. Warrington a new book as soon as possible. But of course, if Jonathan meant . . . *could* he mean . . . ? He had mentioned that he wished her to see a house; why should she do that? She knew nothing about these matters, so she couldn't tell where this talk might be leading.

Jonathan bit down upon an oath. Was the wench merely baiting him with her remark about not remaining idle, or could she not understand his meaning? A bit desperately, he continued, "I've found a small

217

house near Tunbridge Wells about which I should like your opinion."

"Mine?"

"Yes—I wouldn't want to make definite arrangements for it unless I knew the place was entirely satisfactory to you."

Miranda drew in her breath sharply. This talk of not taking a house unless it pleased her . . . this was more meaningful than his earlier talk of finding a house and wishing her to see it. Now he wished her approval. Was he planning to make her an offer? Aside from the flowers he had given her after Almack's and a single ride together, he had shown none of the signs of a man in love.

Or at least, what she thought such signs would be. She was uncertain what she ought to expect. Even when Jonathan had kissed her, she had thought he seemed to be angry with her. At least, at first; then she felt his mood change. Or perhaps because she had been so sleepy, she had misunderstood the feeling she had received from that caress.

They had quarreled more often than they had agreed—but now that he appeared to be willing to accept the fact that there was nothing evil about her writing, that discord would be ended. Perhaps he thought he had best speak soon, before she left for the country. And since he knew she had no parent or guardian, he doubtless thought his offer should be made directly to her. But what ought she to say? Should she encourage him to speak further? Did she truly want him to do so?

Yes, she did. Wanted it desperately, she realized.

She half-closed her eyes, willing him to say . . . to say what she wanted to hear. "I . . . I know nothing about such matters. I'm certain that you'd be a much better judge of what would please you than I might be." The words seemed to stick in her throat.

"Yes—of what would please me—but that's not what I meant. *You* must be the one who is pleased."

She was speechless for a moment. Jonathan *was* offering for her. She hadn't known he would be so shy as to choose such a roundabout way of doing so, but would have spoken out about what he wished. He had never told her that he loved her—but then, she supposed some men were embarrassed to speak openly of love. Men of action, such as soldiers, might find it especially difficult to make soft speeches. But for him to select such a time and such an unusual place as this to make his declaration . . .

She would have to own, of course, that it was difficult for them to find time to be alone together in the house. Sammy would do her best to keep the children occupied if she suspected the way the wind was blowing, but they could be so unruly at times, and Miranda knew it was almost impossible to prevent them from ignoring Sammy's orders and descending upon a visitor, especially someone they liked as well as Jon.

"It's a small place, but not too small." Jonathan wondered why Miranda was delaying so long in accepting his proposition. He thought she would have agreed at once. Had he not made matters clear enough? What else was there to say—except about the men? Surely, she would understand that *that* must stop. "There'll be room enough for several servants; you would wish for your Sammy to accompany you, I suppose."

"Oh yes." Miranda found her voice at last. Had they not been upon the open road, she'd have been tempted to throw her arms about him as she gave him her answer. She did place one hand over his upon the lines. "Sammy has been with me all my life; she would

219

wish to come. And I should want her with me. As my friend as well as a housekeeper, of course."

"Excellent. She'll be good company for you when I can't come."

What a peculiar way for him to speak of his necessary absences. She knew he had hoped to be recalled to the army—but she wouldn't be the first wife who had to face the fact that her husband was off to war. She would miss him, miss him terribly while he was away, but she would write diligently, so that she would have more time to spend with him when he returned.

"A small carriage, of course," he was continuing, "and I think perhaps a pair, would be enough, especially at first, since you're not in the habit of driving. A pair of matched blacks, I think. I can teach you when I come. And I'm willing to be as generous as I can be in the matter of clothing and jewels."

"Oh, I have an excellent wardrobe now, thanks to Lucy's urging, and I can manage quite well without jewels. I wouldn't wish to be a burden upon you."

She was about to tell him that they would also have the income from her writing, but he had caught up her hand and kissed it. *"You* are the one who is being generous about this, my dear. But I'm not exactly a poor man, and I wish to provide for you as best I can. I don't know what sort of arrangements you may have made with the—gentlemen you have been going out to meet. But of course, you realize all that must stop."

"But I thought that you—" Surely he didn't mean that he wished her to stop writing once they were married. No one else need know of it; she was willing for the secret to continue as it now did, but he had to accept the need for her to continue with her work.

"Didn't mind what you have been doing? Of course I mind! And it must stop, immediately. No man would want it to be known that he is sharing his light of love with half of London."

"His—" His meaning struck her like a blow. Not a proposal of marriage, but . . . "I think you had best take me home," she said through stiff lips.

"But I don't—oh, I understand, you wish to give the matter more thought. But don't take too long, my dear. I'd like to have you settled in your own little place as quickly as possible. If there's something else you would like that I haven't mentioned, you have only to say so. As I told you, I'm prepared to be generous."

"Just take me home—if you please."

Obediently, Jonathan swung the team about and headed it toward King Street. Miranda's attitude toward his offer was puzzling. Perhaps she was waiting for him to make a better commitment, but he had told her that she had only to ask if she wanted anything else. He would supply it to the best of his ability.

She knew, of course, that although he was not a poor man, he was not the possessor of great wealth—but he doubted that any of her other patrons was willing to make her a better offer. It appeared that none of them was in a position to offer her a permanent, or at least, semipermanent, settlement. Or was wishful to do so.

Pulling to a halt, he said, "Give me a moment to find a lad to hold my nags and I'll see you to the door."

"That won't be necessary." The words emerged as if they had been drawn through a field of ice, surprising him, for he still considered that he had made her a generous offer.

Aware that she wouldn't be able to keep her control much longer, she slipped from the seat, caught at the side of the vehicle as she once more missed the step, and dropped to the pavement, wrenching her ankle

221

agonizingly. Biting her lips to prevent herself from crying out at the pain, she made her way to the front door.

Jonathan shook his head as he watched her. He knew she had been hurt by her fall, but could also see that she didn't wish his assistance. There was something about Miranda he couldn't understand. Her moods changed so rapidly—but that didn't matter in the least. For all her present show of reluctance, she would soon be his.

Without taking the trouble to remove her pelisse or bonnet, Miranda made her way upstairs, clinging to the banister and pulling herself up step by excruciating step. Giles and Diana, running down after their stint in the schoolroom, stared at her. "What is it, Miranda?" Diana asked. "Did you fall?"

"I—I stumbled when I was getting down from the phaeton," Miranda managed to say. "It's only my ankle."

"I *knew* you weren't well enough to go out again so soon. We should call a physician."

"No—no. It's nothing, truly. I'll lie down for an hour or so with my foot up. Then I'll be fine." She *must* get away from the young pair before she broke down. "You'll see how quickly this will all be over."

Diana looked doubtful, but Miranda should know how she felt. She was about to say more, but Giles tugged at her arm. "Come on," he said. "Don't waste any time. If Sammy sees us here, she may well decide we need more lessons. And I, for one, have had enough of them for today. For many days, in fact."

He clattered down the steps and Diana, recognizing the sense of his remarks, followed almost as swiftly.

222

Miranda gained the sanctuary of her room and, fully clothed, threw herself across the bed.

The door opened, and she knew it must be Sammy, the only one who would have entered without seeking permission. "Just look at you," the woman scolded. "Lying about *again* in your bonnet and shoes. Yesterday, I could understand it, because you had tired yourself with your writing all night. But this . . . You never used to be so careless of your clothes. I don't think London life agrees with you."

"You're right," Miranda said dully, sitting up and allowing Sammy to take her cloak and bonnet. "Let's go home. Let's go at once."

Sammy sat beside her on the bed and put an arm about her. "What is it, my dear? What makes you so unhappy? I was only jesting—I thought you were enjoying yourself here in London."

"I can't write here."

"Perhaps it'll be a good thing for you to take a short holiday from your work."

"No—I need it."

"But haven't you enjoyed going about with your cousin Lucy? The rides in the park, the dances and the flowers you've received?"

The rides, the flowers . . . Jonathan with a rose from her bouquet in his buttonhole . . . Jonathan holding her as he helped her down from his phaeton . . . Jonathan who . . .

Miranda burst into tears.

"What is it, dear? Who has hurt you?"

Held close in the arms that had comforted her through every trouble since childhood, Miranda told her about Jonathan's change toward her, of how she had thought he was willing to accept her writing, of the attentions, his talk of a house in Tunbridge

223

Wells, of the signs—she thought—of his wanting to marry her.

"Instead," she wailed into Sammy shoulder, "he wanted me to become his *mistress!*"

Chapter Nineteen

Sammy was profoundly shocked at what Miranda told her. Captain Murray had always appeared to be a gentleman, even if he didn't approve of Miranda's writing, an attitude which seemed odd to her, but not impossible to comprehend. There were men who boasted of having never opened a book, and would doubtless think writing a foolish pastime, not the thing for a lady. Perhaps he was one of those.

But this . . . this was another matter entirely, if Miranda hadn't misunderstood his words. Could she have done so?

Perhaps he had made her another sort of offer—an offer of marriage. But certainly Miranda, even as secluded as she had always kept herself while she wrote, would have recognized the difference.

"You're certain you didn't misunderstand him?"

"Quite certain. He began with an offer of a cottage, then horses, clothing, jewels—"

"But he could have offered all those without meaning—what—"

"Not when the offer was coupled with the statement that he wouldn't wish for his light-of-love to welcome other men." Miranda attempted unsuccessfully to stop

225

her tears. "Oh, Sammy, I wanted to die when he said that."

Miranda had been correct! There was no way she could have misunderstood a statement like *that*. "I hope that you told him—"

"I couldn't—I merely insisted that he bring me home at once. If I had tried to say anything more than that, I know I would have broken down. And I'd never wish to concede him the satisfaction of knowing how deeply he had wounded me. To think he thought *that* of me. We must leave here at once. I can never face him again."

Sammy rocked Miranda in her arms as she had done when Miranda was a child in need of comfort. "Yes, of course, my dear," she said soothingly. "I agree that you can't remain here after that. The man is in and out of the house all the time, so you would be forever meeting him if you stayed. And you wouldn't wish your cousins to know how he had insulted you. We shall leave at once."

"But how can we do that? They'll ask why we're leaving. What reasons can we give?" Miranda was more than willing to depart on the instant, but she knew her cousins would have a multitude of difficult questions as soon as they announced their decision to go home. And she *could not* have them know the truth about today's scene with Jonathan. To have them know how little he thought of her. Just the memory of what he had said to her was enough to make her feel unclean.

All she had done was to permit him to kiss her— and, she owned to herself, she had returned his kisses, had been content to nestle for a single moment in the welcome circle of his arms. And because of nothing more than that, he had thought her cheap. Cheap enough that she would accept the sort of offer he had made her.

"It will be simple enough to arrange," Sammy said, after several moments of thought. "They believed you were ill yesterday when you kept to your bed. We'll merely tell them that you've had a relapse; it seems that London air and all the gadding about you've been doing hasn't been good for your health."

Miranda managed a faint but watery giggle. "They'll think I'm a weakling indeed—for I haven't gone about nearly as much as Lucy has done. Of course, I have been writing, but they *think* I was resting."

"Yes—but she is accustomed to London, has lived here all her life and is accustomed to running about, to air that is thick with coal smoke. It is a far different matter with you. Your sudden relapse makes us think that it has become imperative for you to return home until you're completely recovered. Perhaps you can make another visit to London when your health has improved."

"Oh no." Miranda struggled to free herself from the haven of Sammy's arms, suddenly turned into a prison by those words. "You don't understand! I couldn't come back here. Never! Not while—"

"Certainly not—but we don't need to tell them why we're going. There won't be anything to make them suspect you have any other reason for leaving except for your health. It will be simpler to allow them to believe that you'll come to them again at some later date when you're feeling stronger. You need not worry, my dear; I shall be able to manage everything."

"Oh, Sammy, you're such a comfort. What would I ever do without you?"

That was the question Miss Sampson had asked herself when Miranda was a small child. The answer

227

was the same as it had always been. Miranda needed her now, as she had done earlier, so she was here. She knew, too, that her own need for Miranda was equally great—without Miranda, she had no life.

Lucy, Diana, and Miss Augusta protested the decision to leave them so abruptly—the younger ladies because they truly liked Miranda; Miss Augusta as much for that reason as because she could see that she might now be expected to share the care of the younger children. Not tutoring them, of course—she knew she could never do that—but they might wish her to accompany them on their outings, as Sammy had been doing. That would be almost as difficult for her to do.

Giles was quite as overset as were his sisters by his cousin's sudden plan to leave, but he felt it beneath his male dignity to say what he felt. Instead, he told her gruffly that he hoped she would be better soon. He didn't feel sad at the coming absence of so strict a tutor as Miss Sampson; he hoped his new tutor would be one who was less strict about lessons, but who would continue to permit him to romp in Green Park. None had done that before, and he knew he would miss those outings.

Mrs. Hemphill wisely agreed with Miss Sampson that she knew best what would benefit Miranda; the housekeeper had no way of knowing what had taken place between Miranda and the captain, either their previous encounters or what was said while she was driving with Jonathan today, but she knew that something had occurred recently to overset the young lady. She hardly seemed to be the same person now as when she had arrived in London. And if Miss Sampson thought that going home would help her, then Mrs. Hemphill felt that was what she should do.

Miranda protested feebly that she did not *think* that she had contracted anything contagious. The air of

London sickened some people, of course, but surely she ought to be strong enough to withstand it. The wording of her statement and the faint cough which accompanied it, were quite enough, however, to keep the others from coming too near her as she prepared to leave.

She could understand how they must feel. Nothing must be permitted to interfere with the remainder of Lucy's all-important Season. Their farewells, although more than a bit tearful on the part of the girls, were said at a respectful distance, and Miranda was helped by Miss Sampson into the back of a post chaise, bundled in a thick cloak—which she threw aside as soon as they were safely out of sight of the house.

"You're tired, as much as anything else," Sammy told her, with an attempt at cheerfulness. "By working at keeping up with your writing at the same time that you allowed Lucy to persuade you to go about with her so many times, you've quite overtaxed yourself. It's a wonder that you did *not* fall ill. Once you're at home and completely rested, you'll feel much better."

"But Sammy, that's not the thing at all. You must understand. When Jonathan Murray—"

"Yes, my dear, I know. When you first met the man, you were wise enough not to trust him because of his attitude toward you. It's only been the past few days that you permitted him to come close to you—close enough that you could misunderstand—"

Miranda sighed deeply, struggling against recurring tears as she remembered those last days with Jonathan. How wonderful he had appeared to her, when she had thought he truly loved her. Then the blow—to her pride, she told herself firmly, not to her heart. "I know—and you're about to tell me that he's not worth weeping over. I know that, too—"

"But when we're home once more and you're thoroughly rested, all this will seem like a bad dream. You'll have your work to think about, and he'll be no more than an unpleasant memory."

She hoped that she was right in making her prediction. Miranda had never been the sort to indulge in schoolgirl infatuations; this was the first time that she felt her heart had been broken, so she suffered more deeply than if she had gone through such scenes before.

Even in the present good weather, their journey was a tiresome one. The chaise they had hired was less comfortable than the one they had taken when they were traveling toward London. Although she continued to protest that she wasn't weary from the journey, Miranda obeyed Sammy's orders to retire to bed at once. For some time, she could still feel the jolting movement of the chaise as it passed over the bumpy roads.

She wouldn't be able to sleep, she was certain, then opened her eyes to the realization that she had actually slept well into afternoon of the following day. "Sammy was right about this, as she always is," she exclaimed, sitting up and looking about her. "What happened in London—" she would not dignify the occurrence by giving it a name, even to herself "—was like a dream. A bad dream. But now I'm awake and it will soon vanish."

Leaping out of bed, she saw that while she had slept, Sammy had unpacked her baggage and put everything where it belonged. Her inkwell, several sharpened quills, and a large quantity of paper had been placed neatly on her desk by the window, her favorite spot for writing.

When words came slowly or ideas refused to come alive, as they sometimes did, she could stop writing for a moment or two and gaze across the field until her hazy ideas formed themselves into another story. Whether her eyes were gladdened by the sight of a carpet of flowers blowing about in the spring or summer breezes, the colorful dance of the falling leaves in autumn, or the snow clinging to the bare branches, each season brought thoughts churning into her mind as if they were eager to have her set them down on paper.

"Luncheon must be well past," she told herself, seeing the angle of the sun. "There's time for a page or two of the new story before I go down for tea."

Tying her robe and pushing back her hair, she seated herself at the desk, drew paper before her, and picked up her quill.

And found that there were no words. No ideas.

Gazing at the field didn't help her at all. It was no more than a weedgrown patch of soil with trees here and there. There were flowers there, as there had always been, but they had no message for her. Where was the new story that she had promised to do for Mr. Warrington? Miranda sighed and replaced the quill.

"Doubtless I'm still too tired from my journey," she told herself—although she remembered that the journey *toward* London had never so wearied her. She had arrived at her cousin's home impatient to be allowed time for her work.

"Of course, I *was* overtired when we left London, and I suppose that we should have taken more time to choose a better chaise for the journey," she told herself, although at the time, she was in too great a hurry to leave to be particular about the vehicle they engaged. "I'll rest for another day or two and then I can write again. I know I'll be able to do it."

As she went downstairs to find Sammy preparing to have tea, she wondered if she ought to say anything to her friend about her continued weariness, to ask if

Sammy also suffered from fatigue due to the journey, then decided not to do so. There was nothing seriously wrong with her. As Sammy had said, she was merely overtired from attempting to do too much. She would soon be as eager to work as she had always been.

For her part, Sammy looked at Miranda anxiously to see if the work of recovery had begun. Miranda would seldom speak about her work while it was in its early stages, but as it progressed, she would occasionally drop hints as to what her hero and heroine, or even her villain, planned to do.

It was too early yet for Miranda to say anything about her plans—but Sammy hoped vainly for some indication that her mind was busy with the story to come. The story that would blot out the unhappy memories of London and return her to the girl she had been.

Every day, Miranda took her customary place at her desk, picked up her quill, and sat looking across the fields in search of the inspiration she usually found there. But the fields told her nothing. Nothing that would help her. The flower-scented breeze brought back memories of her ride with Jonathan. The ride she had found so enjoyable before . . . before . . .

Instead of monks or ghosts or persecuted maidens, the pictures in her mind were always of Jonathan . . . the look in his green eyes that first day, when he had told Lucy he didn't think it a good idea for her cousin to visit her . . . his continued sneers at her writing . . . the roses he had sent her after Almack's, and the bud he had taken from her bouquet to wear in his buttonhole . . . his hands gripping her shoulders while his kiss punished her mouth . . . the feel of his arms holding her against his strong body . . . and always, the worst thought of all, the memory that what she had thought was to be an offer of marriage was an offer of another kind.

"It's no wonder that I can't write when I continue to torment myself with remembering such things as that," she told herself. "I *must* forget that such a person as Jonathan Murray ever existed. Then I'll be free to work again." But saying those words did nothing whatsoever to drive him from her thoughts. Nor did anything else. He was there, and there he would remain.

After several weeks, when Miranda would customarily have been bubbling with the intricacies of her story, Sammy noticed that she no longer made any pretense of writing. She shed no more tears, but sat for hours in her room or on the tiny lawn, staring into space. Jonathan's name was not mentioned, but Sammy feared the man was still in her girl's thoughts.

When Sammy suggested they might enjoy a shopping trip to York or some other diversion, Miranda's answer was always, "I don't think I want to go today, Sammy," or, "Why don't you go?" Never did Sammy hear the familiar words, "Oh, I can't leave my story at this time!"

This was worse than anything Sammy could have thought. There must be *something* she could do, something to end this dreadful apathy into which her girl had fallen. The only thing which came to her mind, however, would doubtless make Miranda hate her when she found out what she had done. "Better to have her hate me than to see her moping about, only half alive." She had always done what was best for the girl, no matter how distasteful Miranda had found it at the time. This was a different matter, however, then forcing her to swallow a mixture of senna and treacle when she had eaten unwisely.

Yet she could think of nothing else to do. And with

Miss Sampson, the time to put her plan into action was the present moment. There was one snag—but she soon saw how that might be overcome. Mrs. Hemphill would help her, and would say nothing to the children. They mustn't know, until the plan was successful.

If it should be.

Chapter Twenty

When Jonathan called at the Owens home to learn what Miranda would say to his offer, and discovered that she had suddenly departed for the country without leaving so much as a message for him, his language was such that Giles looked at him in awe, wondering if he could ever remember all *those* words, while all the females in the household clapped their hands over their ears and took him roundly to task for his behavior.

"In fact, Captain Murray," Mrs. Hemphill faced him, moving her hands from her ears to her ample hips, "I think it would be for the best if you were to curtail your visits to this house until you have remembered how to behave like a gentleman. I refuse to have the children exposed to such vile language."

"Mrs. Hemphill is quite right, Jon," Lucy told him, her tone such an echo of the housekeeper's that Jonathan could almost visualize her as another exactly like Mrs. Hemphill in thirty years. "Merely because Miranda is ill, there is no need for you to be angry with the rest of us. Or with her, either, for she couldn't help it. I think you had best leave."

"Thank you—thank all of you. I shall certainly do so," he retorted, and stalked out, leaving them staring after him, wondering what had made their old friend act like a wild man.

Ill, indeed, he told himself, with more language the ladies would not have approved. Either her "illness" meant that the wench was frightened of his offer—and he could see no reason why she should be, for it had been a perfectly reasonable one, even to his demand that she give up other men—or she thought by running away she could persuade him to make her a more generous declaration.

In either case, it was best that she had gone. He had no need of her in his life. What did it matter that today's drive wasn't to take place? He could drive whenever and wherever he pleased. And if he wished a companion, there were plenty of agreeable ones to be had. Getting rid of Miranda was what he had planned from the beginning, was it not? And that was what he had succeeded in doing. He should be congratulating himself on the success of his strategy.

It was easy to say that, but he found that he couldn't put her out of his thoughts merely because he wished to do so. He remembered how beautiful she was, especially in the blue gown she had worn at Almack's, with her curls piled atop her head, but knew he would think her equally lovely if she were garbed in rags. Her words to him that evening—that she might be persuaded to consider marriage, but that her husband must agree to allow her to continue her "career"—mocked him.

Surely, the jade couldn't have expected an offer of marriage from *him*. He was certain she must have known him better than that. Or she should have, for he had made it plain from the beginning that he knew the truth about her.

Had he not promised her much more than she could hope to expect from any chance-met fellow? And she had spurned him. He might call himself all sorts of an idiot, and did so, but no matter how she had treated his offer, he still wanted her. He would have laughed scornfully if anyone had accused him, but to himself he admitted that he had fallen in love with her.

And what if he had? A gentleman did not *marry* a piece of Haymarket ware. True, Harriette Wilson's youngest sister had snared a lord—but that was an exception to the rule. *Could* Miranda have thought that, knowing her as he did, he would have planned marriage?

He had never made such plans, wouldn't even think of so wild a thing. Not only for his own peace of mind: there was his position in the army—if they finally agreed to return him to service—to be considered. His superiors would have accepted the fact that he had a light-of-love, for that was a common state of affairs among his mates, but if he had *married* her, he would have ruined all his chances for advancement. His commanders wouldn't have permitted their wives to associate with one of her sort. Even his fellow officers would shun him as if such indiscretion were contagious.

"No, Jonathan, my lad, you must own that it was quite the best thing in every way that the little fool ran away when she did. Otherwise, you might well have made a much greater nodcock of yourself over her than you've already done."

Yet he couldn't rid himself of thoughts of her. The day he had been scheduled to return and discover if he was considered fit for service passed without his being aware of it. All he could think about was the way Miranda's lips had felt under his—one would have thought she had never been kissed before—and her softness in his arms. He could even smile at the memory of her falling asleep in the middle of a kiss. Then

237

would come the memory of the man leaning from the carriage window to give her wage, and he would feel his fists clenching, as if he wished he could have the fellow under them.

One afternoon he returned home from an unsuccessful hour at Jackson's Saloon, where he had punished several opponents until the gentleman himself had stropped the bouts and had told him that he was far too dangerous to be going about in his present mood, to find a boy waiting for him, carrying a message from Mrs. Hemphill.

What had gone wrong? Was one of the children hurt or ill? Did they need his help in some way? They had always prided themselves upon being self-sufficient and had never asked for it before. He flipped a coin to the lad and tore open the message to discover that the inner letter was not in the housekeeper's hand.

But why should Mrs. Hemphill forward him a message which had come from someone else? He turned to the bottom of the letter and saw that it was signed "Aurora Sampson."

He racked his brains, but couldn't recall anyone by the name of Aurora among his conquests. If any of them had learned about his connection with the Owens family and had used that method of reaching him, certainly the upright Mrs. Hemphill would never stoop to send him a message from such a source. In the first place, she would never have paid to receive anything of the sort, unwilling to soil her fingers with it.

However, he thought the name "Sampson" seemed familiar, finally remembering that it had been the name of Miranda's "Sammy." But they had barely spoken to one another when she was in London; why should she be writing to him?

"The best way to learn that, idiot, is to read it," he told himself, and turned back to the beginning:

Captain Murray:

If what Miranda has told me about your last meeting is true, I know I ought not to be writing you, ought not to consider you worthy of a word—but I am still hopeful that she misunderstood what you said and that you did not intend to insult her.

Insult her? What had she told her friend about him? When was a straightforward offer of protection an insult to one of her kind?

Nonetheless, I think it only right that you should be informed that the girl is apparently breaking her heart over you. I had hoped she would soon recover from her feelings, but it seems that it isn't to be. Whether she is right or wrong about your feelings for her, there can be no doubt about her feelings for you. I fear that she's going into a decline.

Why a decline? he wondered. If Miranda had preferred someone else, she had only needed to say so; there was no necessity for her to enact a Cheltenham tragedy. He read on:

Day after day, I watch her sitting about the house or in the garden, not speaking, except to answer my questions. Then she says only what she must. I know she has written nothing, not so much as a single line, since we returned home. Since she was a child, I doubt there has been more than a day or two passing without her writing at least a few pages. But although she has not told me, I know she is no longer able to write. Her publisher, Mr. Warrington,

*has written to her repeatedly, to ask her when
he may expect to receive her next book, but
she doesn't even answer his letters and doesn't
tell him there might never be another book. It's
not the loss of the book that concerns me,
however, except that her writing has been her
life until now.*

*If you do care for Miranda, sir, I hope that
you won't hesitate to tell her so. I never
thought the day would come when I should say
anything of this kind—but even the sort of
liaison she believes you have offered her would
be preferable to this continued apathy on her
part.*

*I am writing this out of my love and friend-
ship for Miranda.*

Aurora Sampson.

Jonathan reread the letter several times, attempting
to make sense of Miss Sampson's words. What she had
said about Miranda's strange behavior was difficult
enough for him to understand, for it was *she* who had
deserted *him,* so she had only herself to blame if she
was now unhappy about the way matters stood. But
what was all this part about a publisher—and a book?
Her next book? Was the woman attempting to tell him
that Miranda . . . that Miranda had written books in
the past?

Nothing the Sampson woman said in her letter
sounded anything like the Miranda he had known. Or
thought he had known. Why should Miss Sampson
think Miranda was breaking her heart over him? She
had only to tell him that she was willing to accept his
offer. Or to decline it, if that was what she preferred.
As greatly as he now realized that he wanted her, he
never would have tried to hold her if she had said she

240

preferred someone else. But the Sampson woman said that Miranda had misunderstood him. No, she said she hoped that was so.

But what was all this about books? If he unraveled that particular mystery, the remainder of the letter might be understandable. He made his way into the city as quickly as possible and, after having been given a number of false directions, located Mr. Warrington's publishing house. Once there, he was forced to wait—with increasing impatience—until that gentleman came into his office, inquiring as to the reason for his call.

Was he imagining things? Jonathan asked himself. He had thought so often of Miranda and the man he had seen with her. This man was either the same one, or was enough like him to be his brother. At least, he should be able to clear up the mystery—or one of them—which had been raised by Miss Sampson's letter. "Are you Miss Drake's publisher?" he demanded. "Miss Miranda Drake?"

"Why yes, sir, I am," Mr. Warrington told him. "At least, I'm one of them. I've published all her books, and my brother has been serializing them in his newspaper. He's now printing one of her earlier books while we await a new one. But may I ask how you learned who she was? She's always insisted that we keep her identity a secret. Or perhaps you are the friend she once told me about, who knew all about her work?"

"I knew nothing about her writing. Not until today. And why should it be a secret?" Jonathan was more confused than before. This didn't solve the mystery, but only made it worse than it had been. He had never heard of Miranda's writing, and he knew her cousins would have mentioned it, had they known. Were they speaking about the same person? "Miss Drake is the cousin of several of my friends. Why should she ask such a thing? What secrets could she have? And why should she want them kept from her family?"

"That is the question my brother and I have asked her again and again. We would have preferred to give her more publicity, for we were of the opinion that it might help to increase the sales of her books. But Miss Drake fears that the knowledge that she is the well known Madame V might bring harm to her young cousin. I understand the young lady is making her comeout this Season."

"Yes. Lucy Owens. But—"

"Miss Drake feels that her authorship of Gothic novels—as popular as they have become—might cause certain people to look askance at her cousin."

"I don't understand—"

"We didn't quite understand her reasoning ourselves, but she says she is aware that there are some people—especially those who enjoy reading her books—who might look down upon her for writing them. And would blame her cousin for being related to such an authoress. It sounds foolish, does it not? Yet that was her thought."

"Why should she feel as she did?" *Was this the reason Miranda had said nothing to him about writing books? Had she thought he would blame her for that? Of course, he had never given her an opportunity to say such a thing, had only condemned her for what he imagined she had been doing.*

"I can't tell whether she was right—but Miss Drake may have had good reason for feeling as she did. You have no idea of the manner in which she felt that she was forced to creep around during the weeks she has stayed in London, so that she was able to bring my brother the chapters of her latest book, which he was

242

printing. She gave us only a few chapters at a time as she finished them."

Jonathan once more attempted to ask if the man was certain they were discussing the same Miss Drake, but the other gave him no time for questions.

"I understand that she was forced to write at night when no one could know of what she was doing, and come out secretly to deliver her manuscript. She gave my brother the last chapter several weeks ago, and now I'm happy to say that the bound book will soon be available. I expect it to be more popular than her earlier ones."

Jonathan shook his head, trying to clear his jumbled thoughts. "Do you mean that when she was going about in that furtive manner, creeping out at dawn or at times when no one was about, it was to deliver parts of a *book*? And that the fellow she was meeting . . . the money she was receiving from him . . . ?"

"Was payment for the chapters of her book. And the man you speak of was my brother, the greater part of the time. As I said, she was only able to bring him a few chapters at one time because of the pressures which were put upon her to take a part in the Season's activities."

"I . . . did not know . . ."

"And of course, she did come here on one occasion so that I could give her a share of the income we had received from the increased sales of her earlier books. Running the new story in my brother's newspaper had revived the interest in the other novels, as we had predicted."

Jonathan recalled the notes the fellow in the hackney had handed her. Was this payment for her writing? "She said nothing—"

"No, she would never say anything about it. For her cousin's sake. And now that you have discovered her

243

secret—however you *did* discover it—I hope that you won't betray it."

While Jonathan was seeking for words to express his feelings at this news, the publisher went on. "Do you know if Miss Drake has gone away, sir? Away from her home in Yorkshire, I mean, for we knew she had left London. Soon after she brought in the last chapters of her book, I understand. My brother and I have written to her several times concerning a new book she had promised to write for us, but we've received no reply."

"No—I mean, I don't think she's gone away again. I—understand that she hasn't been well."

"I'm sorry to hear that. If you see her or correspond with her, will you please convey my brother's and my wishes for her speedy recovery?"

"Y-yes—I shall do that."

Looking at the odd expression which had spread across Jonathan's face as he made an attempt to absorb all these previously unknown facts about Miranda's activities, Mr. Warrington inquired anxiously, "Is there anything amiss, sir?"

"Nothing at all, Mr. Warrington, except that I've just come to the realization that I've been the greatest fool in London—rather, in all of England."

"I—I don't understand."

Jonathan shook his head, attempting to make sense of what he had heard, and contrasting it to his earlier opinion of Miranda. "No, I suppose you don't, for I can't quite understand what you've been telling me. But it no longer matters. I'll see Miss Drake—if she'll receive me—and I shall give her your messages."

"That is good of you, sir." Edward Warrington spoke heartily, although he continued to look warily at Jonathan. as if doubtful that a man who would speak so wildly could be trusted. The fellow spoke as if he were a friend of Miss Drake's, but one never knew about strangers. He could well be some sensation seeker attempting to learn the authoress's whereabouts.

He wouldn't wish to be responsible for telling such a fellow how to reach the young lady, if the man didn't already know. She had always trusted his discretion. He had to see that that trust was not misplaced. "We miss her very much," he said lamely.

"So do I, sir—but I fear that I alone am to blame for that." Jonathan strode quickly out of the office, leaving the publisher staring after him and wondering if he should have called someone to look after a madman— or was he a rogue?

Walking at top speed until his wounded leg protested so strongly that he was forced to rest was of no help to Jonathan, for he found that his mind would not be put to rest. He knew now that he was in love with Miranda; he had loved her almost from the beginning, even when he had urged her cousin not to allow her to stay—and he had given her the worst insult any man could offer to a gently bred lady. There was no way that he could ever persuade her to forgive him.

Yet he knew he must try to do so.

His first problem was how to reach her. Miss Sampson, who was usually so correct about matters, had allowed her feeling for Miranda to overcome her good sense. She had begged him to come and help her young friend, but the letter had not contained her direction.

He remembered that Lucy had once said her cousin had come from Yorkshire. Mr. Warrington had said the same. But Yorkshire was a large area; he could scarcely go blundering about, asking everyone he met if they knew where he might find Miss Miranda Drake.

Why had he not remembered to ask Mr. Warrington where he might find her? But then, he had allowed the fellow to think he already knew the answer to that—and if he now admitted to ignorance, he wondered if the man would help him.

"He must do so, whether he wishes or not, for I *must* find her."

He turned back toward the publisher's office, then halted, unaware of the people passing him on every side. He could scarcely force Mr. Warrington to give him the information he sought, if the man did not wish to do so. There was another course he might take, unwilling as he was to lay himself open to ridicule. No doubt Lucy would think his pursuit of Miranda a matter for teasing, perhaps telling the young children as well. He could hear their remarks.

Still, he turned about once more, surprised to discover how far he had walked while his mind had been occupied with thoughts of Miranda, and hailed a passing hackney, giving the jarvey the address of the Owens home.

Chapter Twenty-One

Of course, Lucy would know how to find Miranda, but he found that he was a bit hesitant at first about approaching Lucy. Her eyes were sharp, and he feared he might reveal more of his feelings than he intended. Still, he had no choice but to seek her out, as he hadn't done so since the day that she and Mrs. Hemphill had suggested he leave the house.

With them he exchanged banal remarks about the weather and other matters, happy that they no longer appeared to blame him for his last outburst. He hoped they no longer remembered how he had made a fool of himself that day. Then, attempting to sound casual, he asked Lucy if she knew her cousin's direction. She stared at him for a moment, until he felt his collar beginning to tighten, then began to laugh. Not her usual giggle, which would have infuriated him, but a full-throated laugh.

"I knew it!" she declared. "You and Miranda quarreled, didn't you? That was why she was in such a hurry to leave—and why you were so angry at everyone when you found her gone."

"Yes," he admitted. "We disagreed—rather violently, I'm afraid. The blame was all mine, of course—"

"I'm certain that it was."

"You need not have been so quick to agree with me about that." Even though he knew she was correct, he couldn't help feeling slightly aggrieved at her quick assumption that he was the one to blame. Miranda had said some unkind things to him at times—although nothing to compare with his insult to her. Fortunately, Lucy would never know about *that*.

Lucy laughed once more. "But it would have had to be you who was at fault, Jon. You were unkind to her from the day she came here, although we could never understand your reason; it was so unlike you to be unpleasant to anyone. But I thought that, after the night you escorted the pair of us to Almack's, you felt differently about her. You came to take her driving—"

"Yes—but that was when we disagreed. Not the first time, but later—"

"When Miranda had been laid on her bed with a severe migraine. Did you cause that?"

"I fear I did, in a way." That was after he had kissed her, had felt her responding to him, after she had gone to sleep in his arms. "Then, when we went out again, I know that I said some things that hurt her."

"If you caused Miranda any unhappiness," Lucy's tone was critical, "I don't think I should tell you how to find her. You might do so again."

Jonathan was tempted to shake her—but that would be the wrong thing to do, he was certain. She would never tell him what he wished to know unless he confided in her. And that was what he didn't want to do. Certainly, he could never tell her what he had said to Miranda to drive her away.

He wished again that, instead of coming to Lucy, he had thought to ask Mr. Warrington for Miranda's direction while he was in the man's office, but had already decided that would have been useless. Warrington, of course, had taken it for granted that he already knew where he was to find her. If he had said he didn't know, the man would probably have grown suspicious of his reason for wishing to find her and refused him the information.

So if he must beg Lucy to tell him what he needed to know, he would do so.

While Jonathan had been mulling this over in his mind, debating just how much he could tell her, Lucy had been studying his face. She thought he had changed a great deal since Miranda had left London. He was graver, appearing to be more worried than he had been at any time since he had ceased to worry about the possibility of losing his leg. But this, she felt, was a different sort of worry. "Are you in love with Miranda?" she asked him suddenly.

"I don't think—" he began with a hint of his former stiffness, then saw the twinkle in her eye, and nodded. "Desperately."

"We-ll," she said slowly. "I suppose that if Miranda doesn't want to see you, she can send you away. So here is what you want." She gave him a small folded piece of paper, closely written.

Jonathan opened and read it eagerly. "You intended all this time to tell me what I wanted to know, didn't you?" he accused.

"Of course I did. I was certain weeks ago that the two of you were in love—but I wasn't certain *you* knew it. If you had wanted to find her just to quarrel again, I wouldn't have told you where she is."

"I should box your ears for that, imp," he said, but instead, bent and kissed her cheek. "If you are correct—about Miranda, as well . . ."

Lucy flung her arms about his neck and returned the kiss. "Certainly I am correct about her feelings for you. Everyone thinks that I'm too young to understand about being in love, but I'm not." Her cheeks were slightly pinker than usual as she said this, which made Jonathan wonder briefly if there might be a reason; if, perhaps, she and Colin . . . Yet he had no time to concern himself with Lucy's romantic problems. His own were in such a muddle that he wasn't certain about clearing them up.

"If you marry Miranda," she continued, "then you'll truly be my cousin. And I would like that. You'll bring Miranda back to London, won't you? We've all missed her so very much."

"If she wishes to come, I'll certainly bring her," he promised. To himself, he added, "If she will even consent to speak to me after what I've done to her." He was far from being certain about that, despite Miss Sampson's letter, and Lucy's reassurance.

Before dawn, he was on his way northward, riding his fastest horse, trusting to fate to be able to find good mounts along the way. If Miranda did agree to listen to him, if she agreed to return to London, he would send for a carriage, purchasing one, if necessary; but traveling with a carriage now would be much too slow for him.

"After all, I did promise her a carriage," he said, flushing as he recalled the other things he had said that day. How could he have been so wrong about her—how could he not have seen at once that she was totally incapable of the evil things he had thought of her? And how could he convince her that he had changed?

It was Sammy who answered the door at his knock.

"I wasn't sure if you would come," she told him.

"If Miranda told you what happened, I'm surprised that you would permit me to do so."

"She's told me everything, Captain Murray, as she's

always done. And I own I was exceedingly angry with you—at that time." Unaware that she had neglected to send him their direction, Sammy was certain from his appearance that he must have hurried here as soon as he received her letter. But Jonathan wasn't only weary; he looked almost as worn as Miranda did. She thought that perhaps he had come to regret the scene—the unhappiness he had caused Miranda.

"I agreed with her that it was the best thing for us to leave London, so that she wouldn't have to meet you again. But now, when I see how unhappy the poor girl is, I can only hope that I was wrong and that Miranda misunderstood what you were saying."

"No—she didn't misunderstand. It was I who did so—not to realize that what I thought I had seen and heard was not true." Quickly, he described the scenes which had given him the wrong impression of Miranda's "career."

"I can see how you might misunderstand what you saw. I don't understand how you could have been so foolish as to think such things of her, however."

"I know I shouldn't have done, but her actions looked so suspicious. And when I accused her—but I see now that we were talking at cross-purposes."

"Would the sort of female you describe not appear more hardened? I would have thought one look at Miranda would have told you how good she is."

"It should have done, I know—but it told me quite the opposite."

"You mean that you didn't know that she was writing? That was what she thought you didn't like." She now moved aside from the doorway, motioning for him to enter.

"Not a word, so when she spoke of continuing with what she was presently doing . . . You can see, can't you, that although I should have known that she could do nothing wrong, it appeared quite otherwise?"

Sammy studied his face for some time. "You didn't wish her to remain with her cousins, however, even before you heard and saw these things."

"Because she is so beautiful. I feared she would cause trouble."

"But you knew nothing about her, so that is no reason for not wishing a young lady to be happy."

"It is, I think, when one has just undergone a bitter experience because of another beautiful lady. It seemed to me at that time that beauty and infidelity must go hand in hand. Can you understand that?"

"I think that I do, Captain. You were labeling Miranda as another like the one who had betrayed you. Yes—I can understand. But that may be because I'm an older woman. I'm not certain, however, that Miranda would see matters in that light. It might be best not to mention your earlier misfortune."

"Whatever you say."

"Now, you'll find Miranda in the garden. And I hope you'll be able to bring a smile back to her eyes—and to her heart."

Jonathan went in the direction she indicated, seeing Miranda before she knew he was there. He couldn't see her face, but the dejected slump of her shoulders told him that she was unhappy, and he felt a deep sense of guilt for being responsible for the pain she had been suffering. He had suffered as well, but knew he had only himself to blame for his unhappiness.

He spoke her name and, thinking she had only imagined that the voice was Jonathan's—as she had imagined things so many times before—she looked around vaguely to see how Sammy might have permitted to come into the garden, for her wish for privacy had always been respected. When she saw that it was truly Jonathan who stood there, she shook her head.

This was only another dream, she told herself, one in which Jonathan spoke softly to her as she had once hoped he would do. It couldn't be real, for in real life he had scorned her, thought her cheap. He had offered to give her everything she had ever wanted, she realized too late, then had snatched it away by saying he wanted her for a mistress, not a wife.

Then she knew this was no dream; that he was actually standing before her, looking at her in quite a different manner than he had done before, but it didn't matter now. "What are you doing here?" she asked dully. "Why did you come?"

All the way from London, Jonathan had rehearsed what he was going to say when he saw Miranda. Now those well-turned phrases wouldn't come. "To ask your forgiveness," he said humbly, "if ever you can bring yourself to forgive the hurt I caused you. And to tell you how much I love you."

He would have taken her hands, but she backed away, shaking her head. "Oh yes, I believe you said something of the kind before. Your 'light-of-love'— that *was* what you called me, wasn't it?"

"That wasn't what I meant to say to you," he argued, although he knew that was what he *had* meant, at the time. "I was never more wrong about anything than I was at that time. I should have called you 'love-of-my-life,' or something of the sort. Since you went away, Miranda, I've come to realize that I can't go on without you."

"That's a pity, for that is what you must do. Just as I must—" Her voice trembled and she turned away. For the first time since the day he had told her of his intentions, she was in tears.

Jonathan caught her in his arms and let her sob against his chest while he smoothed her hair, murmuring all the things he had wanted to say to her. At last, she looked up at him, tears clinging to her lashes.

"How do I know you won't vanish again, as you've done before?"

"You mean that you've sometimes thought of me?" Not as often as he had thought of her, he supposed, but that she had thought of him at all was a good sign. Unless, as he feared, all her thoughts, her memories, had been bitter ones.

"Every time I dream, you're there. And sometimes you're kind to me—but then I always wake up and you're gone."

He placed a hand beneath her chin, tipping her face until he could cover her lips with his own, kissing her hungrily, feeling her eager response. "Then let me spend the rest of my life proving to you that this time is real."

Miranda shuddered, pressing herself deeper into his embrace. "It must be real, for I've never felt like this before—not even the other time you kissed me."

"That's because this time is different from that one. I was angry then, and you were sleepy. How do you feel now?" He kissed the last two tears from her lashes, while his fingers traced the path the earlier ones had taken down her cheek.

"I—how can I say it—it's as if I were floating somewhere high above the earth—on a rainbow, perhaps."

"Is there room for two on that rainbow?"

"There must be—for you're here. So if I'm on that rainbow, you must be there, as well."

"I hadn't thought of it in that way. My feeling is more one of suddenly being safe, of having been rescued from a life that would hold only darkness—for that is what it would be if you weren't with me."

He had never spoken to her in this way, but she knew that he was speaking truthfully. Her life, too, had been filled with nothing except dark days and nights.

It seemed so wonderful, so perfect, to be here in Jonathan's arms. The things he had said to her in the past should be beyond forgiveness, Miranda thought—but these weeks without him had been endless pain. She wanted him here, wanted his kisses that she could feel running through her veins like fire, wanted to believe that this time her dream would come true.

She looked into his eyes and saw that the icy greenness had gone. Instead, there was a glow which warmed her to the tips of her toes, that sent her every nerve to tingling with the wish to be held like this forever.

"And darkness for me, as well, without you," she said, reaching up to run her hands through his hair, loving the feel of the strands on her fingers.

Looking at the pair in the garden, Sammy sighed with relief. It had been the right thing, after all, to send for him. The man may have been a rogue, but he had changed. Her girl could be happy now.

Much later, sitting on a bench beneath the trees, with Jonathan's arms still holding her, Miranda asked, "And will you be going away soon?"

"Never," he told her fervently. "Unless you send me—and not even then."

"I meant—what about your request to be returned to active duty?"

Jonathan stared at her for a moment, then began to laugh. "Can you believe that I completely forgot that I had an appointment at the War Office?"

"But it meant so much to you to be allowed to go."

"At one time, it did. But no longer. I've had my share of fighting. Now, my love, I only wish to be where you are."

"You mean here? In the country?"

"If that is what you want. Here—or in London. Or the ends of the earth. By the way, Lucy has asked when you intend to return."

"I—I don't know. Perhaps—"

"Oh, and before I forget—Mr. Warrington wished for me to ask you how your new book is progressing."

"I haven't—" She broke off, turning to stare at him. "I didn't know you had ever met him."

"Only once—but I think I may have seen his brother several times." It was safe to mention that, since Miranda didn't know that he had once—or twice—suspected her of having *liaisons* with the fellow.

"Oh—then—I suppose I should tell him . . . I feel as if I could write again. Would you mind if I did so?"

"I shall mind anything that takes you away from me, even for an hour."

Miranda laughed. "Oh, I didn't mean to start writing at this moment. But I meant—would you object to my writing?"

"You did tell me that, did you not—that your husband—and I intend to be your husband—"

"You do? Have I nothing to say about it?" She would never have believed that she could ask *that* question so lightly.

"That you agree—at least I hope you will. No, my dear, I do not mind how many books you may write. The whole world may know that you are Madam V, for all that I care. I shall buy every one you write—and to prove how much I love you—even read them!"